Aubrey's Journey

D.L. Clarke

PublishAmerica
Baltimore

First printing

ISBN: 1-4241-1572-8
PUBLISHED BY PUBLISHAMERICA, LLLP
www.publishamerica.com
Baltimore

Printed in the United States of America

My *Aubrey*

Braver than anyone I know

And stronger than one could ever wish to be

To you I dedicate this book.

To Whom It May Concern

There were times, you told me just to ignore
All the "certain things"
That baffled you and challenged your heart.
You wanted comfort and the quick promise
That things were "A Okay,"
You wanted me to bury my head also,
In the sand box you so conveniently made.
But what was I to do? Ignore all the "certain things"
That tugged at my gut without relief
Things that pushed me forward and moving,
Despite all of the grief?
But that, I could never have forgiven myself doing,
And will not apologize, remember, my heart was aching too
Such impossible things I was construing
For, it was my daughter, my beautiful child
Being tormented, pulled to pieces, and torn into two.
I moved onward, not trying to hurt anyone,
only trying to find help
And, simply pretending there was nothing there
It was a hand to her, I couldn't have dealt.

D. L. Clarke

You most likely will notice that throughout this book, you do not see me mentioning most family members and medical professionals by their real names, and those that were mentioned, were changed, depending on their personal preferences.

I faced a lot of opposition and had confrontations with family members and the medical community who believed, and still to this day believe, that there is and never was anything wrong with my daughter. The interactions I had with these individuals and the roles they played ended up being such an important factor in the journey, that the *experiences* themselves needed to be told, and not necessarily their *names*. Therefore, I was still able to accurately describe my feelings and experiences throughout the story without pointing fingers and blame.

You know who you are and what roles you did or didn't play, and I actually want to take a moment to honestly thank you. I truly believe that everything and everyone has a purpose, therefore, your opposition and disbelief kept the fires burning in me and helped me find determination to blaze the unbeaten path of truth and discovery for my child. This book is for you.

For those family members and friends that did give their support and believed in my daughter and I as we fought through the battles, I thank you. You realized the emotional journey Aubrey and I had to take to find answers and assistance, and though I often faced isolation and lacked support from some individuals, you were always there.

I had to trust my gut feelings and I justified my efforts and actions to no one except myself and Aubrey, and you somehow, through it all, understood.

I accepted the successes and failures as they came, knowing and firmly believing that at some point I would find a way to provide a better livelihood and future for my daughter. You believed in this too. You know who you are and I thank you again. This book is for you.

This book is especially for all mothers, fathers, care givers, and family members, who may have or might be going through similar experiences with your child or loved one. I hope that by sharing this experience with you, it will give you hope and inspiration to keep fighting in order to find the answers you seek and need. Everything you do *can* make a difference. Please, believe in yourself and your child, trust in your gut, and don't ever give up.

A very special thank you to all my children: Brittney, Aubrey, Austin, Cameron, and Brady. And, to my special homemade family, Carissa, Heidi, Brandi, Janet and Mike, Jen and Jeff, the Wise's, Cynthia and Peter, Kimberly and Erik, and my mummy.

Emily O., thank you for your work with special needs families. You are one of the people in this world that shines your light where it is needed most, and I am so proud to know you.

Thank you, BJ, for being my lifelong friend and always willing to extend a helping hand. Thank you Jen P. and Cynthia M., for "the talks" that helped me to keep writing this story. You, too, are true beacons of light for those with special needs, and I am so grateful.

And thank you to my wonderful husband Gary. Your belief in me helped provide the inspiration and calmness I needed in order to complete this book. I love you dearly.

Take with me a journey, she beckoned
Alas it be one that I did not know.
Come along on this journey, she then promised.
For all you need to see
I will indeed to you, someday show.

D. L. Clarke

Introduction

I can still hear Dwight Yoakam's song "Fast As You" playing on my radio when I think back and allow myself to take an emotional dive into the depths of some of the most difficult nights I ever experienced as a mother. When I think back and recall that song in my head, I feel instantly horrible and terribly guilty. I can see myself rocking my daughter deep into the night trying to comfort her to no avail, questions flooding my weary mind.

After laying down in my bed for what seemed the millionth time that night, listening to that song blaring, and I mean *blaring*, on my bedside radio, I realized that I was dealing with something I neither understood nor had answers to. I also realized that I had no choice but to find the answers and understand them. All along, I had believed that *I* was the one in control. As if the choice was there right in front of me and I just had to decide whether I wanted to dig to find answers to the questions, or not.

But, as I laid there and continued to turn the knob on my radio higher and higher trying to drown out the sounds of my eleven month old daughter screaming for the fourth night in a row, I knew that I was not in control of *anything*. Everything seemed to be spiraling into a dizzy abyss of confusion.

What was wrong with my daughter? Why did she seem so miserable most of the time? And, what caused her to stop talking or responding to me for hours at a time? Why wouldn't she sleep? How come she didn't laugh and play like other children her age? What was making her so angry? Why couldn't anyone but me hold her?

I was out of ideas, strength and sadly, patience. I was completely exhausted and running on empty. All I wanted and needed right then was to know what was wrong with her so I could help her.

But, unfortunately, the only comfort I found that night was in that damned country song that just happened to be yelling louder than what she was at the moment.

Who knew that that night would come back to haunt me later? Had I known then what was wrong with her, I would never had left her side. I wouldn't have had a need for that blaring radio. I should have listened to what my heart and nagging stomach was trying to tell me. I should have held her all night, even though it seemed to be providing no apparent comfort.

Who knew I would feel so guilty later for doing the best I could for her at the time. Who knew that it would take over a hundred medical professionals and therapist three and a half years to start putting understanding to the questions that as a mother, I could not answer that night.

You've got to be stronger, do not give in,
But, when did the strength weaken
And the weakness begin?

D.L. Clarke

Chapter 1

I love thinking back to the warm and beautiful day in July of 1992 at the hospital in Lemoore, California, when my second daughter, Aubrey, was born. She was perfect. Her eyes were deep blue and they were accented by the longest lashes I had ever seen on a baby. Her hair was bright strawberry blonde and her skin was perfectly pink. She had all of her fingers and toes, and a little port wine birthmark on her upper lip. We immediately fell in love with her; our little Aubrey. It had been an incredible day filled with anticipation, joy, and thankfulness.

I also remember the cold and rainy day in Washington eighteen months later when her pediatrician informed me that I really should "for the sake of the family" put her in a children's mental institution. I remember listening through a dark cloud of emotion and disbelief as he proceeded to recommend that I accept, right then, that my daughter was different than other children. He explained that I should never expect her to laugh and play like other children, dance or become a little ballerina. He tried to convince me that she would never communicate normally and would be very unsuccessful and frustrating if she were to attend a "normal" school.

He did mention, however, that she would eventually succeed in destroying the family. I then heard him calmly continue, explaining that I could not possibly have the skills or knowledge needed in order to raise such a child. He then stated matter-of-factly that even if I attempted to, it would just end up causing great distress both physically and mentally to myself and the rest of the family.

I remember the rage I felt and the confusion and disbelief of what I was hearing. I remember seeing the physician's mouth moving with words I could not comprehend. I remember the feeling of the room spinning and the lights fading in and out as the mono-toned doctor continued to speak in a language I could not understand. I remember feeling Aubrey's body squirming on my lap as she tried to get down for the hundredth time without success. I had been warned that I needed to "control my child" or she would need to leave. I guessed that that had meant that I would need to leave too, so I let her squirm as I sweated and tried to somewhat "control" her. I wanted to leave, no, more like bolt for the door.

Something washed over me and before I realized, it had consumed me. It was like a giant nauseating wave of despair that I seemed to have no control over. Attempts to rationalize the situation didn't help. My body swayed in the emotional waves it had created and my mind fell idle of thought. Mental numbness then took its turn and I welcomed the sanctity for the moment it gave. I could feel my eyes welling up with tears.

It felt as if I were about to dive into a heavy fog laden abyss with no escape. I needed clarity and it appeared that none was going to be available. Sudden, immense depression gripped me tightly, allowing my hands to fall from Aubrey's little waist.

Aubrey then successfully hopped from my lap and proceeded to stomp her way over to the door and pound her fists into it. I had just been told that there was nothing anyone could to help my daughter, and if I wanted to do "the right thing" I should take her to someone that could find a good placement for her. *They* would know how to help her, possibly. I was apparently being deemed useless by the professionals. Wasn't *I* supposed to have all the answers? Wasn't *I* meant to be the person that knew her child more than anyone else and know what was best?

What had I done wrong? Aubrey did have some good days and I would be encouraged to the point that I would think I had been reading too much into some of the previously displayed oddities. She could play with her toys and seemed interested in television. I would hear her babbling to herself or to her books. There were days that she went without having the steady flow of tantrums and she would even take her naps without fussing.

So, what was it then? Why would all of that switch and suddenly the bad days would start again? On the dark days, she seemed completely miserable. She would cry constantly and there were raging tantrums several times that would last for hours. She hated to be held and wouldn't play with her toys.

Even the softest of foods would gag her. When she did eat anything that left her hands sticky, she would scream and look at her hands and cry until I could remedy the offending stickiness.

Bath times were a nightmare as she hated having her head touched. No matter how careful I was to avoid her eyes and ears, the second I started to even lightly touch her scalp, she would squirm in the tub and scream as if she was in tremendous pain.

The mystery was impenetrable to me at the moment and the doubts bounced around in my head as the doctor droned on. My neighbors had persistently informed me that I was being too protective over Aubrey and I needed to be 'tougher' and just let her cry. Was I shielding her too much?

But, I *had* let her cry, to the point that neither Aubrey nor I could handle another sob. Did they *really* know what it was like to experience their child screaming into the deepest hours of the night, *every* night?

It was within those late night hours that the doubts crashed in and overtook what little confidence I still possessed. Maybe it had been too long since I had had my first daughter, Brittney. Five years *was* a long stretch between children; perhaps I was just out of practice? Maybe I had just forgotten how to be a mom? Perhaps all I needed was just a little bit more time, a tad more confidence, and maybe slightly more fortitude? Maybe then, things would be okay?

My head ached and my entire body felt heavy. I knew I had to help my daughter, but I was becoming more and more aware by the minute that the doctor's office was not the place I was going to find the answers. So, where were they? I grasped Aubrey's tiny, little hand and we headed for home.

Perhaps I hid the pain, maybe too well,
behind a wide smile.
But, perhaps I had too little to gain
By sharing all the turmoil.

D.L Clarke

Chapter 2

It didn't just happen over night. Instead it took awhile, sort of like a flickering flame that takes on momentum and then eventually becomes a raging fire out of control. Throughout the first few months of Aubrey's life, I had the feeling that there was *something*, but it wasn't ever *anything* I could put my finger on. Unfortunately, I was quickly figuring out that no one else could either.

I was beginning to think, and would often try convincing myself, that everything *was* normal, or that eventually everything *would* be normal. But no matter how many physicians I saw that reassured me she *was* normal, I had the unsettled and restless feeling that could not be extinguished.

Aubrey had *seemed* like a happy baby at first. If it weren't for the episodes of colic that most babies experience, and the nights without sleep, she actually *was* a happy baby, I think. But, I had made so many excuses over the first few months of her infancy that I am now really not so sure that she could be accurately described as a "happy baby."

I became almost impervious to any abnormal behaviors and would just brush them off as "the baby has gas" or "the baby didn't get much sleep last night." Besides, these types of explanations seemed to make everyone around us, a little more comfortable. They could deal with those explanations, and for the time being, so could I.

But, when I actually took the time to think about it and remember, there were way too many occurrences of colic and nights spent without sleep. And, they weren't just simply "nights without sleep," I finally had come to realize. No, instead, they were more like witnessing your child in incalculable and unexplainable pain, writhing and screaming for no apparent reason. Nothing I attempted ever helped and the screaming could last for hours and hours, long into the morning hours.

I eventually began dreading the night hours, for, they had become intolerable. During the day, the tantrums and drama didn't seem quite as bad and I always seemed to find some way to distract myself. It had taken me several weeks that eventually turned into months, to finally start realizing that Aubrey was a very idiosyncratic baby.

I know that all babies are different; personalities and temperament can differ quite drastically between siblings. This fact was something I had been "reminded" of frequently in her early months. and I took all of this into account when I began to make mental notes of what concerned me most about Aubrey.

If it had been simply just "sleepless nights," I could have excused it all on the fact that she was a newborn and that is to be expected of newborns. This, however, was quite different. The nights were often filled with my baby girl twisting and screaming in her little white bassinet, almost like she was in implausible pain. Yeah, it was those, undeniable moments that had definitely caught my attention. After eliminating all sources of possible allergic reactions, (which had also been suggested and then later ruled out), there had been nothing left to blame them on. So, *what was it?*

One of the first *major* things I noticed, other than the sleep issues, was Aubrey's intolerance with breast-feeding. Okay, I know what you might be thinking, but I gave the process the benefit of the doubt and continued for almost two months without much success. I had nursed Aubrey's big sister Brittney for almost four months without problems, so it wasn't like I didn't know the procedure. So, what was the problem?

Aubrey would begin to nurse and then suddenly jerk her head back and start screaming. Once I coaxed her, she would try again, but would stop abruptly within a couple of minutes and scream.

I began to think I wasn't producing enough milk. So, I started on a stricter regimen of drinking water constantly, eating more protein and taking all my major vitamins. Not that I hadn't already been doing all of that, I just made a point of paying closer attention to the procedure. Nothing I did seemed to help the situation and I soon became a nervous wreck at feeding times.

I had done my reading on this as well and knew that once you become nervous and anxious about nursing, it is possible that your milk will not "come down" like it is supposed to and the event would be futile. However, without going into graphics, I knew I was functioning quite efficiently and after realizing it wasn't a glandular malfunction of any sort, I really started to get concerned.

The next morning I would be off to the local grocery store, plucking entire bottle-feeding systems and cases of formula off the shelves. Then, I would drive home, feeling quite comfortable with the thought that at least I would be able to *see* the results of my efforts rather than *guess* with the nursing. Yeah, I knew I was doing the right thing. Or, at least I thought I was.

As I mixed the first batch of formula, my initial feelings of guilt resurfaced. I felt like a breast-feeding quitter. What the *hell* would the La Leche League think of me? What if I *was* on the Oregon Trail with Aubrey and *had* to nurse? What then? Would I just let my baby starve because certainly *they* didn't have the convenient powdered formula and ready to fill sanitized bottles. Oh, such an amazing amount of guilt that tantalized me. Why did I even care? But, curse it all, I *did* care!

First of all, I rationalized, trying to put the guilt in its place as I shook the sanitized baby formula powder in the sanitized bottle filled with pure and sanitized water, if I *had* been on the Oregon Trail, both Aubrey and I would have died during the child birthing process.

Well, actually, to be more accurate, I would have died five years earlier giving birth to Brittney and we wouldn't even be here having this lovely conversation. But, that is another whole scenario that we neither want to recollect nor take the time to dive into, now do we?

Okay, sorry. I actually feel the need to explain myself here, and then we can continue. I am sure everyone has sat through, at least once, a detailed description about some woman's horrific, "I almost died" birthing story complete with blood, crash carts, oxygen masks, and stitches. Sadly enough, no matter how terrible the story seems to be, it could be diminished within seconds with someone else's even more horrible "I almost died" birthing experience.

I, my friends, will spare you all from that drama, for there really isn't a terrible story to tell about either one of my girl's births. They were very normal, except for the fact that they were both delivered by caesarean. Not, by any means, to condense the fact that caesarean's are major surgery. But seriously,

I was one of the lucky few to be up walking within hours after surgery, unaccompanied by any pain medications other than regular Tylenol, with no problems.

So, no major concerns there. I simply had a condition (I found out *after* having Aubrey), where during childbirth, my hips do not do any shifting or make any allowances for a baby to pass through. Great for your future "Levi's wearing days," but pretty bad for your "baby having days."

So, in a nutshell, when you are trying to deliver a nine-and-a-half pound baby by natural process, it does not and *will not*, no matter how many hours you breathe doing the infamous Lamaze, hoo-hooo-heez and the ha-ha-hooooz, or how many pain killers you are injected with, work.

So my simple, yet not scientifically proven, summation of my whole experience is, that had I been one of the Oregon Trail travelers, I would have died screaming and bitching the whole way down.

Or, on the contrary, stayed eternally pregnant, which we all know is impossible, so you do the math. I feel much better explaining all of that. Now that we know each other much more personally, perhaps too much, we can move on.

The bottle-feeding had *seemed* like the perfect solution, but as it turns out, there was an impediment to that as well. There were certain bottle nipples that Aubrey would gag on or just completely refuse which would result in her screaming. I would always check to make sure there wasn't a defect in the nipple and that it wasn't clogged with dry formula. After they passed inspection, which they always did, I would rush to the nearest store to pick up a new assortment of bottle nipples to try.

We ended up going through about a half a dozen, (or more, I lost count) different types and brands of nipples before we found one that Aubrey would tolerate. When I finally found the one brand that she liked, I went back to the store and purchased enough of them to last an entire year. No sense taking the chance of them running out.

Another thing I noticed that really seemed odd and eventually concerned me, was that Aubrey would tolerate being held by only certain people. That list was very short and included just myself. Well, actually, that isn't quite accurate. Others *could* hold her, but she would only allow it when I was in the room within arm's length, and she had an unobstructed view of me.

If she was being held and I wasn't within sight of her, she would often scream and squirm until the captor would release her. This usually took just a few seconds. Grandparents, friends, and neighbors were unfortunately often on Aubrey's "do not hold me" list, and it truly confused everyone, including myself. I tried to rationalize that since the grandparents lived out of state and saw her rather infrequently, they were in a way, strangers to her.

That made perfect sense, but what about my neighbors? I couldn't go a day without running into Janice and Gwen. They both lived with their families across the cul-de-sac from us. We usually ended up doing almost everything together. Evening walks, picnics at the park, we even shared some of our holidays. They definitely weren't strangers, and yet, Aubrey would refuse to let them hold her.

Gwen, the more outgoing of the two, would often try to make Aubrey giggle by tickling her feet or making funny faces at her. Aubrey would shy away and squirm in my arms. Any contact seemed to be too much, unless I was the one providing it.

The more quiet and reserved Janice courageously offered to babysit for me one afternoon during one of my postnatal doctor's appointments, so I took her up on it. It was strict hospital policy that children not accompany adults to their appointments, but I had gotten by with it the first two appointments that I had. However, I was told that the *next* time, I would need to find care for my child for the duration of my appointment.

I had tried the hospital daycare facility, but was paged within fifteen minutes of dropping her off and told to come pick her up ASAP! Aubrey had cried so violently for the duration of my absence that she was gagging herself and the daycare staff had become worried.

So, I logically thought that perhaps Aubrey would be more comfortable at Janice's house. After all, she knew Janice and we had been to her house many times. I feel much better about this arrangement, I thought to myself confidently. I dropped Aubrey off at her house across from ours, got to the parking lot of the hospital, walked in, and was immediately paged over the intercom system. As I approached the front desk to retrieve the phone from the peeved looking receptionist, a feeling of anxiety overtook me. I knew what was going on without even hearing it, but I asked Janice just for the sake of asking it.

"She is crying and I don't know what else to do for her!" I heard Janice's stressed voice telling me. "I tried to get her to calm down by rocking her, but she doesn't want me to hold her. She won't eat; I don't think she is hungry. She actually almost threw up just now because she is crying so hard that she is choking herself!" Janice finished with an anxious gasp.

I could hear Aubrey's frantic screams in the immediate background and my stomach felt sick. As I hung up the phone, the receptionist, who knew me by name because of all the pre-natal and post natal check up's and such, automatically reached for an appointment card and asked when I could reschedule. I took the next appointment available and wondered how in the heck I was going to manage to keep *that* one! I already had cancelled and rescheduled so many appointments that I am sure I was on some "flake" list and flagged as an over anxious mother, but I didn't care anymore. I was confident my uterus could go another few days without being discussed and certainly my bout of postpartum depression was clearing up on it's own. Aubrey needed me so I was off to rescue her.

Another odd thing I added to my mental list was that Aubrey did not like to be messy. She was getting to be strong enough to sit and sort of feed herself in a high chair, but she did not like to have food on her hands or face. There were some rare occasions where it didn't seem to bother her as much, so I tried to ignore it, but after it started becoming more and more of an issue, I realized that I had to do something about it.

Since meal times had become such an upheaval, I tried resolving the situation by providing Aubrey with a wet washcloth at each meal. I would either wipe her hands when she became agitated from the food being on them, or she would grab for the rag and try to wipe by herself. This seemed to be the perfect resolution, unless she got food on her clothing, and then she would scream until the bib or clothes got changed.

Textures of the foods had actually become another issue and it was very difficult finding foods that Aubrey would be willing to touch and pick up to eat. Bananas and noodles gagged her, as did soft canned fruit. I also could not begin to count the many times that I had to do some sort of choking rescue on her because of some cracker or piece of apple that got too difficult for her to manage. I became overprotective and apprehensive each time she ate, thinking that she may choke again.

Family members and friends would criticize me for "watching over her too closely" and "being too protective." Yet, I couldn't help it. The realization that my baby could choke at any given moment scared the crap out of me and still I wondered if somehow the critics might be right.

Was I actually *causing* some of Aubrey's grief by being too careful with her now? Was it *my* fault that she was becoming dependent on the washcloths? I didn't know if what I was doing was harming her in some way or would *eventually*. All I knew was that whatever I *was* doing seemed to be providing her with relief and that was all I needed to accomplish for the moment. I could deal with that for now.

Please don't look too deeply
into finding what has been all the while.
Into something you never wanted to find,
my friend, please don't look at all.

D.L Clarke

Chapter 3

It was during Aubrey's six-month well baby checkup that I finally cracked and began to allow my doubts to take me over completely. I was really starting to realize that things might not be going as well as I had thought they should be. Feelings of anxiety were visiting me daily and I was quickly becoming overwhelmed. I knew I needed to get some help. Confident that the pediatrician would have some new parenting techniques available that would resolve the issues, I warily started spilling a few of my concerns out onto the table for analysis.

The doctor listened to me with one of his ears while tediously checking Aubrey's. After hearing a couple of my concerns, he assured me that everything was normal and that she was progressing right on schedule. As far as the sleep issue, he reminded me to not give in to her crying when I laid her down at night.

I was told to let her cry for ten minutes the first night, and then go in and check on her, reassure her and leave promptly. The next night, I was to let her cry for fifteen minutes, check on her, and then leave promptly. This would only have to continue for about three nights before she would realize her bed time crying was not getting her the attention she wanted and she would discontinue the pattern.

I wanted to cry at this point myself, for I had already tried this technique, *several* times over *many* weeks. I had dutifully done the five minutes, the ten, the fifteen, and had even gone into waiting almost an hour to see if she eventually stop crying. It hadn't worked. All it had really accomplished was a major headache and nausea on my part and a very pissed off five month old, on hers.

No matter what I tried, she could definitely outlast me. I had even started relying on my bedside radio in my attempts to drown out her crying and withstand the minute rules. Guilt riddled me when I would finally give in and retrieve Aubrey from her crib. I wanted to be successful and make it work, but I just couldn't handle it any longer.

I had tried the minute method for almost two weeks and it had gotten me nowhere. The crying episodes never got any shorter; in fact, they seemed to intensify the longer I withheld contact. I would just have to convince myself that I could do without sleep.

I then asked the omnipotent doctor about the other trepidations I had with Aubrey. What about her dislike of certain foods and about having messy hands? What about not wanting to be held by anyone other than myself and not wanting to have her head touched, especially at bath time? Even her skin was ultra sensitive and I had to be so careful what types of detergent I used or she would break out with little sores wherever the offending fabric touched her skin.

Then there was the stroller issue. On most days, she absolutely loathed her stroller. In fact, whenever I even got the stroller within eyesight of her, she would start writhing and screaming. This was a major disappointment for me since one of my favorite exercises was walking.

I was going to list some more concerns for the doctor, but he interrupted me with a smile and flip of his hand.

I heard the doctor say "normal behaviors" after his hand flipped and fell back down to the examining table.

"I'm sure she has good days as well? They can't *all* be bad are they?" The doctor quizzed me. I thought about his question and had to admit that yes, she did have good days. In fact, the days that didn't produce an inundation of tantrums just added to my perplexity.

Was there anything wrong with her, or was it just her temperament? Was she reacting off *my own* moods and feelings? Was I actually the cause of her tantrums? Was I being too overprotective? *What was it? What, What, What?* My mind continued to reel and twist in confusion.

Though it was good to hear that she was normal, at the same time, it made me feel like a complete failure. If I was causing her to be this way, I wished the doctor would just confront me with it. Was he trying to protect my feelings? Why was he *pretending* that everything was just perfect?

It didn't take me but a minute to conclude that I was in fact losing my mind and causing all of the problems. There was absolutely nothing wrong with my daughter. *It was me.*

After I got Aubrey home from her appointment, I didn't waste any time. I marched right over to the phone and made an appointment for me to see my doctor. Even though I could not shake the nagging feeling that everything was not all right with my daughter, I decided to accept her doctor's diagnosis of "nothing wrong" for the time being. I was even beginning to think that perhaps a good and lengthy discussion about my uterus could shed some light on the whole situation.

But, three weeks, approximately 120 tantrums, and one gynecologist exam later, I was still no closer to solving the mystery of Aubrey. My doctor said I looked tired and asked if I was okay. Of *course* I was completely normal, wasn't I? Why did she ask? Did I not look okay? Could she tell that I was going mad? The paranoia was so becoming on me, I thought, but I suppose to someone else it could look a little intimidating. I couldn't tell if she was hinting at something or was fishing for information, so I took the bait and unabashedly swallowed the hook.

I was close to tears by the time I finished describing what had been going on with my daughter over the last seven months. The doctor sat, somewhat awestruck, and then asked if I wanted something to help me sleep. I thought about it for a second and then declined half-heartedly. I had considered taking over-the-counter sleep aides, but I wanted to be able to hear Aubrey when she needed me. There was also Brittney to consider. I had to be alert and on task in order to get her up in the morning and off to school. I could think of a million reasons why I couldn't have anything to help me sleep.

I watched as my doctor wrote in my chart and shook her head in apparent disbelief at my decline for drugs. As she looked up and made eye contact with me, I saw her mouth open and the words "Perhaps I could recommend a good book on parenting to you?" come cascading out and billowed in thunderous exclamation. If you add the look of being dumbfounded onto the paranoia, you now have an accurate description of what my face looked like at that moment. It was a very good thing that I didn't have a clue right then that I would hear that same sentence from another fifty or so professionals in the next few months.

I suppose it was safe for me to assume by now that the professionals actually did think it was my fault that my daughter was having so many problems. A parenting book indeed! As if I could actually be the cause of all of Aubrey's discomfort and misery? Who the hell did she think she was anyway? Did *she* have any kids? I secretly bet to myself that she didn't, but somehow thought from her elucidation, that she might.

"Do you have children?" I asked her. I could feel my pulse beating in my face. Great, I was probably getting ready to have a stroke or something. Didn't my body know that I didn't have time for a heart attack or stroke, or that even an episode of hypertension would be too time consuming?

"No, but some day maybe," she replied weakly, her face flushing slightly.

I considered that I was possibly making her think twice about enduring such an endeavor of having children. But as she gracefully handed over a piece of paper that had the titles of three books about how to be the perfect parent on it, I reconsidered. I heard her state that they were very good books and that I would definitely find them helpful.

"I am just amazed at how many different behavior modifications are available for the wide variety of problems we as parents face today," I heard her say in her perfect voice.

We? As parents? Didn't she just tell me she didn't even have kids? The heartbeat in my face pounded on. *Good for her*, I thought. Great to be prepared and know how to ward off any problem situations even before they occur. That is what I should have done I suppose, but I hadn't. Instead, I had relied on what had worked with my first child and was left floundering in the wake of confusion. *Next time* I would be the perfect parent because I was going to read the books and find out how it was possible, I decided vehemently.

I was aware that the pounding was moving upward into my head. Yes, definitely a stroke, I thought. Or, maybe it was a tumor of some sort? I then wondered what it would be like if I did have a stroke? Hmm... no chores, no laundry, no responsibility. Damn! I had to scold myself harshly for thinking like that. I knew I was fatigued so I kept the scolding short.

I watched her flip her blonde hair to one side and continue to write in my chart. I glanced down at the book list and saw, at the top of it, "How to Raise the Difficult Child." Well, I surmised, at least she realized that my daughter was a bit of a challenge. Or did she? The next book on the list was a psychology self-help book for individuals that are overwhelmed with life. Wow! Okay, she seriously thinks I am nuts. Could she see that I had started to sweat? Probably. I am sure she had 20/20 vision inside her perfectly blue eyes. I could feel my protuberance expanding in my head as it pounded on.

I don't know why I had immediately started hating her. Was it because she talked in a way that created feelings of self-loathing within me? Was it because I saw how organized and seemingly perfect her life was and I was jealous because mine was falling apart into chaotic disarray?

Or was it her blonde hair and blue eyes with the perfectly pressed white coat and the manicured nails? Perhaps it was the fact that she appeared to be judging me and my integrity as a parent. I didn't care why actually, but I couldn't help the thoughts from running rampant in my head as she told me my uterus appeared to be quite normal.

Happy to hear that at least one organ in my body was functioning normally, I walked out the hospital door and to my car. On the way, I spotted a penny on the ground. Knowing how lame the whole "lucky penny" belief was, I still picked the stupid thing up and stuck it in my shoe. I drove home feeling drained and a bit pissed off.

Janice was waiting by the door holding Aubrey and swaying side to side as I drove up to my house and got out of my car. My pulse quickened with anxiety, but lessened when Janice told me she was just trying to get Aubrey down for a little nap. I was relieved that I wouldn't be needing to make any more appointments for myself.

The whole babysitting issue was such a problem that I dreaded having to leave her for *any* length of time. Sure, it was nice to get away for an hour or so, but normally the anxiety and stress that followed once I got home, was not worth any comfort the outing temporarily gave.

As I retrieved Aubrey from Janice's arms, she caught my eye and noticed the tears that were welling up and getting ready to spill over in a torrent.

"What happened?" Janice asked gingerly as she wrinkled her already dismayed look and watched me circumspectly.

"Same stuff, actually," I heard myself quietly reply. "Nobody knows what is going on with Aubrey and they seem to think it is all my fault somehow," I continued, ready to let the tears loose. "I think I must be in the beginning stages of a stroke or tumor or..." my voice trailing aimlessly off.

Aubrey began wailing at that point and Janice said she was sorry but really had to get going. I understood. She probably had enough of Aubrey's crying while I was gone and was ready to head back into the quietness of her own home.

I wanted to go with her, to be somewhere quiet too. Wait a minute! Hadn't I just come from somewhere quiet? Hadn't I just spent an hour away without the crying and tantrums? Guilt flooded me and the tears overflowed the dam and, without a sound, fell to the floor. I stood watching Aubrey scream in my arms, and my tears kept falling. I vowed silently to never leave her again.

So many questions filled my head and seemed to overwhelm every part of me. What was I going to do? Had I exhausted all my resources already? Was everyone at the hospital convinced that *I* was the creator of everything that ailed my daughter?

As the tears shot down my cheeks in hot rivers, a small part of me began to believe that I was in fact causing Aubrey's anxiety and tantrums. I had done something terribly wrong somewhere along the seven months of her life and somehow she had responded to that, and was now miserable. If only I could put my finger on exactly what it was that I had done, perhaps that would help solve the mystery and I could fix everything.

I immediately started picking myself apart. I studied and scrutinized everything about myself. My mind quickly filtered through past moments and situations, decisions and directions.

What had it been? Where had I steered wrong? Was I too much of a neat freak, which caused Aubrey to dislike change? Even moving her crib from one side of the room to the other had been such a crisis that I had moved it back within a couple of hours. Had that been it?

What about the time in the middle of the night when she was four months old that I wasn't able to retrieve her right away because I was battling some sort of intestinal bug and was stuck in the bathroom for a half hour? I knew she was sensitive and perhaps that incident had sent her over the edge? I know it had almost done *me* in!

Maybe it had been the trip to the mall when I didn't rescue her out of her stroller right away. I had wanted to counteract the tantrums by not giving into them, but it just seemed to make things worse. Perhaps that was the moment when Aubrey figured that I *would* eventually give into the tantrums and she just simply had to wait me out.

But, was I giving into the tantrums? Or was it simply a timing issue? The episodes could last for hours. At some point during the tantrums, lunch would have to be eaten, diapers would need changing, and naps would need to be taken. Did that mean that I had given into her constant demands? It was hard to even remember why or when one would start and another would end.

My mind was a neatly wrapped mess by the time I had quieted Aubrey and laid her down for her afternoon nap. She was sleeping so peacefully that I officially decided that I must have gone insane to believe there was anything wrong with her. I mean, look at her! How could there be anything wrong? She was only seven months old!

I looked around her room and examined the jungle motif that decorated her walls. Elephants and zebras danced amongst the palms and a monkey swung from one tree to the next. It was a happy room filled with bright colors and stuffed to the brim with toys. It was also full of memories. Sleepless nights and sounds of crying bounced and seemed to echo silently from the colorful walls that surrounded me.

Being careful to not make a single sound, I quietly made my way across her room and shut the door halfway as I left. My legs ached from standing so long and I felt an impetus nudge of hunger from my stomach. I wanted to sit down and let my mind drift aimlessly from thought to thought. The pile of laundry on the sofa reminded me that sitting wasn't on the agenda, and there certainly wasn't any time available for aimless thinking either.

I prepared to tackle the list of chores by kicking off my shoes and plopping myself on the floor by the pile of unfolded towels clinging to the edge of the sofa. As my shoes flew across the room, I switched the television on with the remote and let the sounds of Oprah's voice soothe me.

Just a mere fifteen minutes or so into her discussion about love and relationships, I was brought out of my tranquility by a loud wail from Aubrey's room. She had been asleep for a measly twenty minutes, hardly a proper definition of a nap!

I retrieved Aubrey and sat her on the floor next to my unending pile of laundry. I would need to change her diaper, and Oprah was just finishing up a segment before she went to commercial break. Perfect timing! I had to know if the couple, whose marriage was on the rocks, was actually going to end up staying together. I hurried into Aubrey's room to grab the diaper changing necessities, and was back out into the living room within seconds.

I heard the commercials blaring as I laid Aubrey back onto the changing mat on the floor and started to change her diaper. Just as the commercial ended and Oprah's voice resumed on the television, I heard a choking sound from Aubrey. I hadn't given her anything to eat, so what was she choking on? I immediately lifted her and opened her mouth for examination. She had stopped gagging and was breathing normally so I was able to gently run my finger along the sides of her little mouth and then under her tongue. As my finger swiped below her tongue, it revealed the culprit. Out of her little mouth, I pulled my 'lucky penny.'

Part away from the midday masses
People streaming here and there
Come away, gently, feeling the solitude.
Grasping it into the night as it quietly passes.

D.L Clarke

Chapter 4

I tried letting the idea that there was something terribly wrong with Aubrey fade and disappear just as the engulfing valley fog had a few weeks prior, but it proved to be an impossible task. As the weather turned warmer and the sun shone brighter, my mood turned cold and dim. I was running out of hope and was giving into the idea that I may never be able to help her.

Aubrey was now nine months old and spring was doing it's springing. The warm months were definitely arriving, and though I was happy the gloominess of the fog was gone, there was another feeling that consumed me, panic.

The holidays had come and gone. Busy shoppers had long disappeared from the stores, the shelves had been restocked with wares for summer, and the roads were having a reprieve from the deluge of heavy and anxious traffic. Everything, in a sense, was back to normal and settled in ready for the embrace of summer. Except for me. I was still reeling from the madness of it all.

I summed up the whole holiday shopping fiasco as being my gaffe. I had been ill prepared, but I had to give myself a break. Then I thought about it more and gave Aubrey a break. I knew she hated malls. What had I been thinking anyway? There had been so many outings to take and every single one had turned into a disaster. All I ended up with was a few wrapped gifts and a stomach ulcer.

The routine of the holidays had become a new definition of stress. Every store we went to, Aubrey would scream and cry. Often, she wailed so loudly that shoppers would stop binging at the bargain bin and stare at us. As I would silently wish and beg for them to stop staring, they would blatantly demand that I "do something" to get her to calm down. Heck, I was open for suggestions, but did anyone have any that didn't involve "spanking the spoiled brat" or "making it shut up and sit still somehow?" No.

I thought I had been prepared for the challenges, but I wasn't. No matter what I thought we needed and packed accordingly for the outing, it was never the right thing, or there was never enough of the item to keep Aubrey content and quiet.

A box of animal crackers would last a few minutes and then there would be a tantrum the second the last rhinoceros had been consumed. I had thought one box would be enough, I was wrong. Once, the washcloth I had packed wasn't big enough to clean the messy off of her hands and once all the clean areas of the cloth had gotten sticky, it was useless, thrown aside, and another tantrum would ensue. I had packed the car full of her few favorite toy items to keep her busy, but they were later hurled forward into the front seat with me when we had to stop for gas on the way home.

Everything I did seemed to make her angry. If I tried to soothe her in a crowded store, she would buck against me and scream. Sometimes just entering a store would cause her to start screaming. Soon I became afraid to go out into the stores at all for fear of a huge public display. Even grocery stores were a nightmare and I would put off going until I absolutely had to.

I was thankful that I had gotten a few gifts purchased and mailed. I dreaded even thinking about the next holiday season, so I didn't. One moment, one hour, one morning, one afternoon, one night, one day, became the aphorism that kept me going. I couldn't bring myself to dwell on the what ifs and I didn't dare approach the notion that things would never improve. They had to get better. Aubrey was going to be fine, I reminded myself; she was going to be happy someday.

Baby girl, tell me
Why do you look so sad?
What in your life so far my child
Has been oh so bad?

D.L. Clarke

Chapter 5

Easter came and went, and the next big event on the calendar was Brittney's sixth birthday party in the middle of May. And, because I was completely insane and didn't want to "leave anyone out," we ended up inviting her entire first grade class of thirty kids, and even hired a clown for the big day. It amazingly went perfect to plan and without a hitch. Aubrey slept through the entire three-hour afternoon event.

As summer got into full swing, Aubrey's first birthday was on its way. There would be a party, but fortunately, since she was just a baby, there would be far fewer people to invite. That meant less of a crowd and hopefully a lot less chaos than Brittney's party.

Don't get me wrong, Brittney's party had been a blast, but with thirty kids under the age of six being chased by Bubbles the clown, you can probably imagine what the scene looked like!

Although I tried to not think too much about it, I was honestly worried about how Aubrey would handle having a party and being the center of attention. I considered not having a planned event at all, but was quickly chastised by Gwen and Janice.

"You have to have a party for her! I cannot believe you are even thinking of not having a party! Oh, my God!" Gwen had snorted at me one afternoon as she and Janice stood in my yard and then began interrogating me on the party details.

Janice had been equally aghast, but wasn't quite as animated as Gwen had been about the situation. When I tried to explain my reasoning, they just guffawed and said that I worried too much, and I needed to relax.

So, there would be presents, friends, a crowd of kids and, of course, a cake. I stopped short and thought about that. Baby's first birthday cake. I knew what was expected of babies on their first birthdays. It was tradition that the cake or a piece of the cake be sat in front of them and destroyed by their little hands. Of course it was always much more entertaining if the baby actually smeared the cake all over their clothing, and in their hair, ears, and nose.

I knew how Aubrey felt about messes and I also knew how she felt about crowds and noise. The party was a disaster in my mind before I had even considered whom to invite. Maybe Gwen and Janice were right? Maybe I was actually thinking too much about things and I just needed to relax? Trying to shove all the anxiety aside for the moment, I sat down at my kitchen table and started to write out the party guest list.

As I wrote down the names of my neighbors and friends, my mind drifted. I imagined the kids staring at Aubrey and crowding her while she opened her gifts. I saw neighbors and friends reaching for her expecting to give her a hug or hold her and being denied by her screams of objection. I imagined the cake scene and I shuddered. Wasn't everyone going to expect her to make a huge mess of her cake and smear it everywhere? Everyone would think I was being a neurotic mother if I didn't let my one year old have her way with a birthday cake.

First of all, did I really care what other people thought? Well, I did, sort of. I was tired of being judged by everyone, especially by everyone that seemed to have all the answers inside their parenting books. I realized then, as my mind snapped back out of its solitary sashay, that by Aubrey's first birthday, I was void of most of my confidence as a parent and was relying on mere instincts.

And just exactly what were my instincts telling me to do? They were screaming at me to protect her from everything that made her uncomfortable; to shield her from the people that made her scream in fear. They second guessed my natural sense of motherhood and re-directed me in a way that was unfamiliar. In order to get me to depend on them, they forced me to believe that they were right. My instincts had me convinced that they knew what was best. No one else wanted to listen or believe in them, so I had to.

I glanced down at the list I had scribbled and was startled by how many names I had managed to think of to invite. A whopping total of twenty-two names stared up at me and challenged my will. Panic almost settled in, until I examined the list and realized I had written some of the names as many as three times, in a row. I held my hand to my forehead and felt a huge sigh escape from my body. I needed a vacation.

Ribbons and bows, my love
All for you they say
But, take away the chaos and tape
For all that it is to you
Is a craziness that you cannot possibly take.

D.L. Clarke

Chapter 6

It was the morning of July tenth, and I was actually feeling confident and calm, not at all how I had expected to be feeling the day of Aubrey's first birthday party. She had been doing so well in the last few weeks that my confidence had begun to restore itself slowly and my mood was definitely encouraged by the progress we seemed to be making. The tantrums had slowed, or at least lessened their intensity, to where they were manageable, and I had actually had the opportunity to relax a little. I even had some free time on my hands to finish a novel I had started reading a couple of years prior and had been neglecting since. Things were looking up!

I couldn't have been more wrong. On the surface things appeared to be normal and I wanted to believe so badly that they were, but, as soon as the party had started outside in our yard, I couldn't ignore the look of panic that was growing on Aubrey's little face. Her eyes widened and she frowned when the kids crowded and gathered around her. When they hit the piñata and the candy spilled out, the kids screamed with glee, and Aubrey's anxiety seemed to grow. When they tried to push their gifts toward her, she cringed away from them and started to cry. I wanted to pick her up and take her into the quietness of our house, but I didn't.

Everyone kept laughing and telling me that she was just tired or was in a "bad mood," and that I shouldn't worry so much. 'I really needed to relax,' they would all chime in.

When it was time for the big cake moment, I carefully placed it on her high chair tray and stood back and waited. Aubrey stared at the offending treat on her high chair tray, then gingerly started to daintily pick at the very outer edges of the frosting. Being careful not to get any more frosting on her hands than absolutely necessary, she began to shove tiny blobs of it into her little mouth.

All the kids watched and giggled at her as she continued shoving more and more cake into her mouth. Then it happened. She caught a glimpse of her hands and saw that they were covered with sticky frosting and cake crumbs. As she started to cry and look dismayed at her hands, then down to her dress where more of the cake and frosting had landed, the crowd of party goers laughed and thought it was cute and funny that she was getting so upset.

"Look! Look! She wants to be so tidy like her mom!" I heard someone say while laughing and shoving a forkful of cake into their mouth.

"Yeah, better not get anything on her dress huh?" I heard someone else chiming in.

Oh God. I *was* neurotic. It *was* my fault that Aubrey was the way she was! I had created all of her problems by being such a neat nut, and everyone knew it. I would change, I convinced myself on the spot. No more Ms. Tidiness. No way. She had died and gone away as were all the washcloths at meal times. The need for routine would vanish out the window and we would become a very relaxed family. Wow. That had been so liberating.

It only lasted a moment, though, because my nagging gut cursed at me and dared me to second-guess it again. It seemed to have gotten really pissed off this time because I was in the process of discounting everything it had been trying to teach me thus far about my daughter.

"How dare I think that I am so powerful to create such a mess! Who the hell do I think I am anyway? Why does your daughter need a washcloth at every meal, huh? Do you think it is because *you* insist that she stay clean? Or is it because *she* insists on it?" My stomach churned and gurgled with glee as I reached for my stashed supply of antacids I had hidden on the gift table.

I thought about the answers to my gut's demanding questions as I chewed down some antacid tablets. Mmm. Tropical flavor, nice touch. Hum, I wonder what that flavor was? Papaya? No. I think mango. Yes, definitely mango. Suddenly I felt like a small child with a packet of lifesavers wondering what flavor I would come up with next. Pathetic how I let my mind wander away like that. I continued to pop the antacids into my mouth, chewing them until the grit was gone. They honestly needed to do something about that grit,

I thought as my tongue swirled in my mouth to retrieve all the particles.

Aubrey was screaming and wanted down from her high chair. I had succeeded in doing nothing to intervene for about ten minutes; it was all I could handle. I had waited long enough and I didn't care now what the crowd would think when I pushed them away to rescue my daughter.

Between the swarms of party guests, I could see Aubrey sitting in her high chair staring and screaming at her hands that were covered with white frosting. The crowd huddled more toward her and I could only catch brief glimpses of her face.

When I did finally get a good look and saw into her eyes, they told me all that I needed to know. I sat my bottle of tropical flavored antacids down, walked over to my daughter, released her from her high chair and took her inside our quiet house. I then proceeded to dutifully wipe her little hands and face clean of any traces of the offending cake.

Outside I could hear the continuation of the party while I changed Aubrey out of her little pink party dress and into some cooler shorts and tank top. Apparently one of the adults had ended up in the kiddy pool and while the parents were shrieking with laughter, the kids were yelling to each other to get the hose!

I heard the outside water faucet being cranked open and figured they were trying to replenish what the tsunami had destroyed. I chuckled to myself, thinking what might have taken place if I had actually given into Gwen's request for her "must have Corona's and lime" request for the party!

My thoughts were interrupted by the sounds of someone coming into the house and walking down the hall to where I was with Aubrey. I looked up to see a very wet partygoer come into view and as I grabbed a dry towel from the cupboard and handed it to him, he thanked me sheepishly.

"Having fun, Blaine?" I asked him with a smile as I continued to dress Aubrey.

"Yeah, but my wallet got all wet when I fell into the pool," he replied, laughing as he pressed the towel onto his clothes to dry them.

Hmmm, was about all I could think of to reply at the moment, so I said "hmmm..." and looked over at Blaine. He then replied that he needed to gather his kids and head home. His wife was going to kill him for getting his wallet wet, he added. I wondered silently why she would care, but I wished him good luck and thanked him for bringing his kids to the party. As he headed down the hall and out the door, he threw his head over his shoulder and quipped, "Same time and place next year?"

"Ha!" I hollered back trying to laugh without success. "You'll have to bring your swimming trunks next time!"

As I heard the front door slam shut behind him, I couldn't help but wonder what next year would be like and if we would actually still be living in the same house. Aubrey's dad was due to graduate from radiology school in the fall and we knew the chances of a move to a new base station were highly likely.

A hot wave of fear washed over me for a minute as I pondered the thought of moving. I immediately discarded the thoughts, picked Aubrey up off the changing table and took her back out into the sunshine and warm breezes of the afternoon.

Everyone was either getting ready to leave or was chasing kids down to prepare for their departure. I was happy that the event was finally winding down. Aubrey surely had had enough excitement for the day and I was feeling a little ragged myself. Glancing over at the pool, I could see where the "Blaine incident" had occurred.

Part of the pool frame was caved in and water flowed easily out and over the rim. I could hear Gwen and Janice laughing and going over details of the "fall," and when they saw me, they made their way through the departing guests and recounted the entire event for me. It was a "should have been there" event and it was a "so funny I almost wet my pants" occurrence, they both jabbered.

I couldn't help it, but I was a million miles away in my thoughts. I wanted to lay Aubrey down for a nap and there was a huge mess in the front yard that needed to be picked up. The piñata had strewn its candied guts out onto the lawn and there was paper ribbon everywhere. Whose idea was it to have a piñata anyway? I knew it had been my own, but it helped to think momentarily that possibly it hadn't been. I guess I hadn't realized they would make such a mess!

Janice saw the look on my face and I guessed that my despair was apparent, for she immediately suggested to Gwen that they help pick things up. I thanked Janice for offering and heard myself tell her that they really didn't have to help, I could do it.

"Yeah, riiiight!" Gwen scoffed at me. "You have to take your baby inside. Look at her, she is tired and even getting sunburned!" Janice and Gwen exchanged glances.

Oh God! I hadn't even thought of sunscreen in the chaos of getting everything ready! I looked at Aubrey's little face and saw that her cheeks were definitely pinker than they normally were and I immediately felt like I was failing again. How could have I forgotten something so important? Aubrey was so fair skinned that I always put sunscreen on her, even if we were going to only be in the sun for a short while.

"Damn! Damn!" I cursed to myself silently as I headed for my front door. I heard Janice telling me that she and Gwen would take care of everything outside and not to worry. I heard myself hollering a "thank you" over my shoulder and that I would be out again in a little while to help.

After rubbing some aloe into Aubrey's reddened cheeks and changing her diaper, I offered her a bottle, which she readily accepted. I then situated us in the rocker and ever so gently began to rock, barely moving from the force of my big toe pushing on the carpet. Aubrey's eyes started to fade and close as she drank her warm bottle of milk. I watched her face. All the earlier expressions of fear and anxiety had drifted away and were now replaced with calm and peacefulness. I watched as her little body sighed heavily and then fell into a deep sleep.

Brittney and her little friends were outside riding their bikes and I could hear them laughing and giggling as they raced around the cul-de-sac. I sighed and stood up as the sounds of laughter continued to filter into the living room.

I carried Aubrey down the hall and into her bedroom. After laying her down carefully in her crib, I walked back out into the living room and looked out the window. Brittney was zooming by on her little pink bike and there were about six kids following on their bikes. She had a big smile on her face as she turned and did a full circle before coming to a stop. I watched as the others followed and came to a stop in front of her. She was the leader today, I surmised.

I continued to watch out the window, and I caught a glimpse of Janice throwing a wad of paper into the trash container. I knew I should go out and help them, but it was so quiet and calm inside that I hated to relinquish it.

I glanced back over to where Brittney was sitting on her bike and saw that she was looking at me. Our eyes met for a second and she gave me a quick smile and then took off again on her bike, giggling as the pack struggled back onto their bikes to follow her.

She was a happy child, I was convinced of that. Her smile and laughter confirmed it. As I watched her glide around on her bike, I knew that I had done something right as a mom, and at that moment that was all I needed to know.

Chaos is here, I will have to admit
But what is to be had of the gentle spirit
That bites impatiently at the bit
Sitting in the stable silently waiting
Is the course of which the quiet one will sit.

D.L. Clarke

Chapter 7

Time seemed to stand still on some days, and fly by on others. Weeks quickly turned into months and the summer breezed by. After Aubrey's first birthday, things seemed to calm down a little and I was beginning to think that maybe she had just experienced a rough first year of life. It sounded logical enough, but then again, what would have made it so rough?

The doctor visits had all but diminished, other than her well baby checkups and immunizations, so the battle that I had been waging inside of my head weakened. I found that I was no longer so consumed with what I had done wrong or right as a parent and the lack of dissection felt wonderful. I had somehow convinced myself that I wasn't to blame for the unusual behaviors that Aubrey was experiencing and my degree of worry faded.

As the autumn days passed, and the tantrums lessened and became few and far between, I reassured myself that it had "just been a phase." It was good timing, for I had just discovered that I was expecting my third child. With the tantrums subsiding, I had confidence that things would be smoother and I would have an uneventful nine months of pregnancy.

Unfortunately, Aubrey's "calm phase" only lasted a few weeks, and the tantrums came back to life like a volcano waking after a few hundred years. My parents had come to California for vacation during the week of Thanksgiving and I linked the return of her tantrums to their visit. There was someone new in the house and Aubrey's routine had been thrown off.

There were new sounds and new people trying to play with her. Lunch was late sometimes and the wet washcloth that needed to be on the highchair tray *before* lunch was served had been late as well. I knew the lack of the washcloth could provoke a tantrum, but with all the distractions at times, it had gotten left temporarily behind.

It didn't take long for me to become frazzled and my confidence to all but disappear yet again. My parents kept asking me, "what was wrong with Aubrey. Why, being almost sixteen months old, doesn't she sleep through the night, and how come she cries all the time? Why did she walk on her tiptoes all the time?"

I didn't know how to answer them. I thought she had been doing so well, hadn't she? It didn't take long before the doubts started circling like vultures ready to pounce and rip me apart. What had happened? Why all the tantrums and sleepless nights again? Was it just because my parents were in the house? I secretly believed that was the reason, but I wisely kept that to myself.

On one of the days during their visit we all had gone into town to shop at the local mall. Aubrey screamed the entire ten miles into town. We were in my parent's car. It was a different car with different smells and I could see the look of panic on Aubrey's face the minute I buckled her into her car seat. I placed my hand on her little knee to try to comfort her and she kicked her leg and screamed until I removed my hand. There was no conversation in the car other than Aubrey's demands to "Get out! Get out, NOW!"

Once inside the mall, she continued to scream and struggled violently in her stroller trying to free herself from it. Everything I attempted to do to calm her just seemed to make her angrier. I knew if I let Aubrey out of her stroller, she would quickly flee on her tiny legs and be intermingled in the clothes racks and lost within seconds. I know this because I had mercifully released her from the stroller several times prior, only to have to go on a search and rescue mission within seconds of her escape. After I would finally find and retrieve her, it was then nearly impossible to get her back into the stroller.

Aubrey was a strong little thing and would do everything possible, which included kicking me in the face, to prevent herself from getting strapped in the stroller again, so I knew that letting her out of the stroller was not a sensible option.

Everyone who approached us had to stop and stare at the little toddler screaming and bucking madly, back and forth, in her stroller as if she was some featured display. Some even had the courage to ask what was the matter with her, and I retorted with the statement that she was almost two. That seemed to satisfy the crowd's need for an explanation, for the time being. But, the staring continued, no matter how much I silently begged for them to stop, their eyes would glare on.

It did not take us long before we all decided to call it a day and head back to the house. Brittney and her grandpa led the pack out of the mall and back into my parent's car. I wished that I had driven my car, at least Aubrey would have been more comfortable and they wouldn't have had to listen to her screaming. It was a bit unnerving and I could tell my dad wasn't too happy about all the screaming while trying to drive.

Aubrey was a sweaty mess and I was completely nauseous and rattled. My parents were trying to keep the conversation light, but I could tell from their faces that they were deeply concerned there was something very wrong with their youngest granddaughter. I knew the tantrums would subside once their visit was over, but again, I didn't tell *them* that.

After enduring another night of Aubrey's tantrums and her refusal to even attempt to sleep, my parents were packed up and ready to make the trek back to Oregon. They had had a wonderful time they said, although I highly doubted their claims. I felt exhausted, wiped out and very ready to have things get back to normal around the house.

Perhaps it was because my nerves were already on edge and worn thin, that, when my step-mom turned to me on her way out the door and asked, "Do you suppose Aubrey might be autistic?"

I replied hotly, without a moment's hesitation, that there was no chance that she was. What the hell was she thinking anyway? I immediately got very pissed off and really wanted them out of my house, now!

How dare they think that their granddaughter was somehow flawed? "Autism?" I snorted to myself. "No way!" My stomach turned and gnawed at me for a moment, then I realized that no, it was actually nagging, again.

I breathed a sigh of relief as I watched their car pull out of my driveway and be on its way. Aubrey had already started taking her nap and it wasn't even afternoon yet! See? Things were already going back to normal. I felt another twinge in my stomach and realized I hadn't eaten yet that morning. Yuck! A wave of nausea flooded over me and I felt the urge to vomit. Not being a happy-to-vomit type of person, I ran to the bathroom and struggled through deep breathing and heavy self-convincing that I was "just fine" until the wave subsided. It took almost an hour.

By the time I had composed myself and realized that I was never going to allow myself to throw up, Aubrey had awoken from her midmorning nap and was ready for some lunch; so was I. I retrieved Aubrey from her crib and we went into the kitchen to warm up some noodles. She was clinging to me tightly and I snuggled my arms around her little body. I heard her sigh and relax against me.

Somehow I knew she felt that everything was going to be okay now. The strangers had left and we were all back to normal. How odd was it that Aubrey's own grandparents seemed like strangers to her?

I pondered that thought while I started cooking the macaroni noodles on the stove. It was the same situation with Janice and Gwen though too, right? They saw Aubrey daily, and yet, after a year and four months, they were still people that she was not comfortable being around.

There was a chewing sensation in my stomach and though I tried to ignore it, it wouldn't go away. Dammit! It was definitely back. It was what my step mom had said, autism. Did I know much about autism and all it involved? If I allowed myself to think about it, would it make it real? And, did I want it to be real? No! I couldn't dive into the depths of what that word and possible diagnosis would entail.

I had seen the movie "Rainman" and knew that Aubrey wasn't even close to being like the character Raymond. It was really obvious in the movie that he was suffering from autism. Aubrey's behaviors weren't so obvious. There were hints of some similarities maybe, but nothing compared to Raymond.

There was nothing consistent with Aubrey's moods or behaviors. She could have really good days when she would laugh and somewhat interact with toys, and then there were really bad days when nothing made her happy. Instead of playing with her toys, she would sit and shred paper into tiny pieces. Although I desperately tried to figure out why her behaviors had shifted so drastically, there was nothing that I could ever pinpoint as the reason for setting her off.

Well, just hold on a minute now. What about when the washcloth wasn't on her tray at the beginning of a meal? Then, there was the fact that she hated to be messy. That was consistent, I knew of *those* things. Of course, there was the fact that she hated loud noises, shopping malls, grocery stores, and any type of change in routine.

My thoughts taunted me as I stirred the now burning noodles. Ugh! I was going to have to start lunch over again! I put Aubrey down on the carpet in the living room and went back into the kitchen to throw the burnt noodles out and start a new batch. As I reached into the cupboard to get another box of macaroni and cheese, Aubrey started to cry. I knew she was hungry and I felt bad for burning her lunch.

My stomach turned again and I had to run back into the bathroom for yet another cheerleading event to get myself talked out of vomiting. As I leaned over the toilet waiting for the inevitable, unless of course I was successful in my "prevent the vomit" breathing technique, which I almost always was, I could hear Aubrey's sobs turning into a raging fit. I hurled myself forward and let out a tiny little burp. Gawd! Pathetic. I couldn't even puke correctly!

With that, I hopped up, washed my hands and headed out of the bathroom, only stopping briefly to scoop up my wailing daughter, and continued onto the kitchen to prepare the second batch of noodles of the day.

Lagging on behind is the head that wants to follow
But waits, alas, for instruction.
Shall it come along, it always wants to know
But somehow solemnly, you always tell it no,
you are not ready, you try to explain
To hear the echoes vibrating within it
that only seem resonate your pain deep within its hollow.

D.L. Clarke

Chapter 8

Things didn't go back to normal after my parent's departure. If anything, they got worse. Aubrey was awake all-night and screamed and cried for the better part of the daylight hours for weeks. The weeks soon turned into months and before we were ready for it, we were loaded in the car and moving to Washington State, courtesy of the U.S. Navy.

Though I was a bit apprehensive about the huge change, I couldn't help but be excited as well. We had lived in Lemoore, California, for two years and in San Diego for four months before that, so we were happy to get back up into the Pacific Northwest and closer to our home state of Oregon.

Brittney was excited to live closer to grandma and grandpa, so there were a lot of positive things about the big move that sort of outweighed the negative, for the time being anyway.

The only obvious downside was that Aubrey's dad was going to be stationed on a ship in Bremerton, Washington, rather than at the hospital on shore duty, which had been his assignment in Lemoore. And, I suppose you know without me telling you, but I will anyway, the ships go out to sea for several months at a time.

I was a bit worried about taking care of the kids all by myself, but I knew that I didn't have a choice and was mentally trying to prepare for it. I accomplished this task easily by sticking my head deep into a sand pit and not thinking about it. I found that using this tactic was quite useful if used sparingly and you remembered to pull your head out before getting trampled. Yes, better to be blindsided and almost trampled, than spend your time worrying.

Upon our arrival into Bremerton, we ended up being one of the fortunate few families that received military housing without having to be put on a waiting list. We settled quickly into a three-bedroom townhouse that happened to be just up the street from where Darrin's brother and sister-in-law, Kyle and Tanya, lived! They were also a military family and, like Darrin, Kyle was also stationed on a ship.

They had two kids of their own which were about the same ages as ours, and we often ended up spending time picnicking together and we took turns having each other over to our homes for dinner and games.

I also appreciated the companionship, especially once the Naval ships set sail taking our husbands with them. I came to rely on getting together with Tanya, when we could, for walks in the evening as well as the brief trips we took to the park with our kids. It was also really nice having someone to talk to.

Although it took a few weeks for our furniture and belongings to arrive, we seemed to be settling in and making do without it, for the time being, and things were falling into somewhat of a routine.

Brittney got started at her new school and was quickly on her way to making new friends. Darrin was working every day on the ship preparing for a two-month outing, and I was frantically learning the ins and outs of the city in my attempt to memorize all the crucial locations.

The grocery store, gas station, and ship dock were all at the top of my list. I had a way with maps, which included not using them, so my best bet in the learning process included getting lost quite frequently and then, by some grace of God, eventually finding my way back to my townhouse. It wasn't the most efficient of methods, but it worked, and I was soon buzzing around the city running errands like I had lived there all of my life. Well, that might be a slight exaggeration.

I was quite pleased on one of my location discovery outings to find that the hospital and doctor's offices that we would be utilizing were within a few blocks of our house. It turned out to be very convenient, especially since we owned just one car and I would often end walking to several appointments.

One of our first visits to the doctor's office was for an appointment to have Aubrey's ears checked. She had been tugging at her ears all morning and I thought it would be best to have them checked in case there was an infection. I made the call to the pediatrician's office and was told to come right in.

Armored with the statement that they would "get us right in," I felt that we were definitely off to a good start with the new doctors. I was excited to meet her new pediatrician, actually. I was still a little apprehensive, however, thinking back sullenly to some of the experiences we had with the doctors in California. We needed a change and I desperately wanted some new opinions on some of my concerns about Aubrey.

Darrin had taken the car that day, so Aubrey had to ride in her stroller, which she was actually beginning to tolerate somewhat, but only on her good days. I was hopeful that the stroller ride that morning would go smoothly, since I was getting hugely pregnant and didn't want to contend with a squirming, kicking, and screaming sixteen-month old that refused to ride in her stroller.

Letting Aubrey walk was not an option, in case you were wondering why I didn't just go with that mode of transportation. She still possessed an uncontrollable desire to run, quite quickly, as far away from the stroller as possible without so much as a look back or a single thought to the traffic zooming by. She was also not fazed one bit by my hollering for her to "come back right now!"

As luck would have it, the stroller ride went well and we ended up a few minutes later at the receptionist desk of Aubrey's new pediatrician. Since we were worked into the doctor's schedule, she informed us then that we might have to wait "awhile," but she would "do her best to get us right in." My hopeful mood sort of slipped a notch or two, but I reassured the receptionist that I understood and Aubrey and I took a seat in the waiting room. I offered to read a book to Aubrey and she happily went along with my idea.

We ended up waiting an unmerciful amount of time finishing off several story books, and both Aubrey and I were getting very restless by then. We had gotten up earlier than usual, since sleep had been interrupted several times the night before, which was not uncommon, and it had proven to be less frustrating to just get up and start the day rather than toss and turn trying to manufacture sleep.

The morning seemed horribly long because of the unusually long wait, and breakfast seemed like it had been ages ago. My stomach let out a loud signal that it was very ready for something to fill it. Aubrey heard it and twisted in her chair, hopping down to get another book. She loved books and I was silently thanking the staff for having such a large selection available. Truly it was the least they could do for making us wait for so long, I silently added.

Glancing at my watch, I saw that it was almost noon which in translation meant, lunchtime. The timing couldn't have been worse. You don't mess with lunchtime as far as Aubrey was concerned. Not that she actually liked the *eating* part of lunch so much, she just loved to *ask* to eat a lot. When I say a lot, I truly mean repetitively, sometimes as much as forty times in the span of an hour or so.

The confusing part of that whole thing was she often would start asking to eat right after she finished eating! So, when she was told she couldn't eat again until the next snack time, she would fly into a rage and demand food even more loudly. I cringed thinking about what might be in store if a physician's ear scope didn't distract us in the next few minutes.

It was not my lucky day after all. We ended up waiting past the noon hour and well into Aubrey's "after lunch" potential naptime. Aubrey had started demanding food, and I was at my wits end after she had asked for the eighth time in the course of a few minutes to *eat!*

I had begun to sweat and I somehow knew I most likely looked like a wet, sweaty, goon in a bulky fuchsia colored maternity sweater. Not a good color choice when you are hugely pregnant, trust me. This only added to my anxiety and I pondered the ramifications if I were to suddenly demand that we either see the doctor this minute or we would walk out. I scolded myself knowing that they really didn't care if I walked out and they were not going to give into my demands to see the doctor before he was ready for us.

Surely their waiting room would be much more peaceful without the squalling toddler demanding food over and over, and the doctor would have a little bit longer of a lunch if we deserted our appointment. Still, I decided to wait him out, screaming toddler and all.

I was so buried in the vocal demands for food from my toddler and my own thoughts of escaping the waiting room, that I barely heard the nurse call Aubrey's name. Another glance at my watch told me that we had waited for almost two hours for the appointment. I was amazed Aubrey and I had stuck it out this long. It was nearly 1:30 p.m. and way past potential lunch and naptime.

The day's schedule was blown to pieces, but it had had to be done. You didn't risk not treating an ear infection. I had read that bit of info in the "Childhood Illnesses" book. See? And you guys thought I was *just* relying on pure instinct and my nagging gut!

As it turned out, Aubrey did *not* have an ear infection and was in perfect health, other than the obvious sniffling that I tried to explain to the doctor had come from the trauma caused from lunch being late, not a cold. I was told to watch for cold and flu symptoms anyway. As we left the office, and headed outside, I added his bit of cautious advice to the brisk wind that was now blowing from the north.

The exam had gone as expected. Quick and non informative. Back at home, I thought about the visit as I made Aubrey's lunch. The new doctor hadn't time to hear of my list of things that concerned me and I was firmly told that if I had further discussions that I needed to make another appointment. I gently sat Aubrey into her booster seat and watched as she readily gobbled down her sandwich.

Poor little thing. I felt bad for the morning's outing, but how was I to know that her ears were okay? I wasn't a doctor, but secretly wished I were, but then again, not really. I did know that it was a really good thing that the military doctor's visits were, how do I say this eloquently, *free* to military families, or I would have seriously thrown a gasket or ruptured some vital organ.

There had been no time to discuss anything other than Aubrey's perfectly healthy ears and potential cold and flu she was apparently coming down with. Okay! I would just have to wait and do as he said and make another appointment. I could do that. I didn't work. I had nothing better to do with my time than sit in doctor's offices and wait… and wait…and wait.

So that would become my new profession, "mother who sits in doctor's offices waiting." My humor truly was becoming an annoyingly sarcastic trait that I was actually beginning to rely on to get me through the day. It rarely let me down, and today was no exception. I allowed a small giggle to escape my lips, and then stuffed them full of animal crackers.

Would it shatter you to not have the answers I seek?
Or would it not be bothersome
If my questions rendered you weak?
Please just tell me something, if you can
That will calm my aching heart
Be honest for I believe I am reaching for something tangible
Though you might see it differently
being oh so very, very far.

D.L. Clarke

Chapter 9

Within three weeks of our arrival into Bremerton, Aubrey's dad was shipped out to sea for two months. It was some sort of "practice" drill, preparing the crew and ship for the three-month tour in the early summer. We knew it was coming, but we were hardly prepared for it. All of our household belongings had been delivered just a few days prior and the evidence was still scattered throughout the house.

I only had the opportunity to go through just a few of the boxes and unpack, but most were still tucked in corners or stacked down our hallway. It was a cluttered chaotic mess, and, needless to say, I was freaking out. There was so much to do, and I was feeling very tired and lacked motivation to even start the daunting tasks of getting the girls' beds put together, let alone mine.

It didn't take me too long to change my mind, however. One more sleepless night on Aubrey's part, and I was knee deep in bed frames and nuts and bolts. The rest of the house followed suit, one box at a time until it was finally all in place.

"I can rest now," I exclaimed out loud with an over exaggerated sigh. It was a nice thought for a second, but it only lasted a second.

Brittney and Aubrey had both been vying for my undivided attention during my frantic unpacking phase, and I felt bad for not having the ability to grow several more arms so that I could provide them both, simultaneously.

But I, not being a member of the starfish family, quickly forgave myself and carried my expanding belly into the kitchen to go make dinner.

Aubrey's behavior had gotten understandably worse during the time it took me to get the house put together. I chalked it all up to me not being as attentive as I should have been. There were hourly tantrums on most of the days and many sleepless nights that accompanied them. I desperately tried getting things back into a routine that we could rely on, but it seemed impossible.

Walks to the park were tossed aside due to a tantrum, as were the very much needed trips to the grocery store. It was just easier to stay inside and out of the public eye than to take her out and have the judgmental stares and comments from people passing by.

Most mornings would start with Aubrey screaming from her bed at six o'clock, after being awake for most of the night. When I didn't retrieve her, she would climb out of her bed and stand at the baby gate across her door and shake it violently. The screaming fits would eventually wake Brittney up, thus would begin our morning.

I had tried both responding to and ignoring the tantrums and screaming in the early morning hours, but neither had worked, and as usual, I was out of ideas. My third child was due in a few short months so I *had* to get a handle on this; but how?

I was thankful Aubrey's next pediatric visit was just a few days away. I knew I *had* to get some answers and advice and I also had decided that I wasn't going to leave his office without it. After a few long days and a very short car ride to the pediatrics office, Aubrey and I once again found ourselves in the ever-so-familiar pediatric waiting room.

We chose our seats and sat down. I couldn't help but notice that Aubrey had chosen the very same set of chairs we had sat in a couple of weeks ago. Rather cute, I thought. As she hopped up on my lap to read the book she had grabbed from the table, I realized that it too was the same book we had read during our last visit. Again, I thought it was cute. That was just Aubrey. She just liked things to be the same.

Once that book was done, she hopped down and grabbed another book. I have no clue if it was the same book as in the previous sequence, but knowing my daughter, it probably was. We only had time for two books that day, for we were called back in a remarkably short amount of time. The doctor was also quick to arrive after we got settled into the exam room and had explained the reason for our visit to the nurse.

"What is the reason for today's visit?" I heard him ask me as I watched him reading over the nurse's notations of 'our reasons for today's visit.'

"Well, it is the same set of problems that I was wanting to discuss with you a few weeks ago," I sort of stammered. I knew I had to pull this off by sounding professional, not dim-witted and unintelligent and I also realized that I was not off to a good start.

Clearing my throat, I continued, "My daughter has behaviors that really concern me."

"Such as?" the doctor quizzed, scratching his graying head of hair.

"Well, I am worried about her walking on her toes all the time. That can't be good, can it?" I hesitated momentarily before continuing. "There are times that she will sit on the floor and stare off into space for long periods of time. I can't seem to get through to her when she is like that. I try to ask her questions, but she just looks right through me without answering. No matter what I say or do, I can't get her to respond to me and it almost seems like she doesn't hear me. I have had her hearing checked, so I know her ears are fine. She hates the radio on in the car most of the time, but sometimes she actually *likes* the stereo on at home, but most of the time not." I hesitated for a moment, realizing I probably wasn't making much sense at this point. But, after seeing the doctor's gaze intently on mine, I continued.

"She won't sleep for more than a couple of hours at a time, and she has tantrums, which are more like rage attacks." I stated glancing over to the doctor to make sure he was listening. He was. "She asks for food constantly even after she just ate, and she often sits and shreds paper into tiny little pieces for no apparent reason. She also likes to crush crackers or bread into minuscule crumbs, and again I don't know why." I paused, then to let that all soak in and watched as the doctor scribbled hurriedly in Aubrey's chart.

"Is there anything else?" he asked, looking up from the chart. Worry struck me then. Did there *need* to be anything else? Wasn't *that* enough to raise some serious alarm? Uh, apparently not.

But, I did have more concerns and I poured them out in a jumbled mess of questions and statements: Why did she scream when I gave her a bath and touched her head? And why would brushing her hair send her into a shrieking fit? I used de-tangle spray and I was so very careful, but still, she would scream as though I was pulling it all out!

What about the fact that she did not like being messy? She was a toddler; don't most toddlers enjoy getting their hands into messes? Everywhere we went, she had to have her hands rinsed and dried thoroughly after contacting something sticky or messy. She would scream and flap her hands on the sides of her legs until I could figure out a way to get them cleaned. I learned pretty quickly to bring along wipes and dry towels whenever we left the house.

Aubrey also hated her car seat, despised riding in her stroller, screamed continually while at the mall or grocery store, didn't like to look at me when I talked to her, and didn't enjoy being held or touched. I finished up with, "There are just too many things that don't make any sense, aren't there?" I then took a deep breath and waited. I almost felt lighter somehow, as if some of the weight had shifted off of me.

The doctor seemed to have listened intently to everything I had said and after taking several painful minutes writing and thinking, he finally started to speak.

"I would like to recommend that you take a visit to our onsite library and check out these books that I have listed here for you," he said reaching forward to hand me the list. Looking down at the book titles listed I saw, through the tears welling up in my eyes, the words *defiant child, difficult child, hyperactivity, attention deficit, and stubborn* all mixed up in a jumbled heap of ink.

Didn't he know that I had already read most of the books about difficult, defiant, stubborn, and hyperactive children? Did he think I was a resourceless moron? It was obvious this visit was not going to be of any help and it was a huge waste of time. I almost laughed when, as I was leaving, the doctor requested that I schedule a followup visit in case the books didn't provide any relief.

Since that had been the first *official* time that I had taken Aubrey in to see her pediatrician with *the list of things that concern me*, I shouldn't have been surprised to receive in return the list of books to read that would cure her problems along with several hundred other ailments, including, I am sure, world hunger, but I was.

I was realizing quickly that the doctor didn't have any more clues as to what was going on with my daughter than what I did. On my way out, I went ahead and scheduled a followup appointment, knowing damn well the books would not be providing any immediate relief.

Several more weeks passed and as Aubrey's dad returned from sea we made another attempt to get into a normal routine. However, no matter how organized or settled we tried to be or thought we were, Aubrey's tantrums just kept getting larger, louder, and longer.

At each consecutive pediatric appointment, the doctor would reassure me that he "would get to the bottom of it." Aubrey and I would then be promptly shuffled to the door, along with an armful of "helpful" books, and scheduled for yet another "followup" appointment. I was beginning to think I should qualify for some sort of frequent visitor's award, or red carpet program, or even just a VIP pass at the clinic, but sadly, none was ever offered.

Occasionally, Aubrey's pediatrician would invite another colleague of his into the exam room to offer their professional opinion. Unfortunately, they would become baffled within a few minutes and the questions would re-emerge.

"Have you read some of the terrific books about children with difficulties and different temperaments?" When I reassured them that I had in fact read *all* of the books, what else was I supposed to do in the wee hours of night when my daughter was flipping light switches off and on repeatedly, they would cast a doubtful eye my direction and ask, "Do you have any *other* children?" To this question, I would then answer, "Yes I do. I have another daughter that is five years older than Aubrey, and she is actually quite a happy child and seems perfectly content."

End of story. That would pretty much baffle them and they would shuffle me on my way home with a dumbfounded look and remark that I should call in a couple of months if the books didn't help.

The problem was that Aubrey never fit the description of any of the children that were described in the books they recommended. *Some* parts and descriptions would make sense, and I would think that I was really onto something, but there were so many other behaviors Aubrey had that never fit into any specific category.

Perhaps I had missed something in one of the books? Maybe in my haste to absorb as much as possible I had skipped over something crucial? I hated doubting myself, but I was getting so good at it. I would reread the books on the list, all of them, I told myself with determination.

What is lacking, can be learned
What has been learned, utilized
What is it then
That cannot be tapped?
Is it the stubborn entity that claims itself to be
Within itself true,
But undeniably trapped?

D.L. Clarke

Chapter 10

So, on one sunny afternoon, after laying Aubrey down for a nap, I plopped down on the couch and flipped open the first book I grabbed from the shelf. It happened to be *The Difficult Child*, by Stanley Turecki, M.D. After staring at the table of contents and deciding to re-read *Part One: Some Children Are Born Different*, I took a deep breath and flipped to page number eleven.

Matthew has trouble going to sleep at night and staying asleep. Trying to get him to go to bed in his own room can provoke a pitched battle.

After silently agreeing that my child *did* seem to fit *that* description so far, I continued on reading skimming and searching for any information that would be useful to me.

Whether laughing or crying he is always very loud. He gets revved up very easily, especially in a noisy room filled with people or in brightly lit stores and markets. In the playground he gets overexcited and can push or hit other children. His mother is very embarrassed by such behavior but finds it hard to be firm because she's not sure of herself.

Yes, again I could relate to this situation and I felt comforted that I wasn't the only mother out there that had some of the same feelings that I did. I continued to flip through the pages until another paragraph caught my eye.

But Rachel can do more than just cry and cling. She will, at times, publicly tantrum, and her mother does not know how to handle that. She stands by helplessly as her child "makes a scene." Simple transitions from one activity to another can cause power struggles—"

I put the book down in my lap for a moment and thought about what I had just read. Aubrey had a lot of the same behaviors that these children did. So how did *they* get "cured?" I knew the answer to that question and hated even asking it.

Behavior modification. That is how they were cured, simple as that. In fact, after reading through to the bottom of the page, I was reassured that the *difficult child* is not *abnormal*. It didn't mean that they were emotionally disturbed, or mentally ill either. I was also reassured not to take into account the comments from well-meaning relatives that "*something must be wrong with her.*" I felt my grip tighten on the book and I firmly decided that I would use the last line of page fourteen as my new mantra. "*Difficult is very different from 'abnormal.'*"

I continued to thumb through the book trying to ignore the headache that was coming on strongly. I couldn't help but realize that none of the children in the book walked on their toes, disliked being held or touched, repeated certain words over and over, continually asked for food and water, or had episodes of no communication. Maybe I had missed a page or two? Perhaps I had overlooked a crucial paragraph?

Nonetheless, I was rapidly beginning to realize that I was dealing with a child that was very complex and not just simply difficult. We would obviously have to attend yet another "non-successful, followup to the useless books," pediatric appointment. I got up, scheduled the appointment, and in a few days that seemed to last forever, we found ourselves back in the doctor's office.

After looking over Aubrey's chart like he had seen it for the very first time, (I later concluded that he was just stalling) he finally blurted out that he had come to the realization that whatever was wrong with my daughter, was "out of his hands." He said he was going to refer us to someone "who might have a better grip on things."

It was then, directly after that statement that he began to inform me that my daughter was definitely a very different child. It was then that I heard that she should never be expected to dance or play, talk or walk right, and should absolutely never attend a regular school.

It was then that he stated he didn't know what else he could do to help me because he didn't know what was wrong. All he did seem to know was what he thought Aubrey never could or would do. She was just eighteen months old, and was apparently already being considered hopeless by her pediatrician.

I don't even remember the trip home from that appointment, nor do I remember the doctor handing me the business card that I shoved into the now stuffed full junk drawer the second I got in my door. All I really remember is the rage I felt and the agony of utter helplessness that consumed me.

There never was going to be an answer that could magically turn things around. But, I couldn't even fathom the idea that things would never get better, that Aubrey would never be happy. I remember the heavy blanket of helplessness engulfing me as the questions and doubts swirled in my head.

What was wrong with my daughter? Why couldn't anyone figure it out? Her pediatrician recommended that I get her "mental state" tested. That comment had immediately made me mad, no, let's not diminish this; pissed me off, and I was in total shock. Mentally my daughter was *fine, wasn't she?* It definitely had nothing to do with her "mental state," did it? Why wasn't he able to realize that she was just probably suffering from the terrible two's syndrome?

As the weeks passed and nothing seemed to be improving at all, I would go to the "junk drawer" and look through all the medical professional's business cards I had collected. There were so many! After looking over several of them, I would always shut the drawer, with all its contents intact.

Although I would consider calling one of the recommended professionals, I never actually could, yet. I was so tired of being scrutinized and picked apart, and seeing Aubrey getting poked and stared at like a zoo animal was getting very frazzling as well.

It seemed like I wasn't getting any closer to discovering anything that would help and it was exhausting dragging my daughter all over trying to find something that possibly didn't even exist. I was coming to the conclusion that there wasn't anyone out there in the professional world that could help. I was just going to have to find a way myself.

Every month that passed became a huge accomplishment for me. "Yeah! I didn't lose my mind this month! "Yippee!" or "Wow! I can't believe we actually got through almost a whole month with only a few nights of sleep! Amazing!" Crossing the days off on the calendar at the end of the day had turned into a ritual. Every day that was crossed off represented another twenty-four hours that I had gotten through without the assistance of a "professional" and/or their advice. The big X's on the calendar also encouraged me that everything was going to work out and Aubrey was going to be okay.

But, just when I had gotten comfortable with the new calendar ritual, (I had even purchased a new set of jazzy pens for making the X's), the doubts began to resurface.

It was shortly after Brittney and Aubrey's little brother, Austin, had been born. I was sitting on the living room floor, Austin was sleeping in his little bouncy chair, and Aubrey was flipping through a picture book. It was serene and calm and I had really convinced myself by now that all along I had just been over analyzing things.

I mean, seriously, since I had been trying the technique of not reacting too much when Aubrey acted out, things had been going a bit smoother, well somewhat, I think. I also knew that because I had been stressing out over her actions that maybe I had actually *caused* some of the bad behavior on her part. It is funny how we try to explain things away, and make it make sense somehow. But at that minute, it did all make sense to me. Things were going to be *fine*.

I smiled as I watched Brittney playing in the backyard with the neighbor girls. Things were so peaceful at that moment and I allowed calmness to completely engulf me. But, the very second that it completely wrapped around me, Aubrey rose from the floor, marched over to her brother, grabbed at his face with her little hand and squeezed.

It happened like lightning, striking out when you least expect it and choosing the most vulnerable thing around. Austin immediately woke up and started screaming, Aubrey began shrieking, I ran to get a cloth for the wound, and Brittney dropped her dolls and came crashing into the house.

As I stood holding a cloth to Austin's forehead to stop the bleeding, I tried to comprehend what had just happened and how everything turned into such a chaotic mess so quickly. I had not been fast enough. I had not been able to foresee and prevent this from happening. I pulled the cloth away from Austin's forehead and observed the scratch. It was deep and long, centered between his two eyes. I took a deep breath, thankful that the attack had not damaged his eyes. Austin was calming down to sniffles and I was able to bandage the wound. I was shaking, as Brittney looked at me and then over to her little sister in disbelief.

I had to discipline Aubrey. I had to show her what she had done and that she had hurt her baby brother. There needed to be a consequence for her actions. Being one of those parents that do not like to spank, (it just never made sense to me to tell a child not to hit, and then proceed to hit *them)*, I had to figure out another method of punishment that would get through to Aubrey.

Time out, as we previously established, did not work, and yelling was pointless. So, I decided to talk to her, and try to explain that what she had done was wrong and hurtful. I know, she was only a two year old, and two year olds are not really too predictable and do crazy things, but I still had to do *something*.

Aubrey had retreated to her bedroom and was in the process of tossing her stuffed animals from one bin to another pile across her room. I got down on the carpet and started to talk to her calmly as I could, still shaking.

"Aubrey, do you know that Austin has an ow-wee now?" I asked. She kept tossing her stuffed animals, avoiding all eye contact with me. This time I was firmer with my speech.

"Aubrey! Look at Mommy!" I was getting anxious. There was no response from her. I did not exist. "It is not nice to hurt your brother," I said as I went over to her and stopped the migration process of her stuffed animals. She defiantly grabbed another animal and tried to toss it to the other side of the room. I stopped the baby lion in mid-air and firmly sat Aubrey down on the edge of her bed.

"Do not touch your brother," I stated bluntly. Her face was right in front of mine, but she would not look at me. Her brown eyes were glassy and there was a distant look to her face. "Did you hear me, Aubrey?" I asked, standing up. I had to leave to go and check on Austin. He had begun to cry again and it was obvious that I was not getting anywhere with Aubrey right then.

I hurriedly made it down the steps and back to where I had left Austin in the living room. The bandage had soaked through and needed to be replaced. As I went into the kitchen to retrieve another band-aid from its box, I glanced in the direction of the "junk" drawer. As soon as I had replaced Austin's bandage, I found myself pawing through the drawer in earnest.

I had made a promise to myself long ago when the very first problems had started to surface, that I would do absolutely everything, exhausting all means, if that is what it took to help my child. My pride marched out the door, taking the marked up calendar and jazzy pen set with it. I firmly decided not to let them back in, at least not yet.

You say you have the answers
To all that I question.
But what I query you with
Is not all that I lack.
For what I need most from your answers
Is the meaning behind the subject I question
Not just your facts.

D.L. Clarke

Chapter 11

"What brings you into my office today?" The child psychologist wanted to get right to the point. That was good, because I was prepared. I pulled *the list of things that concern me* out of my purse and gave it to him. This doctor did not waste any time, thank God since it had cost me my right arm, okay, let's not be frugal, my left arm as well, to see him!

He asked a million questions, which was great, I was very much into explaining everything to him and he seemed truly interested. I kept my guard up, however, waiting for him to reach over to one of the stuffed bookshelves that adorned his beautifully lush office, and hand me a *great* book on "how to be a proper parent." It didn't happen. Hmmm. I was impressed, so far.

He asked me if Aubrey was a "planned child" and yes, I assured him that she was. It was an *uneventful birth,* if you can call a cesarean *uneventful.* It had something to do with a hip condition, I explained, so it had not come as a shock to anyone when Aubrey was also delivered surgically. I also reassured him that I had never smoked and I had made sure that I didn't even drink caffeine while I was pregnant.

I had taken all of my vitamins ritually, even when they made me feel like I wanted to puke. And, I had listened to classical music. I read somewhere, in one of the other million books I read *before* Aubrey was born, that classical music is "supposed" to make your baby smart. I left nothing to chance. I did it all.

After asking the millionth question, and writing down pages and pages of information that I was feeding him, he asked if I would leave the room.

"Just me or—" I was not able to finish before he interrupted me.

"Yes, just yourself, please, I need to observe Aubrey without *the mother* in the room," he stated, obviously unaware of my heightened anxiety at the thought of leaving my daughter alone in a strange place with a stranger.

"She will be fine, ma'am, I just need to do some observations and you will be brought back in within a few minutes." He looked up at me and gave me a hurried half smile. I was wasting time with my stammering. Shame on me! Now move it!

I gathered my purse and asked for my *list of things that concern me* back before leaving the room. He reassured me that he would have his receptionist make a copy. With that, I left the room and went through the notorious professional's office maze, and found myself back out in the waiting room.

I passed the time by watching the fish in the overcrowded tank swimming around frantically. I wondered if they were all mentally stable, and immediately after *that* thought, wondered if *I* was mentally intact.

Gazing around the room at the other "patients," I wondered why they were there. No one had a child with them. He was a child psychologist after all. It was a valid thought. I sat back and continued to watch the fish while I kept my ears on alert listening for screams from down the hall where I had left Aubrey.

After what seemed too long for my liking, a nurse-like person opened the door and let me back in to the room where I had left Aubrey and the psychologist. Aubrey was sitting at a desk that was covered with plastic numbers on it, staring out a nearby window.

"Hi, Aubrey!" I said, letting her know I was back. There was no response. I sat down in the chair across from the psychologist and waited for him to begin talking. I heard him sigh heavily as I sat my purse on the floor.

As I looked up at him, searching for answers, he leaned forward and handed me some papers. I though it was odd that he had not said a word up until this point. He must have been deep in thought, I presumed. He began to talk as I looked at the numbers and enormously long, complicated words on the page, trying to decipher what they meant.

"Aubrey is a special kind of child, like a puzzle, if I can refer to her as that?" I supposed he was going to whether I wanted him to or not. He moved slowly forward in his chair and I thought for a second he was going to whisper something to me, instead he slapped his hand down on his desk and leaned into it. He seemed to be searching for words, thinking ever so deeply.

Another sigh, this time even heavier than the first. He was a very large man, and the sigh seemed to envelope the room. It made me nervous and tense.

"We need to do some more testing. I would like to administer the Stanford-Binet, and the Boyd Developmental Progress Scale can be performed as well," he stated. I had read about these tests, but did not really know exactly what they were and how they would help, but I was willing to give them a try and find out how Aubrey would do.

As directed, the testing was completed, and two weeks later we were back in the psychologist's office waiting to hear the results. Aubrey was called back almost immediately upon our arrival, and I was asked to remain in the now familiar waiting room.

As I sat and waited, I again watched the fish swimming in the tank. I knew that the tank had been strategically placed there to help people in the waiting room relax, but there was no chance they could help me relax at all today. My hands were cold and I had that nervous clammy feeling all over my body. I could feel my heart beating quickly and loudly against my chest.

I knew that quite possibly, this could be the day that I found out what was going on with my child. I had high hopes, but I was also fearful of what they might find. I tried to shove all the "what ifs" away and continued watching the fish. One was swimming maniacally around the tank; I *knew* there was an insane fish in there somewhere.

"You can come on back now," the nurse-like person said as she beckoned me to follow her. She never smiled and I couldn't help but wonder if she liked her job.

This time I was directed to a different room, and once inside, I realized that Aubrey was in another room behind one-way observation glass. I could see her sitting at a small table with a woman that was handing her toys and wooden blocks. As she grasped the objects from the lady, Aubrey had no expression on her face and was completely silent.

"That is part of the Boyd Developmental Progress testing. She completed it last week, of course, but we are just seeing if she will interact differently with another tester," the psychologist said as he entered the room.

"It doesn't appear as though Aubrey will interact with anyone today. No eye contact, no verbal responses, it makes it very difficult to reach accurate results," he continued.

"However, on the Boyd testing, she did come out, as far as we can tell, in the appropriate limits for her age," he stated as he sat at his desk and roamed through piles of paperwork.

"Okay," I heard myself begin to speak and I wanted to sound professional and knowing, but not having really a clue what he was talking about.

"So, that part is good then, the motor skills are okay at this point?" I was stammering slightly, watching my daughter sit in silence staring at a block in the other room.

"Like I said, with her not responding and interacting, it is difficult to get accurate results, but this is what the Boyd scores show as of last week. Also, her Stanford-Binet was unscorable due to the fact Aubrey could not obtain a basal score," he cleared his throat and sighed deeply again.

I wanted him to stop sighing. It was *really* beginning to get on my already frazzled nerves. I felt myself tensing up and becoming cold all over. What did that mean? Why couldn't she attain a basal score? What was a basal score anyway? I wished I had paid more attention to some of those nonsensical books!

"What does all of this mean?" I asked finally.

The psychologist proceeded to inform me again that she was indeed a "puzzle" and he could not figure out what was causing the rage attacks, the hitting, the kicking, the biting, the periods of time where she would not speak. He paused and then continued in a confused voice stating that he didn't know why all the child management strategies had been proven ineffective. He said he was sorry and that he truly wished he could be of more help.

As far as I was concerned, he should have stopped right there, but he had more to say, yep, he definitely needed to finish this thing up. A chill coursed down my back as he went on to say that perhaps my child, my little Aubrey, was the youngest child schizophrenic that he had ever encountered.

He also thought, in his professional opinion of course, that perhaps she would be better off if *the father* and I would place her in an institution. (I am sure that *the father*, who at the time, was across the ocean in the Persian Gulf, wouldn't have minded *me* making that decision on my own.) As *if* I were to even consider it!

He carried on as if I weren't even sitting in his office, explaining in the next breath that perhaps Aubrey was, "what he liked to call" an opposite polar, or in simpler terms, "bi-polar." The fine doctor also wanted me to carefully consider the possibility that Aubrey could be suffering from a multitude of disorders, including a split-personality.

I was stunned, shocked, pissed off, scared, ready to cry, and almost did. (I am not a violent person, nor do I ever intend on becoming a violent person, and lets just say that he was probably lucky I wasn't!). What in the world was happening? I had wanted answers and this is what I got. I knew immediately that this 'official' assessment or his 'findings' were way off the mark, and I just wanted to get the hell out of there as quickly as possible.

I thanked the psychologist ("With a PHD, no less!" his receptionist had gushed) for his time and paid the three hundred dollars for all the testing, gathered my child and left the office.

Aubrey screamed all the way home, which happened to be only thirty miles, no sweat. She was giving me hell I thought for putting her through all of that turmoil, I deserved it, and I knew somehow she was right. Here I was dragging my child all over the state of Washington trying to find answers and getting absolutely nowhere.

Again, I was ready to completely give up. I was too tired, depressed, too exasperated, and way too confused to go any further. What I had intended to do was help my child, and what was happening in the process? Subjecting her to strangers who tried to get her to do things when she didn't want to, watching her behind one way mirrors like some criminal in an interrogation room. Nothing good was coming out of this and I was quickly running out of options.

After putting Aubrey down for a nap, ironically, she had fallen asleep during the last mile of the trip home, I made myself a cup of hot tea and sat down on the couch. I needed to pick Brittney and Austin up from my sister-in-laws house, but Aubrey was asleep and I didn't want to wake her.

Besides, I needed time to sit and think, and most of all, allow myself to cry. So, I did. The tears wouldn't stop, and for once, I didn't try to stop them. They turned into sobs and the sobs turned into silent wails of desolation.

I realized at that moment that I had failed somehow and realizing it made my body ache all over. I didn't want this pain, but it wouldn't leave. I didn't want to be weak; to feel sorry for myself. And, where did that strong woman, who at one point could do anything she set her mind to, go? I knew without answering, that she had vanished along the way and sadly, I didn't even have the strength to care anymore.

I trudged up the stairs to check on Aubrey. My legs felt like I had weights on them. Her tears had dried and her little face was peaceful and angelic. I felt my eyes well with tears again and I silently prayed for more patience, then quickly prayed again for more parenting techniques, and once again for even more patience.

Believing half-heartedly that I was the cause for all the disarray, I turned to leave the room, and my big toe snapped. In an instant, Aubrey was wide-awake and screaming at the top of her lungs. I walked her down the steps, gave her some juice, and once again opened up the "junk" drawer.

Please don't be right, my love, at least not tonight
don't start to argue once again with me, my dear.
Let your mind wander off, my sweet, into the moonlight.
I promise that beautiful things can happen there,
Beneath the shadows it casts in the night.
They will keep safe with your thoughts, my love.
For my thoughts alone, my darling dear,
will raise such mayhem themselves, I so dreadfully fear.

D.L. Clarke

Chapter 12

The mind does strange things when it is tired, well, at least mine does. It had been days, actually four to be exact, since Aubrey slept more than a few hours at a time. I was borderline crazy and praying again for answers. With another night falling, I sat on the couch and started to think back to California, when Aubrey was born. I wondered what could have caused all of her stress.

There had been so many times that she seemed just like a normal little toddler. She spoke well, very coherent for her age, I credited all of the story telling and book reading for that. And, there were times that Aubrey would crawl onto my lap and actually give me a hug. Not the "pat, pat" on the shoulders, which was her trademark, but a real, genuine, wrap, your arms around, hug. It felt so good, but I had to be careful not to return the hug with too much restraint. If I held on too tightly, she would arch her back and squirm away. The hugs definitely had to be on her terms.

With one ear tuned into listening for sounds of the kids waking, I continued to look out the window, stare at the stars and ponder. I had absorbed everything that anyone had ever said about Aubrey's "condition," and there was that one particular statement that kept haunting me.

It had been what my parents had said back in California during their visit. I knew they had immediately realized that something was atypical about

Aubrey. They hadn't seen her since she was born, and now she was almost a year and half. It made perfect sense to me that she seemed inimitable, but they assured me that that wasn't what they had meant by being "different." I remember bluntly defending everything they had said about her.

"Why does she cry all the time?" my dad would ask. I would fire back that she was just a baby and that is what babies do.

"Why does she start to tantrum so severely, and then within seconds, start laughing? And why does she follow you around harassing you to give her something to eat? She can't be hungry *all* the time, *can she*? It doesn't make sense, something is wrong," my step-mom would say.

"Isn't it odd that she walks on her toes? Maybe her tendons aren't long enough?" they would both say.

I reassured them that I had had her tendons checked and that Aubrey just *preferred* walking on her toes. Besides, the professionals had promised she would grow out of it. A set of sturdy soled shoes should help the process, they informed me. So, that is what we bought, at a meager fifty dollars a pair.

They just don't know her very well, I would infer. If they were around her more, then she would be more comfortable and she wouldn't be like this. She just needs to get to know them better. During the week of their visit, my daughter ranted, kicked, screamed, bit herself, pulled her hair, laughed hysterically, and repeatedly asked to "eat" over seventy times one of the days, even though we had just had lunch.

She wouldn't sleep, paced the floor, and would not allow them to touch her. Even when my parents tried to speak to her, it seemed as though that too had been "off limits" to Aubrey.

But, what truly haunted me the most was that moment by the door as they were packed and heading back home to Oregon. I remember vividly the vacillation in their voices as they tried to somehow think of the "right words" to say, and then, without further dithering, heard them, "We were just thinking, wondering actually, if you had ever thought of...perhaps...Aubrey is autistic?" come spilling out of their mouths.

I remembered watching them as they shifted their uneasy glances from Aubrey, back to me, and then finally to the exit door. They had had difficulty saying all of that out loud, but they still knew somehow that their granddaughter was flawed, and had felt the need to express their opinions with me.

I remember immediately firing back, "Autistic? Uh. No way!" I remember thanking them for their thoughts and had arduously told them to have a safe trip home.

What had happened *exactly* that had them convinced that there *was* something different or wrong with my child? Had it been the chaotic grocery trip scene when Aubrey had thrown things from the cart and screamed at the top of her lungs? Or maybe it had been the horrific mall scene where Aubrey screamed again non-stop for almost an hour while arching her back and biting herself. I was so tired of everyone staring and pointing fingers, and I had really tried to keep our shopping entourage as inconspicuous as possible, with apparently no luck.

I remember how angry I was at my parents as they finally pulled out of my driveway and headed their car toward home.

Autism? What were they *thinking*? What did *they* know about autism? Wait a minute, what did *I* know about autism, nothing. End of story.

I had ended up burying that thought and not thinking about it again until now, this moment. Sitting in the dark, watching the clouds slowly cross over the moon, it emerged and came at me with full force. Why hadn't I ever looked into my parent's un-official diagnosis for Aubrey? I snorted. Because there were my *parents*!

I had emotionally decided, back in California, that they were just like all the others that gave their opinion and had no solid foundation for giving it. They didn't have a clue, I remembered thinking. Besides, Aubrey only behaved her worst in front of my sister-in-law, my neighbor friends, my parents, and me.

Some members of the family saw Aubrey as a little angelic child that could do absolutely no wrong. How could I possibly explain it to them what she was really like when they wouldn't admit to ever seeing *anything* out of the norm? Venting and voicing my concerns was pointless. Aubrey was perfect and completely normal in their eyes.

Then again, maybe Aubrey just knew how to play me, my parents, and friends? Maybe she *was* normal and okay? Was it just *me*? Was *I* a bad parent? Around and around the questions repeatedly swirled and my head ached and begged for answers and relief.

The thoughts caved in one after the other, leaving me even more confused than before. I pulled the blanket off the back of the couch and covered myself up in its warmth.

What if my parents were actually *right* about Aubrey? It wasn't that I didn't want them to be right, I just didn't want *anyone* in my family or the world for that matter, looking at my daughter as if she were somehow defective.

Their statement had made me defiant, and since I am so stubborn, it hadn't helped matters any. But the statement was there, it always was, just buried deeply. Yet, it continued to dangle mercilessly, catching momentary and fleeting bits of light, in the depths of my tangled and tired mind.

What was I going to do with it now that it was swinging right in front of me? It was now staring me in the face and there was no more escaping it. I was completely exhausted and out of hope. I was alone with my children and I needed answers.

If I could rock you to sleep
Would you perhaps let me try
No? It's alright, I understand for
Deep within me, the true answers lie.
Go to sleep now little one,
No more tears tonight, my sweet, to cry.

D.L. Clarke

Chapter 13

I was startled out of my foggy, no sleep for days, deep thought process by Aubrey screaming upstairs. Glancing at the wall clock, I saw that I had actually dozed off and it was now almost midnight. It was going to be another long night, I thought as I despairingly pulled the warm blanket off me. The sounds of her waking were becoming more apparent and I knew from the sounds of it that I had just a few seconds to get upstairs to retrieve her, or there would be a full-blown explosion in store.

I jumped up from the couch and raced as quickly and quietly as I could up the stairs and into Aubrey's room. She was sitting up in her little bed, her auburn hair wet with sweat, looking dazed as she came more out of her sleep. I gazed over at the crib where Aubrey's brother lay sleeping.

Although he had become very familiar with the tantrums and upheaval that lay across the room from him in the other bed, I was still very thankful that he was able to sleep through most of her less tumultuous tantrums.

"*Shhhhhh*...Aubrey! Quiet now, shhhhhhhh...We don't want to wake brother up, do we?" I was almost begging. She looked at me and I could tell she was getting more and more agitated.

I gently picked up my sweaty little bundle, and started to quietly leave the room. We were almost to the bedroom door, when she threw her back into an arch and repelled against me. I hung onto her with firm grip. If I let her down, she would immediately proceed to Austin's crib and start shaking it until she successfully woke him. Once he began to cry, she would leave the room. I knew this, because it had happened many times before when I had not been fast enough to stop her.

The pandemonium could evolve into raging hysteria within minutes. Aubrey would often throw herself onto the floor screaming and wriggling as if she were being attacked by killer bees or something, and Austin would be in the background screaming as I would try to calm her in any way that I thought would work.

I had tried everything, and I mean *everything,* that I had either heard as advice or read in one of the recommended parenting books, in my attempts to calm her down. Behavior modification, ignoring the tantrums (I actually think I was perfecting *that* one), time out chair, time out corner, time out times a million in other areas of the house, and good ole' fashioned scolding. Nothing was working and things were once again obviously escalating out of control.

"*Shhhhhhhhhhhh!*" I whispered firmly and then I began to hum as I clung onto Aubrey's arched body. I had to remain calm. If she sensed that I was getting upset, the scene could last for hours. It was almost as if she *liked* making me mad. Not wanting to let her win, I had long ago decided that I would just not let it faze me.

But it *did,* how could it *not?* Here was my beautiful child, spending her days in apparent misery and screaming for no obvious reason. But, maybe she *did* have a reason and I just wasn't seeing it?

I wondered why there had to be so much chaos? It seemed to have gotten worse since Austin's arrival a few months ago, so maybe *that* was it? Maybe she was having trouble adjusting to the new baby? It would make perfect sense. But when I thought about it, she was having the raging tantrums well *before* he arrived. She seemed to flourish on the chaos and would create it when there wasn't any, just to have it around.

I made it successfully down the stairs and into the living room before letting Aubrey down. She then scurried from room to room, flipping the lights on and off, muttering in her little voice. I followed her, wanting to do something to calm her. If I picked her back up, she would scream, if I let her roam, we would be up all night. I felt helpless and I wanted to cry. What was I doing wrong? Brittney, Aubrey's older sister, had the "terrible twos" tantrums, but never acted like this. I must have done *something* right, *right?*

Once again, the antagonizing questions flooded my mind as did all the doubts. It had been four years since Brittney was this age; maybe I had lost the magic "mom" touch. What was I doing wrong now? The questions and doubt set-up camp in my mind, as I sat in the rocker and opened up a children's storybook.

Aubrey still loved her books and I was thankful for that. Since she was old enough to sit on my lap, I would open the pages of books and she would gaze at them, intrigued. Now, she would often sit with a book for short spells, she was a toddler after all, and flip through the pages seemingly enjoying them. It was the one thing she was truly attached to that could sometimes even thwart a tantrum.

"Hickory dickory dock, the mouse ran up the clock—" I started to read out loud into the moonlit room. Aubrey stopped flipping the light for a second and looked at me. I kept reading, pretending not to notice.

"Mary had a little lamb—" I kept reading out loud, a little quieter than before. I could sense that I had definitely gotten Aubrey's attention. She was coming closer to me and finally crawled onto my lap and grabbed the book from me. We were through the book in two seconds. Aubrey hopped down, went to the bookshelf and came back with *Jack and the Beanstalk.*

"You want to read about Jack?" I asked her in a quiet, soothing voice. She nodded, and I started reading to her again. As I read, I began slowly rocking the chair back and forth. I rocked and read about Jack over and over, letting Aubrey flip the pages back and forth, for more than an hour. It was now two o'clock in the morning. Finally, the page flipping stopped and I felt her little head fall against my chest. Thumb in her mouth, she fell asleep. But I couldn't be sure. I had to wait the extra few minutes to be sure she was asleep, for if I was wrong, the whole process would have to start over, and I was exhausted.

After determining that she was indeed fully asleep, I ever so gingerly got up and carried her upstairs to bed. As I laid her down and covered her with her little quilt, I felt a lump form in my throat. She was so precious, and I adored her. The tears started flowing before I could stop them and ran down my cheeks in hot rivers. I had to find out what was going on with my little girl. I absolutely *had* to help her. I quietly tiptoed out of her room and went into my bedroom across the hall to lie down.

My eyes fluttered shut and my mind started to drift off, listening to the sounds of a train in the far off distance. As I fell deeper into relaxation, I became a bit aware that the train sounded like it was getting closer. "That's impossible!" My mind woke itself up to challenge the ears. All of a sudden, it was obvious to me that the sound hadn't been a train whistle, but an emergency vehicle siren!

I sat up in bed with a jolt, listening as the sounds of the siren as it proceeded to intensify. "Please, please, pllleeeaaassseeee just let it go on by!" I pleaded silently into the air. Late night ambulance arrivals were the one major downfall of living so close to the hospital. As luck would have it, the sirens kept getting louder and louder and as it passed by on the street in front of our house, Aubrey awoke screeching. I do believe I swore under my breath a little then, but since I don't want to zing this up too much, just fill in the blanks as you wish!

It took me approximately two seconds to fly out of my bed and reach Aubrey. I know what you are thinking, but I had tried that too, remember? The "no response" routine had been diligently carried out in the past until it almost make me physically ill to the point of puking, and we all know that I hate to puke.

She would cry when I put her down in her crib, I would then go in reassure her *once*, and then leave. Each night, and/or episode for that matter, I repeated the same ritual. Reassure and comfort, then leave. I was *definitely* not going to come running back like a Tasmanian devil into her room to retrieve her. But, it obviously hadn't worked for I had undeniably and quite obviously become just that.

I got double duty when I reached Aubrey's room, for Austin was up screaming as well. He needed to be fed, and good ole' mom that I was, had actually stuck with the nursing thus far. But now I was in a dilemma. How was I going to get Aubrey back to sleep and feed Austin at the same time? I really wished at that moment that my husband were home from his Navy duties across the ocean. I could really use an extra set of arms, let alone, some mental respite! But that wasn't going to happen, and I had two screaming children that sounded like peacocks calling and answering each other in the night.

Sitting up in bed with her blankets thrown on the floor, Aubrey was wet with sweat and very agitated. I grabbed Austin out of his crib, and I was thankful that he momentarily stopped wailing. While taking him over to his changing table, I told Aubrey that she needed to night-night again. No, it wouldn't work, but soothing voices are nice in the middle of the night amidst out of control screaming. It helped *me* to talk to her softly. It kept *me* calm. I began to hum.

Austin settled down to his job of nursing as I situated myself in the rocker across the room from Aubrey's bed. He was getting the hang of tuning out the screaming too. I kept humming. Aubrey was still sitting up, but her crying was diminishing to a few snappy outbursts. She wanted me to look at her, observe her bursts of tears and then, amazingly, she would burst into sudden laughter. I gazed out the window and kept humming.

This too was part of my new and improved "behavior modification" technique. Completely ignoring the tantrums. Obviously there was nothing physically wrong with her. I remembered back to all the times I used to drag her to the physicians office, thinking there must be a raging double ear infection going on for her to wake up howling so violently in the night. But, her ears always proved to be just fine.

I remembered too all the attempts to try to feed her, thinking that perhaps she woke with a raging appetite, but even a bottle would very rarely comfort her. During one of the doctor visits I dragged her to, the physician had coached me to "ignore the tantrums at night" because 'she will eventually learn that it doesn't do any good to scream all night. Really? When? When she turned twenty? Oh, how the sarcasm kept me such good camaraderie in the night hours.

Knowing that she was physically healthy, and realizing that there was *nothing* I could do to help her, did help me to remain a bit calmer, I think. I knew she would eventually enervate herself by screaming. Even though I knew it could take several hours of on-and-off screaming occurrences, I would just have to wait it out.

Austin was eating very methodically and we had the procedure down pat. I was so thankful that nursing was a no-brainer and that we were being so successful with it. I think it was possibly a factor in keeping me sane during all the upheaval that was going on around us. I was doing *something* right.

After settling Austin back into his crib, I stood and was able to rock Aubrey back and forth in my arms for almost an hour. She was relaxing against my touch and actually allowing me to hold her. It had to be on her terms only, and because I knew this, I refrained from pulling her any closer. But, oh, how I wanted and needed to feel her mold into me just for a moment. And, oh how sadly tempting it was to just grasp her little sighing body and pull it so tightly into my embrace. But I couldn't, I didn't dare.

My arms felt as if they were falling off, when I was finally able to lay her back down into her bed. It was now almost six o'clock in the morning and I would need to get Brittney up and off to school. She could sleep through an earthquake and, at the moment, I was *very* happy about that!

It arrived today on crisp white paper
So formal it seemed to be.
Answers to questions I thought that I needed
Some things I thought I just had to see.
The words, however scribbled, were not all that clear.
For what I thought they had said
Were nothing compared to what I feared.

D.L. Clarke

Chapter 14

Brittney woke in her usual exultant self and trod off to school with a small group of her neighborhood friends. I watched as she disappeared down the path and onto the school grounds. On the way back into the house, the mail handler came by with a stack of envelopes and handed it to me. Right on top, was an envelope that bore the name of the child psychologist.

"Gaaawwwdd!" I heard myself exclaim out loud, and then in a more whining type of voice, "What the heck does he want *now?*" I really hoped that none of my happy-go-lucky neighbors were within earshot.

Then, I immediately thought it was probably a billing statement saying I owed more money for his useless, *professional* diagnosis. Then thought that perhaps it was an apology for being such an ass when he referred to my daughter as his "youngest patient with childhood schizophrenia."

"Ha!" I snorted, and once inside the house, tore the envelope open and read the contents.

After careful consideration, I have recommended your child, Aubrey, to be screened and possibly placed in the Clover Ridge Early Intervention program. This facility is dedicated solely to children with developmental delays.

It is my opinion that this facility can assist Aubrey with her speech and language difficulties, as well as offer other remedial services that may prove helpful.

There is normally a lengthy waiting list for these services, however, I have forwarded information to Clover Ridge, and they are expecting your call.

It took me approximately two minutes to read the letter and another minute to let it soak in. Then I re-read the entire letter again. I couldn't believe what I was seeing. It was a light. Another flicker of hope ran through my veins and coursed its way upward into my brain.

Even though I felt a bit apprehensive, I was still eager to get the process started. Sure, I knew my hesitations could use some much needed validation, but I still knew that I had to at least call them and find out how they could help Aubrey; to, at the very least, give them a chance. I also knew that I had to enervate every lead I got, just to be sure.

I called Clover Ridge Center and was greeted by a very pleasant lady on the other end of the phone. She explained to me that they see all types of developmental, and physically challenged children, from spinal cord injuries, to mild and severely mentally delayed children.

I liked the way she spoke to me. She was very informative and reassured me that they would see my child and try their best to assist us in any way they could. No miracle cure. No "getting to the bottom of it." No promises they couldn't keep. It was just assistance, someone there to listen and help, and that was exactly what we needed right then.

Aubrey's first visit to Clover Ridge came quickly. I had prepared myself for another professional visit the days leading up to the appointment. I already had my guard up. Even though they had been so nice on the phone, I had to be prepared to defend my daughter and my parenting skills.

While I was waiting to be called back for the initial interview process, I strolled down the entry hall and noticed hundreds of small photos wallpapering the walls. I was shocked at first to see that most of the children in the pictures were either in wheelchairs, had downs syndrome, or looked disfigured in some way.

I suddenly thought I was in the wrong place. Somehow the information had been confused and we were not supposed to be here. This facility did not look like the place that could help my child. Aubrey didn't need a wheelchair, and I knew that she wasn't delayed mentally, nor retarded. So what were we doing here? I didn't have much time to ponder that thought for we were called back to the assessment office for the interview.

On the way down the hall, I glanced down at my purse and double-checked to make sure I had my *list of things that concern me* onboard. I did.

Of course I would not have even considered not bringing it. I had double and triple checked that it was in my purse before even leaving the house and once again when I was in the car. It was my security blanket, if you will.

We were seated in a very small office that was decorated with pictures drawn by children. It was like a giant refrigerator door plastered here and there with pictures brought home from school. It was messy, all mixed up and crazy like, but it was comforting and beautiful too. A smiling lady interrupted my gaze as she went behind her desk and sat down. She folded her hands on her desk and welcomed us to her school. School? That made me feel instantly better. It was a school! Ah! I breathed a little sigh of relief.

"Read!" Aubrey demanded as she climbed up on my lap. She shoved the book into my face and had I not instinctively moved my head back, she would've poked me in the eye.

"Aubrey loves books!" I informed the nice lady who was still smiling behind her desk.

"Oh! Good! We have lot's and lot's of books here, Aubrey!" she exclaimed.

Aubrey did not look up from her book, instead buried her head further into it.

Just don't hand me one of your books, I thought to myself very silently. Which almost caused me to snicker but I didn't dare. You had to keep a sense of humor and it was nice to realize that mine was still intact.

The smiling lady asked me if she could go through a checklist with me as part of the interviewing process. I agreed eagerly, and we began. We went through several pages of questions and she would either make a check or write a small comment next to the box. She showed genuine concern, and it was nice to have the sympathy for once. It amazed me that she truly did seem to understand what I was telling her! And, for the very first time since beginning to go to see the professionals, I did not need to produce my *list of things that concern me*. She had practically covered them all and I felt a weight almost start to lift off my shoulders. The light began to flicker a little brighter inside my head.

One week later, I got a letter informing me that Aubrey was accepted into the Clover Ridge program for developmental delays. They had determined after looking over all of the test results, that she was functioning socially at the equivalent of a twenty-two month old. Because she was now thirty-one months old, that significant delay more than qualified her for therapy in socialization skills as well as more testing for motor skills development.

I began taking Aubrey to Clover Ridge twice a week, and being the child-loving place that it was, I was able to take Austin with me, which proved to be extremely convenient.

A typical therapy session would involve Aubrey and a tester, a.k.a. "new friend," behind one-way mirrors again, but these sessions were more like play time rather than testing. I was hesitant at first to put Aubrey into that situation again with a stranger, but the therapists at Clover Ridge were wonderful.

They would come out, try to engage Aubrey in a book, they learned quickly what made her respond, and then lead her back to the "toy room" to play. I was able to follow and watch through the one-way glass.

Some days were better than others as far as Aubrey's response to what was going on around her. Sometimes she would play quite well and it was encouraging to watch her examine the toys and try to push the trucks on the floor. She appeared to be in her own little world, and it seemed like a happy place for the time being.

For most of the sessions, the tester would perform some exams with blocks of color and patterns and on the other side of the glass, another therapist would write down what they observed. Other times, the tests would be more physical where Aubrey would have to try to walk on wooden beams, bounce a ball with her hands, and jump over lines on the floor. After a week of observation, the therapist informed me that they believed that Aubrey was almost up to where she should be with her motor skills. There were, however, a few areas that still concerned them and they wanted to offer some therapeutic assistance. It was in the form of Occupational Therapy.

Don't tempt me with your snares
Your coils and your ropes
I cannot begin to reckon
With all that you wish
I cope.

D.L. Clarke

Chapter 15

All of the previous testing and exams seemed like a walk in the park once Occupational Therapy began. It involved, I figured out quickly, going beyond Aubrey's comfort zone, which was already extremely small to begin with.

Aubrey started going to her sessions on a cloudy Thursday morning, and I should have been more aware of the foreboding clouds and perhaps rescheduled to another day.

She was in a mood, which her dad and I used to call, not to her knowledge of course, "Zardar." It was a name that just popped up one evening as we watched our little child transform into a raging, then hysterically laughing, screaming, biting being, that did not seem to be of this planet. It was imperative, please realize, that at those particular moments, that we kept our humor.

We arrived at Clover Ridge right on schedule. I made it a point to never be late to anything and this, of course, was no exception. The smiling lady led us to a large airy room that was full of large bouncy balls, balance beams, gymnastic mats, a mesh swing, ropes and pulleys, and jungle gym type equipment, as well as a small table and chair.

"Wow, Aubrey! Looks like you are going to get to really play today!" I was trying to be enthused, although I felt a bit apprehensive.

Aubrey hated swinging, and a large meshy swing hung smugly in front of us. She hated to be off the ground, and there were so many ladders and things off the ground that I could easily see that we were in trouble. I knew that there was going to be a major scene, I could feel it. I dreaded it. In fact, I almost gathered her up, kicking, screaming, or not, and headed for the exit sign.

But I didn't. I had to trust this method and at least give it a try. I could not stop this process yet, not now. I watched Aubrey look at her surroundings. She had a blank look and I knew that it was definitely one of her "off days."

Just then, a woman with long gray hair emerged through the door and shut it with a loud thump behind her.

"Good morning!" she exclaimed and walked over to me with her hand out. "I'm Jackie, Aubrey's O.T."

I shook her hand and greeted her. Aubrey watched us, and Austin crawled around on the floor. I had no idea what to expect. The anticipation was really getting to me.

Then, possibly sensing my apprehension, the gray-haired woman, who had introduced herself as Jackie, reassured me that we weren't going to use *all* the equipment today. *Today*. But it *would* be used then, *some day*.

That was what bothered me. How were they going to get my child, who would rarely swing at the park without screaming and crying, into that huge mesh swing without putting her in a straight jacket first? Maybe *that* was the idea?

The rest of the equipment sort of had that restraining feel to it. Again, definitely out of the comfort zone of most human beings, let alone my child who already had issues!

Jackie was not shy. Quite the opposite indeed! She started explaining her ideas as far as Aubrey's therapy and as she talked she got closer and closer to my face. I kept trying to back up without it being noticeable, but soon I was backed up against the windowsill with nowhere to go. I had avoided crushing Austin crawling on the floor as I maneuvered backward, thank goodness. But now, I was trapped.

What she had to say was definitely intriguing and if it hadn't been for the small wad of spit that formed on her bottom lip and kept getting larger, eventually creating a bridge between her upper and lower lip, I could have paid closer attention. How could you *not* notice that? I felt a little sick and figured it was the mixture of nervousness, apprehension, and finally the spit mass that was doing me in.

"Okay? Sound like a plan?" She was asking me a question, and I didn't know how to answer her. Jackie had invaded my bubble and I was at loss for words.

"Uh. Yes! That sounds like a plan! However, Aubrey does not like to swing," I informed her. Somewhere in the spit mass conversation, I had heard the word "swing" come up. I knew that it wasn't a good idea to put Aubrey on a swing, especially today.

"Oh, that is all right, like I said, we are just going to try some things out today!" she said as she crossed the room to where Aubrey was. She was tracing a circle on the floor with her hands, oblivious to the approaching Jackie woman.

"Hi there! My name is Jackie!" She held a hand out to Aubrey as if she was supposed to know what to do with it. Aubrey looked up and then back down at her circle.

"And your name is Aubrey?" she coaxed.

It wasn't working. Aubrey could have not cared less who this person was and she was not about to leave her circle any time soon. Jackie walked over to the balance beam and hopped onto it.

"Hey, Aubrey! Why don't you come over here and try this! It's really fun!" she said as she proceeded to balance-walk her way across the beam. I was waiting for an Olympic dismount, but was sorely disappointed when Jackie merely hopped down, with a thump, onto the mat. I gave her a measly five for her attempt though.

I rolled my tongue inside my mouth. I was suddenly out of saliva; I guessed Jackie would have some to loan if I needed any. Oh! I just felt so out of control in this place! I wanted to just leave and go home and forget the whole idea of occupational therapy. It was obvious that Jackie was getting nowhere with Aubrey, and Austin was getting just as cranky as I was.

"I am going to try something else! She doesn't really interact with strangers well, huh?" she said as she hurriedly breezed by me.

"No, she doesn't. I guess that's good though, you know? I always taught my kids to *not* talk to strangers!" I said trying to manufacture some saliva so that I could swallow easier. Where had that lump in my throat suddenly come from? Clearly this Jackie was going to need some interaction from me in order to get my daughter to comply with her requests. I did not want to tromp on her toes, however.

I weighed the options, and decided that I would intervene; at least until Jackie shot evil glances my way, which didn't happen to my relief. I watched Aubrey across the room and asked her to come over and look at the birdie out the window. She stood up, came right over to me and pointed out the window then asked, "Where is the birdie?"

"See on the branch? It is a bluebird!" I said as I looked over at Jackie who had set several clear bags full of various objects on top a small table. Gently taking Aubrey's hand, I guided her over to where Jackie was sitting. As I got closer, I could tell the bags were filled with various uncooked legumes and some contained several different colored sands. Sitting next to the bags were armies of plastic zoo animals. I was thinking that this looked fun, and Aubrey reacted similarly, sitting right down and picking up a stray zebra.

"Do you think the zebra would like to hide in this bag?" Jackie asked Aubrey, pointing to a bag full of uncooked split peas. Without waiting for an answer, Jackie picked up the zebra's mate that was lying on the table and dunked it into the bag of peas.

"Ooops! Where did the zebra go?" she asked Aubrey with a very animated voice. "Better save him, Aubrey!" Jackie continued, exclaiming encouragingly.

I watched as Aubrey gingerly put her hand to the top of the bag and touched the very top of the dried split pea pile. She would go no further. She pulled her hand back and wanted no more to do with that zebra or the peas. Apparently, the zebra had to find another guide out of the jungle today.

But, Jackie was persistent. She grabbed another animal and plunged it into a bag of uncooked rice. Only this time, she left the head of it exposed at the top of the rice pile. With Jackie's coaxing, Aubrey again reached her hand over and into the bag. This time, however, she ended up retrieving the elephant without touching a single grain of rice.

"Yeah! You saved the elephant, Aubrey!" Jackie exclaimed.

I heard Aubrey giggle. It was little, barely audible, but it was there. She thought Jackie was funny. It looked as if we were going to make some definite progress and my hopes continued to rise, ever so slightly.

The game went on for several more minutes until Aubrey got tired of it and went over to the large rubber balls that sat along one wall in the room. Jackie informed me that she thought that we could be done today. But then she saw Aubrey approach the mesh swing.

"Do you want to swing now?" Jackie said in an "I am not going to give up" voice.

She unfurled the mesh and began to arrange the ropes that held the swing to the ceiling. Aubrey was watching her intently.

I felt my eyebrows up into my hairline. This wasn't happening was it? But before I knew it, the mesh swing was ready for action. Jackie coaxed Aubrey into the swing and the very second Aubrey sat down into it, the meshing completely engulfed her. She started screaming and clawing at the enclosure like a crazed cat in a cage. Aubrey started biting at herself and continued to scream as I jumped up as fast as I could, managing to get Austin off my lap and over to help her in the same instant.

Jackie said she was confused and looked completely flustered. She said that most children find the mesh comforting because it applies pressure to the body and makes them feel secure. She didn't understand why Aubrey was reacting this way!

It seemed like it took forever to get her out of the swing. Aubrey was flailing her arms and screaming so loudly that a supervisor type person appeared at the doorway to see if "everything was alright." NO! It wasn't all right! Look at what this evil beast had done to my child! Trapped her in a mesh bag and then thought she was strange because she didn't react the "proper" way.

I was furious and frustrated and knew that this whole Clover Ridge thing had been a huge mistake. I didn't know what I was thinking anymore. I kept heading in different directions, looking for some hope and finding more chaos and *professional* opinions that proved to be meaningless.

After freeing Aubrey, I hurriedly gathered up Austin with one arm and wrapped Aubrey around my other. We departed the building without saying goodbye. I was happy that the drive home took only ten minutes, for Aubrey and Austin both screamed the entire time. I shook my head and knew that I had screwed up again. Causing more pain for my child, all the while thinking that I was doing the right thing.

As soon as I got in the door of our house, I heard the telephone begin to ring. I felt like screaming myself then, but decided not to, well at least out loud. I rushed in, sat my screaming children on the living room floor, and answered the phone.

"Hello?" I queried.

"Yes! Is this Aubrey's mother?" I heard the other voice ask, and I assured them that I was.

"This is Clover Ridge Center, I was planning on just leaving you message, but it looks like we forgot to schedule you for Aubrey's next O.T. visit," I heard the lady who smiled all the time say. I knew it was she; there are very few people on the planet that have her type of extra chipper voice. It is the kind of voice that you know shouldn't annoy the crap out of you, but still does.

"I have Monday at 9:00 a.m. with Jackie, and Claire will be here so Aubrey can meet her too, she is the pre-school teacher with our program," I heard her explaining in her happy voice.

A million thoughts were going through my mind at the time. They all crossed each other and faded then came back again. And, they all wanted their turn at getting answered. I couldn't answer any of my thoughts. So, when the smiling lady continued to ask if Monday at 9:00 a.m. was going to work out for us and I numbly agreed, I really don't know what was going through my mind at the time.

I hung up and sat down. Aubrey was just over two-and-a- half years old and we still had no definitive answers. Was pre-school going to be the beginning of something wonderful for my child? Or would it end up badly as everything else seemed to? I didn't know, and unfortunately there was not a soul I could ask.

As I looked over and saw my little girl rocking back and forth on the floor, with her hands tightly clamped over her ears screaming, "Stop it, Stop it!" into the room, I leaned forward and laid my head onto my kitchen table and started to pray.

Where have you been
All of her life, so far, not there
Alas I have found you
Or you, rather, found she there.
Take her now, and mend her little broken wings
Help her become whole again, I beg of you now
Can you possibly do onto she these things?

D.L. Clarke

Chapter 16

Occupational therapy continued at Clover Ridge. I somehow decided to rule against my initial plan to keep Aubrey at home and quarantined from all of the therapist and professionals that challenged her to do things she did not want to. Even though I knew it was uncomfortable, and it often didn't seem fair or nice making her go, I still couldn't help but trust my gut and kept taking her.

During some of the sessions, it looked as if Aubrey was truly enjoying herself, and her progress encouraged me. She had actually started digging her hands *into the center* of the bags of rice and beans to retrieve the animals! It was a big step, and I was proud of her. She had gone beyond her comfort level and that is what the therapists had wanted. They promised me that she was making remarkable progress.

We were well into the first month of therapy, when, after several re-scheduling attempts, we were finally able to meet Claire. I had heard so many good things about her from Jackie, that I was very anxious to get Aubrey into her classroom. Jackie had described her as an energetic, special education teacher, that taught both Clover Ridge and South Kitsap pre-schools. She was someone who truly loved her job.

"Good morning!" Claire said to me, and I swear her eyes were twinkling, no kidding!

"Hello, little Aubrey!" I heard her say as she got down on her knees and handed Aubrey a book of nursery rhymes. That was it. She then stood back up, and I could see that she was still smiling. All the interaction she demanded of Aubrey was done. For the time being, anyway. I liked her non- demanding style, and how at ease she was. It was truly comforting.

Claire sat down on one of the couches in the reception area of Clover Ridge and beckoned us to join her. I complied eagerly, and Aubrey followed behind me holding the book Claire had given her. As soon as she had sat down, Aubrey buried her face in the book.

"Is that typical?" Claire whispered gesturing toward Aubrey.

"Yes, it is," I replied, nodding my head. "Especially around strangers, and when she is not comfortable. She tends to hide behind books quite a bit actually," I continued.

"Aubrey, is that a good book you are reading?" Claire's soothing voice asked. There was no response from Aubrey.

Claire's smile did not fade; in fact it broadened when she announced to me that she had an opening at the Silverdale pre-school. Aubrey could begin on Monday and a bus would take her to and from school. My smile immediately disappeared.

"A *bus?*" I questioned Claire uneasily. I knew already that that was absolutely not going to work. The occupational therapy was turning out to be an okay move on my part, the pre-school sounded like a great idea too, but a *bus*? No way!

"I think I will just take her to school actually," I hastily replied. "She hasn't ever ridden a bus and I know that it could cause some *issues*," I wrapped that argument up nicely I thought.

"Are you sure?" Claire asked as she stood up. Her brown eyes were seeking out an answer from my direction. I wondered if she was thinking what I had meant by *issues*. It didn't really matter though; there would be no bus.

"Right, I will take her," I said really thinking we had exhausted that topic.

"Well…okay…the school is fifteen miles out, two or three times a week, depending on what program we get her into. But, you are really sure you do not want us to provide transportation?" Claire stated.

I reassured her that it would be no problem at all for me to drive her to pre-school. But, in reality, there *was* a slight problem. We didn't have much money. I wasn't working at the time, and the military pay was nothing to brag about. Just the gasoline alone was going to be an expensive venture, not to mention the forty dollars a week it was going to cost for the pre-school. But,

I firmly convinced myself, this was an opportunity to possibly find some help for Aubrey, and we had to do this. Whether we could afford it not.

"So! I guess we will see you on Monday!" I exclaimed enthusiastically to Claire.

"Yes! I am looking forward to having you in my class, Aubrey!" Claire said as kneeling to be eye level with Aubrey. I saw Aubrey look up at her for a second and then down at her book.

"You can keep the book," Claire said sweetly, as if reading her mind. "See you next week!" she said offering her hand to me to shake. I shook her hand, thanked her for seeing us, and more importantly, for making room for my child in her class.

I turned to begin the departure process, but Aubrey had decided that she was staying.

"NO! YOU go!" she demanded. I did not want a scene, especially here. They would realize in a heartbeat that this child had control over me, and decide that *this* was the reason for all the behavior problems. We would be dropped from their program, and sent on our merry, screaming, way.

Aubrey threw herself on the floor and turned into a noodle the minute I tried to pick her up. Trying to hang onto Austin, and pick her up at the same time, I had begun to sweat. Oh! I must have looked like a raging lunatic. I am quite sure at that point the staff at Clover Ridge was exchanging knowing looks and casting their vote as to whether I should be escorted out by security or…no?

I let go of Aubrey's hand to adjust Austin on my hip. If I let *him* down, he was likely to crawl off into the maze of offices, and *that* would be a whole other story. At the moment I released grasp of Aubrey's hand she got up and tore off down the hall with her little, fifty-dollar shoes thumping madly into the distance. I wanted to say, shiiiiiiitttttt! really loud. I actually wanted to say every cuss word ever invented, not that I could profess to knowing them all, however, I really think that, under the circumstances, I could have easily made up a few at the moment.

I also thought about crying, but didn't. No need to get entirely hysterical, yet. Nor did I swear. In the midst of the mass of children that had gathered to watch the scene, that surely would have brought in the security team.

At the end of the hall I saw the smiling lady emerge. If halos were real, *and* they were visible, she definitely would have been adorned with one. I watched her as she caught my child and stopped her mid-run. Aubrey did not know what to do. She didn't know this smiling lady. She had *seen* the smiling lady many times, but she was still a stranger. That worked toward both my and the smiling lady's advantage. Aubrey fell apart with *me*, not strangers.

I was already halfway down the hall, which suddenly appeared to have grown several football fields long, when the smiling lady and Aubrey caught up with me. Aubrey's face was streaked with tears and the hair on her forehead was wet with sweat. I was so upset at the situation, but I demanded myself to stay as calm as possible.

There was no sense showing her, let alone telling her, that I was upset about what she had done. It seemed like she really didn't notice when I had scolded her sharply in the past for running away from me. And mind you, in a crowded grocery store parking lot, it had been completely justified for me to yell at her to STOP! Then when I caught up with her, scold her and repeatedly tell her NO!

I would be such a shaking mess that I am sure the astronauts could notice it from space, and there would be no reaction from her. Nothing except more kicking and screaming, biting, and writhing out of control in her car seat all the way back home. However, there were often times that she would return my frustration and fear with just a blank stare.

Aubrey's habit of running off in all directions without warning had become such an issue that even at our house I had installed pins in all the sliding glass doors high enough so that she couldn't reach them. On every doorknob heading outside, I had placed child safety devices, as well as safety chains as a backup.

I know that when you have children in the house, it is *normal* for these things to be installed, but since Aubrey would just take off running without prior notice, sometimes in the middle of the night, and would *not stop* running, it had become a major problem. No matter how much I scolded, yelled, ranted, sat her in time out, put her in her room, nothing changed and absolutely no form of "behavior modification" helped. Yes, she was just a toddler and I knew that toddlers ran from their parents, but, like I said, this was different, believe me.

Take for example, Brittney. When she was about Aubrey's age, there had been moments where I wanted to pretend that the child who had just thrown herself onto the department store floor was not *my* child. I know that might sound terrible, but I know there are other parents out there who can relate. At least I surely hope so, if not, you may now call security.

When Brittney chose to tantrum in the store, it was usually over wanting something and being told "no." When she didn't like my answer, she would proceed to throw herself onto the floor and scream as if *she* was being attacked by killer bees.

It took approximately three times (oh how the mind forgets! I am sure it was more like three *months!*) for her to "get the idea" that she was not going to win me over by screaming nor get her way by flopping on the floor of Target.

My method as follows: as she lay on the floor, kicking and screaming, sometimes oddly, face down, (if she knew that *now* she would be entirely disgusted at the thought of all the germs she must have come in contact with!), I would look at her in the calmest way possible at the moment, and tell her she was not embarrassing *me*. (Ha! big fat fib *that* was!). However, she was probably going to embarrass *herself* if she kept it up.

I would then inform her that I was now leaving and she would have to get up and follow, or be left behind. I would then begin to depart the store. (Of course I would never have actually *really left* her and gone to the car). I hope you know me well enough by now to realize that without me telling you, but I thought I would throw that in just in case you still had any doubts.

Within seconds, she would be following right behind me, sniffling and whining, but nonetheless, I had gotten through to her that I meant business. The next time we went to the store and I had to tell her no on something, there might be a tantrum, but it was more manageable. Not the grand mall seizure type as before. The tantrums got less and less until she realized that they really had no point. Sure, it was a struggle, and it took time and patience, but I felt each time *I was getting somewhere.*

Which brings me back to Aubrey. It never felt as if I was getting *anywhere*, so it made disciplining her a huge challenge. Somehow, I knew that she didn't realize the effect she was having on those around her. I sensed that she was not doing it on *purpose,* although at times, I seriously had my doubts.

Especially, when she would dump baking soda all over the inside of the refrigerator, then scatter the rest of the box in a path-like pattern onto the carpet, en route to the sliding glass door. I would scold her about the mess, and she would laugh at me in return.

It never made sense to me. It was hard to make her laugh at the things she was *supposed* to find funny and at the things that *weren't* supposed to be funny, she would laugh hysterically. Cartoons weren't funny to her, and neither was Barney. Even Aubrey's baby brother at age one, would giggle at Barney's antics on television.

I would tickle her sometimes and she would laugh, and what a wonderful sound that was! But, it was rare that I could produce a tickle. Her dad was better at it than I, and she actually allowed him to do it.

She liked to squeeze live animals, thinking it was funny when she produced some of their hair in her fist. Then realizing there was "icky" on her hands, immediately scream and want it off. I repeatedly told her to be "nice" to the doggy etc. I had reminded her of that so many times around animals (especially those whose owners had them out on a friendly walk at the park) that eventually, she began to call *all* animals "nice." She would see a dog and say, "nice," even cows in the field were "nice." And, it was so rewarding when she would sometimes pet the animal in the method I had taught her, and say "nice." You can imagine the look of surprise when she finally learned that the furry things we had been calling "nice" all this time were actually dogs and cats!

As I pulled out of the parking lot of Clover Ridge, Aubrey melted in her car seat. Her hair was matted and wet with sweat, and she had her thumb firmly planted in her mouth. I heard her let out a collective sigh as we drove further away from the school. It had taken the intervention of both the smiling lady and Claire to finally get Aubrey into her car seat. By that time, Austin had begun to cry and the entire car seemed to sob as we wound our way down the little road that led away from Clover Ridge. Thoughts crashed and collided in my mind again. Doubts drifted and faded, then became stronger and more invasive as I heard Aubrey begin to squirm in the backseat of the car.

Was pre-school the right decision, or would it turn into yet another roadblock creating more stress for Aubrey? I longed for a crystal ball that held all the answers. I guess even *some* answers would suffice.

I wanted reassurance that the decisions I was making *now* were the right ones that would help Aubrey with her future. Some of the therapies seemed helpful, and then there were some that just made things worse. I grimaced as the mesh swing image came slamming into my mind.

I feel lost, can you help me find the path?
How sad it is to feel this way
When I see you feeling so much more than I can imagine
What more possibly can I say?
You are a light that I have been given, true
I take it unwillingly, but still I do
Let me light your path someday
I promise faithfully.

D.L. Clarke

Chapter 17

Monday morning came as the weekend jolted to an end with another sleepless night brought to me exclusively by my little Aubrey. I sent Brittney off to school, and loaded Aubrey and Austin into the car. Too exhausted to worry, my mind went into a deep fog the entire fifteen miles to pre-school.

Before I realized it, we were pulling into the parking lot of the school and I was preparing for the disembarkation of Aubrey and Austin. Other mothers were arriving also, and I couldn't help but notice all the handicap parking spaces were rapidly filling up. Large vans with lifts arrived and mothers began pulling their children from the vans.

Most of the children were in wheelchairs and those that weren't, used the assistance of crutches to walk up the path to the school door. I felt foolish for standing there with Aubrey who had legs of steel that could surely outrun me any day. I knew this firsthand for they did almost daily.

Aubrey was tugging at my hand trying to wiggle hers free from mine as we walked the path to the school door. Anticipation grew as we entered the school and saw the halls lined with doors to classrooms. I hadn't bothered to ask Claire which room Aubrey was supposed to be in. Any hesitation now on my part could be a fatal mistake. Aubrey would bolt if I didn't tell her our plan of attack, and at the moment, I had none. I really hadn't thought this through and I felt like kicking myself. This needed to go off smoothly. The transition for Aubrey had to uneventful, which meant, there was no leeway for getting lost.

Out of nowhere, Claire appeared right in front of me at the moment that I had decided to wander nonchalantly down one hall in search of her.

"Hi, Aubrey!" she said, smiling down at her. Aubrey merely shifted her feet and looked away. "The classroom is down this way." Claire gestured in the opposite direction of the way I had intended to begin my search. "Room number twenty-two, just go ahead and go in and pick a spot on the carpet. I'll be down in a sec!" Claire said, still smiling. Then, off she bounced down another hallway and out of sight.

With Austin on my hip, and Aubrey still holding my grasped hand, we headed down to room number twenty-two. Upon arrival, I immediately noticed that there were only six other children in the room, and they were unusually quiet. Come to think of it, the entire school was unusually quiet. Definitely not your typical preschool mayhem madness that usually greets you. I let Aubrey lead me to a spot on the carpet and we sat down.

A middle aged woman with jet black hair that was graying in sections, came over to us and introduced herself as Claire's assistant, LeAnn. She was friendly and possessed a soft face that was absent of makeup. LeAnn was, as I like to put it, "earthy" and "granola-ish." She didn't appear to fancy the secrets that Olay supposedly held, nor did she seem like the type that would spend any amount of time in front of a mirror worrying whether her jeans made her butt look fat. She was simple and sweet, and like I said in not so many words, down to earth.

As she walked away from my little trio on the carpet, I began to take inventory of the other children and their mothers. Almost every one of the six other children there had an obvious physical handicap of some sort. One boy had a tracheotomy and could not walk. He used his arms as legs and drug himself from toy to toy, smiling as he scuffled by.

Another boy had Down's syndrome and could not talk other than soft babbling. A little girl sat in a wheelchair silently with her mom, as my eyes continued scanning the room.

To my surprise, Aubrey was being extremely quiet and still. It was Austin that was beginning to fuss and I was actually happy for the distraction. It was uncomfortable sitting there waiting for Claire to arrive. I didn't know what to say to the other parents. I am sure they wondered why I was there, just as much as I wondered silently why the few children that weren't physically handicapped were there.

Were they like Aubrey? Maybe those kids were like Aubrey and the mothers and I would eventually be able to talk and share experiences, while we sat watching our children play behind one way mirrors.

Claire finally arrived and all eyes turned to her as she began to speak. As soon as the first word came out, her hands came up in front of her and she used sign language to accompany her spoken words. She articulated her words and animated her hands. Her face was a bundle of expressions and emotions. I could feel a glow of positive energy shooting across the room.

After Claire introduced herself and LeAnn to all of us, she asked that the parents tell their students good-bye and that we would see them right after class. As I stood up, Aubrey looked at me and her expression was a mixture of confusion and blankness. I could tell that she was scared to be left and I hated having to leave her in the strange room with kids she didn't know and teachers she had just met. I convinced myself that this was necessary, and hugged Aubrey as much as she would let me and walked out into the hall. I sat on a long wooden bench and placed Austin on my lap. It was going to be a long two hours.

One of the mothers came over and sat relatively close to Austin and me on the bench. I decided to let my bubble issue pass, this time, and gave her a brief smile. There was an uncomfortable silence that followed and the only noticeable sound was Claire's happy voice seeping under the classroom door.

I shifted slightly on the bench and heard the mother sitting in my bubble ask slowly, "So, what is wrong with your daughter?" Followed by, "My boy is here because he was born with spina bifida, so he can't walk."

I looked at her and told her I was sorry. I then told her that I didn't know what was wrong with my daughter. I elaborated that I hoped we could find out soon so that we could start helping her. Just then her boy scurried over to Claire and gestured to his throat.

"Ooh!" I heard the mother next to me exclaim as she rose suddenly from the bench. "I gotta get in there, John has a tracheotomy and I have to suction it when it gets plugged," she hurriedly explained. And then she paused for a very brief second, placed one hand on the tracheotomy kit that hung permanently around her neck, looked at me and said, "I am so very sorry about your girl, at least I *know* what John has. I feel really lucky." And with that she disappeared into the classroom with her suction kit.

Why do you do those things you do
They upset my balance so
Motions you make in my direction
Only confuse me, split me in two.
Take me into another direction I beg, I beg of you.
Or is it something that absolutely, you cannot do?

D.L. Clarke

Chapter 18

School continued and became a regular routine for us just like everything else eventually had. Two times a week I loaded the kids into the car and drove Aubrey to see Claire. She was becoming my hero, and Aubrey seemed to have taken quite a liking to her as well. The way she spoke to her class caused even the deaf children to respond with gales of silent laughter and joy. Everyone seemed to look up to Claire. The school staff, the assistants, even Joe the janitor talked highly of her.

I saw changes in Aubrey that gave me hope. For instance, I had started using some of the hand motions that Claire used in class, along with short phrases that I articulated. I noticed that it got Aubrey's attention and the short articulated words and phrases *held* her attention. Using direct tones along with the articulation also achieved results.

Instead of saying, "Aubrey, put that toy down and come over here." I would say, "Toy down, come here." I remembered the first time I had heard Claire talk that way, I thought she was a little too blunt for pre-school age children. But after trying *that* method at home, and getting results, I completely clung to *everything* Claire did in class.

If she calmed a child that was having a tantrum, I watched how she did it. If someone threw a toy and needed discipline, I observed Claire's intervention and would try it with Aubrey. Her methods were making things a little smoother at home. However small the difference, it *was* a difference and I knew it was helping.

Aubrey began interacting with the other children in the class after the first two weeks had passed. She was hesitant to talk and would not initiate any interactions with them, but with Claire's urging and instruction, Aubrey had begun to slowly respond a little.

I was also beginning to relax a little more when another child would approach Aubrey. Her normal response a few weeks prior would have been to throw sand at them (on the playground), or if they asked for a toy that she had, she would scream violently, which would successfully terrify the child into running away forgetting all about the wanted toy.

That had always been a huge deterrent when deciding whether or not to take the kids to the park. I hated trying to be the referee in such instances because nothing I did made anything better. The parents would be angry at me for *allowing* my child to throw things at their precious Molly or Janie or Jacob or…you get the picture, and it was fruitless for me to try to explain why my child behaved the way she did. (Where was that stupid T-shirt that would explain everything, when I needed it?)

I didn't even know what was making her behave the way she did. I just let the other parents look at me in disgust as they gathered up their children and remarked loudly that, "they would find another park to play at." Uh, no need, you see, I am gathering up my children and leaving too. I would often cry all the way home from such adventures.

I was so encouraged by Aubrey's progress in Claire's class that I didn't even mind, well, too much, having to get acquainted with all the other mothers that were slowly invading my very large safety bubble. I think they were puzzled by my reluctance to share my "story" about Aubrey with them. It had not been my initial intent to hold back from explaining why I had enrolled Aubrey; it just had always seemed the wrong time to speak up.

Most of the mothers had tragic stories about their children. I heard story after story of their tortured birthing experiences. How they had almost died and then when their child was finally born, then to find out that they were challenged with Down's Syndrome, or did not have a closed spinal cord, or had been born without arms and legs.

Their stories were tragic and sad, which made me more aware of how lucky I was to have such a healthy child. After all, who was I to sit and moan about my sleepless nights and months of putting up with 20-30 tantrums daily? I suddenly felt ashamed and out of place out there with all the mothers who desperately were trying to give their challenged children hope for a successful future.

Was I being too hard on my daughter? Expecting her to be something that she was not or could never be? Maybe she was just a shy toddler. Maybe she was angry because she had to share space with her new brother? Questions mounted themselves and rode gallantly across my scattered mind, while I listened and absorbed another tragic story from a weeping mother sitting next to me on the bench.

"Why don't you tell us why you are here?" I heard her say after she blew her nose violently into her Kleenex. I looked at her swollen red eyes and felt suddenly a little defensive.

"I am not sure what is wrong with Aubrey," I said cautiously, thinking they would all groan and turn away at my pathetic response. "Claire wanted Aubrey to be here," I continued as the mothers leaned in closer to me. "She thought that she would be able to help us," I threw in adding to my defense.

"So you don't know what is wrong with her at all?" one of them asked. They all looked at each other and I was waiting for the groan and turn away. But they didn't. Instead, they peered at me intently wanting to know more. I told them how foolish I felt whining about my problems when they had such difficult challenges of their own. They did all finally groan at *that* and insisted that I "spill."

Even though I knew it was going to be undoubtedly difficult for me to let loose and "spill," I still felt as if I needed to. Perhaps these people could help me? I needed to find out. Exhausting all resources to help Aubrey had been my agenda all along, and this situation and these people could be no exception.

As I began to talk to the mothers, it felt like a dam burst inside of me. I had six pairs of eyes staring at me with sincere emotion. It was refreshing when I explained the tantrums and they all could relate. They were all sympathetic and truly listened to the words I said. They would often interject how sorry they were and how they wished I knew what was the matter with my daughter. Then they would all glance around and tell each other how lucky they all felt because they *knew* what was wrong with their kids.

When I told them about the times when Aubrey seemed to close herself into a shell and not talk, one of the mothers interjected that her son Ryan does the same thing. When I related the sleepless nights, the odd behaviors, the toe walking, sensitivity to textures, and her intolerance to touch, the same mother whole-heartedly agreed with me.

"Yep, Ryan is the exact same way! I can't even give him a bath without him going through the roof when I try to wash his hair!" she said. Then she told me that we needed to get together and talk when we had more time. I completely agreed. Somehow we both knew that we needed each other. What we didn't know was that the stories we would share were going to be little lights that would eventually grow into hope and guide our paths to better understanding our children.

Now that I had made an acquaintance at Aubrey's school, I looked forward to going even more as it had turned into somewhat of a therapy session for Ryan's mom, Heather, and I. When she had a bad morning, she would tell me about it and we could laugh and relate. When I would come into class after a sleepless night, she would offer to bounce Austin on her knee to give me little break. It was wonderful having someone to talk to who was going through the same type of things with their child as I was.

What it also meant to me was that whatever Aubrey had, might possibly be something that could be found and hopefully treated. Now that Heather and I had discovered that both Aubrey and Ryan apparently shared the same type of problems, we both found it to be comforting in a strange sort of way. It also enabled me to become more focused and lose some of the feelings of despair that had tagged along with me on the first day of school.

One morning after class let out and children found their mothers and vice versa, Claire motioned to me that she wanted to talk. I gathered Austin up and we walked over to where she was standing. She asked LeAnn to take Aubrey out into the hall to hang her drawing up. I was beginning to get a little apprehensive by the look on Claire's face.

"I am concerned about Aubrey," Claire stated. "She rarely makes eye contact, and when she does, it is very brief. She has also been begging me for food all morning! We had snack and she still persisted. It is almost like she is getting "stuck" or fixated on certain things. I also thought she would be getting better with the social aspects by now, but it has been four months. It really has not improved much at all and it confuses me," she said, sighing. "Aubrey won't interact with the children unless I take her over and begin the contact, and she is very reluctant to maintain contact at all with the other children," she added.

"Is there something that I can do at home to help?" I asked hopeful.

"Well, maybe, but I do have a suggestion that I would like you to consider, " she stated. "And, of course, this would be entirely up to you, but I think it may help get some answers," Claire said smiling cautiously at me.

"Yes! Anything to help!" I agreed wholeheartedly, then suddenly remembered the mesh swing incident. "Actually, exactly what did you have in mind?" I proceeded, deciding I would need clear details before plunging forward.

"I think it would be wise to have Aubrey evaluated by Dr. Daniels at Clover Ridge. She is known statewide for her expertise in children with developmental delays. I really think she might be able to help you fill in the blanks as to what is going on with Aubrey," Claire said matter-of-factly.

I wondered where this Dr. Daniels had been for the past year of Aubrey's life? Why wasn't she beckoned before now? What was the magic potion that had caused her to appear and answer all our questions? And then, as if she were reading my mind, which I wouldn't doubt included in one of her many talents, Claire said, "Dr. Daniels has just began accepting new patients again after eleven months. There is a very high demand for her and it is pretty hard to get in to see her," Claire said.

Now that I knew she had mind reading abilities, I tried clearing my head of all thoughts that did not pertain to the subject at hand, which I found nearly impossible. I thought about what Dr. Daniels might do to my child that the other thousands hadn't already, only to end up empty-handed. I thought about the tests that she might have up her sleeve that would make my child frantic and uncomfortable. (Again, the mesh swing incident came to mind, followed by the Ritalin incident). I wondered how I would feel if she did in fact hold the answers to my daughters mysterious condition. What if she ended up not finding anything out at all? What would I say or do if I was informed that something *had* been discovered? And what if there was nothing that could be done? My mind continued to drift away, deep in thought and worry.

What, what is this maze you put me through
Am I such an idiot that I cannot trace
This path this apparent ridicule?
Stop it! I want to scream, scream it loudly
Right in front of you
Though you are wise, possess such charm, such wit
Such grace such power, for shame am I
That oh bother, I did go and forget
For just a moment though, for
unfortunately for you, am I no fool.

D.L. Clarke

Chapter 19

I had always held out hope that there would be a magic pill that would take the tantrums away from Aubrey and make her comfortable and at ease. I do not think I fully realized how ridiculous that fantasy sounded or was. My mind drifted back to when I had given the fantasy legs and let it run off with my child.

After hearing another opinion from yet another professional, ADHD had been brought up as a possible diagnosis for Aubrey. Because she was only two years old at the time, the doctor said the only way to really see if she had ADHD was to do a trial of some medication. My gut told me that she was way too little for medication trials, but the plaques on the doctor's wall suggested that he knew otherwise. So, we were given a prescription for Ritalin. This was supposedly going to be the magic that took away Aubrey's strange behaviors, along with the rage attacks and tantrums.

I was hopeful, but worried. Drug my child? Did she truly need it? Would the behaviors stop? The tantrums as well? I desperately wanted something to help her, but I was also scared of doing the wrong thing. I should have trusted my gut, but I didn't. I listened to my neighbor Cheryl instead.

Though she lived just a door away from me, the conversation we usually had just consisted of a brief "hello." If I were in a really talkative mood, I would summon up a "have a nice day," much to her surprise. Then the topic of

Ritalin came up. I hadn't even wanted to discuss it with her, but there was one particular afternoon she seemed to be bursting with something enormously wonderful to tell me.

I could tell immediately that the usual "hello" wasn't going to suffice. No, today she just *had* to tell me all about her newly found cure all for her son Timothy who was suffering with Attention Deficit Disorder with Hyperactivity. She felt obligated, she gushed, to spread the word. Cheryl became more and more enthused throughout her success story and I remembered feeling a bit relieved hearing what wonders Ritalin had done for her son.

Apparently, Timothy had gone instantly from being completely out of control to extremely manageable, according to his mom. Yes, Cheryl was definitely convinced that Timothy would no longer be the tyrant he once was, now that she had Ritalin. "I am sure you have noticed the changes in Tim, huh?" she had quizzed me. I honestly hadn't, but I told her I had anyway. No need for me to burst the enormous joy bubble she had formed around herself.

Cheryl was so convinced that the medicine had definitely made a huge and helpful difference that she repeatedly encouraged me to give it a try, after all, she almost guaranteed I would see instant results! Boy! Did that ever sound great!

Right after dinner, as prescribed, I gave Aubrey 2 mg of Ritalin ground up in a small spoonful of applesauce, and began to wait. I went about my nightly chores of dishes, laundry, refereeing tantrums, etc., while watching for signs of immediate improvement in Aubrey's condition. I eventually loaded Aubrey into her stroller, (without the usual *stroller drama* she normally provided), and headed outside with Brittney for a walk.

The anticipation of the "wonder drug" was making me nervous and doubt tugged at me in every direction. We walked around the neighborhood until the sun went down and then headed for home. Aubrey was her same ole' self and I was beginning to think the Ritalin had been useless.

It was soon bedtime, and oddly enough, it proved completely uneventful. Maybe the drug *was* working after all? I kept waiting for more signs of her recovery. Unfortunately, they never made an appearance.

I should have trusted my gut. Instead, I put my trust in everyone around me and just ignored what it was trying to tell me. However, when it woke me up quite abruptly one hour after I had fallen asleep, it was time to listen to it.

I heard Aubrey screaming and I automatically jumped out of my bed and raced into her room. I could see her standing up in the middle of her bed screaming and pulling at her hair. I tried to grab her to take her out of the room, but she recoiled at my attempt and slammed herself onto the bed. Aubrey writhed and her body buckled. When she rolled onto her back, she would flip and be on her stomach the next instant. She looked like an alligator in the death roll. Over and over Aubrey tossed and turned, wriggling and squirming wildly. I knew I had to get her out of the room and calm her, if I could.

She was oblivious to everything around her. I spoke to her calmly. Then, when that failed, tried being more firm. Nothing worked. She was completely out of control and nothing I did seemed to help. The writhing and rolling would not stop and I thought that Aubrey was possibly having a nightmare that she could not wake herself out of. I had to do something to help her!

I was afraid that she was going to hurt herself by thrashing her body on the wall and headboard of the bed. I was surprised and thankful that she had not fallen out of her bed during all the rolling. I grabbed Aubrey as gently, yet firmly, as I could and held her. I could feel her heart racing a million miles an hour. Aubrey's chest was heaving in and out and her hair was again matted with sweat and tears.

Shit! What had I done? I knew then that this was a reaction to the wonder drug. The doctor had warned me that Aubrey might have an "adult reaction" to the medicine if she was not in need of the Ritalin, and to expect some "excitability." Obviously, this was what was happening. The dosage was tiny, but so was she. I hated myself for trusting that damned doctor! Where was he NOW?

I sat beside Aubrey's bed all night, my hand gently resting on her chest, and watched her. She was restless off and on, but she had calmed down considerably after the initial episode and was able to sleep off and on throughout the night. I left her bed only long enough to use the toilet and check on Brittney. If anything were to happen to Aubrey because of this medicine, I would not have been able to forgive myself.

In the morning, as Aubrey woke up and trod down the stairs for breakfast, I stopped in the bathroom long enough to grab the bottle of Ritalin, take the lid off, and toss it's contents into the toilet. I watched the water carry the "wonder drug" around in circles and then finally downward and out of sight.

Once I got into the kitchen, I picked up the phone and called Aubrey's doctor's office. With my voice trembling and my hands shaking on the receiver, I respectively requested that my daughter be released from his care. I would pick up her records later, I concluded.

As my head spun from the recollection, I was brought back to the present by Claire asking me if I would like to give Dr. Daniels a call and schedule a consultation. I guessed that I would. After reliving the nightmarish Ritalin incident and then the morning phone call to Dr. Johnson, I thought I should probably keep trying to see if I could get some answers, but in another direction.

"Yes, that would be just fine," I heard myself agree. I drove home in a daze.

I called Dr. Daniels precisely three hours after I got home from Claire's class. It had taken me that long to decide what I should do. When I did finally decide to call her, it was almost five o'clock in the afternoon. Their office would be closing in ten minutes. Claire had warned me about their strict cancellation policy, therefore, once the appointment was made, there would be no backing out without money exchanging hands.

Dr. Daniels' office had an opening to see Aubrey a little sooner than I had expected. Before I knew it, Aubrey and I were sitting in her office waiting for her arrival.

Such quick things you notice, take heed
Then disappear, you do
Upon me you grant one wish
But oh if you could grant me two?
Wish upon such things, I need, I might,
Be able to give
my little one some peace tonight.

D.L. Clarke

Chapter 20

The décor in the office was basically certificates of achievement and I noticed her name had several different members of the alphabet tagging behind it. It appeared that she really would know what was going on with my daughter. I took in a slow cleansing breath and shifted in my seat.

The doctor almost exploded through the door. I say this because, in one instant there had been just myself and Aubrey in the room, then suddenly there was the blur of a person, a whirl of paper and then the doctor sat twirling in the seat behind her desk. The door slammed behind her as the papers settled. Dramatic, I thought to myself. *So much* drama.

Dr. Daniels spoke in a heavy accent that made it difficult to understand what she was saying, and she spoke very fast. What I did get out of the conversation was that she was going to visit with Aubrey and then give me her assessment. Wow! I was impressed! Here I had been dragging my daughter all over Timbuktu searching for answers, when this little, black haired, pointy nosed, too well dressed, superstar had them all. I could hardly wait to hear what she had to say.

As suddenly as she had arrived, she was gone, flapping down the hall toward the "intake" room. I was instructed by another lady that appeared suddenly at the door (where were all these people hiding anyway?), to head down the hall with Aubrey and take a right at the end of the *first* hall. *That* hall would then lead to *another* hall, which I would take a left at the end of and finally end up at the place where Dr. Daniels was waiting. I needed a map.

After pausing a second, to think about all the lefts and rights I had to make, I shrugged my shoulders and headed off in the wrong direction. Another woman, who suddenly appeared in a doorframe, immediately redirected me. " No, honey, you need to go down *that* hall!" she said with a plastic smile. Maybe it wasn't so plastic. I think I could have been possibly overanalyzing the moment due to my intense stress of getting lost in the doctor maze. I secretly hoped it wasn't an indirect test of *my* intelligence.

I could just see them all now, with their number two pencils, sitting behind one way glass, knowingly filling in the blank circles next to "dim wit," and "no sense of direction." They would all concur that this was indeed why my daughter had difficulties, and I would be sent down *another* hall, toward the exit. It would save them all a few hours' time and they could all have an early Friday.

I *somehow* found the room where Dr. Daniels was waiting. I think she had a smirk on her face, but I will let that go for the time being. She instructed me to leave Aubrey in the room with her and sit out in the hall in the observation area. I knew what that meant, for you see, we had been through this many times before. Different place, same type of deal.

Aubrey sat in a little chair in the room across the hall from me, fiddling aimlessly with a block of colored wood. I watched as Dr. Daniels presented her with various wood pieces and then proceeded to begin a conversation with Aubrey. Although Aubrey did not respond, Dr. Daniels kept presenting sentences and asked Aubrey to point out pictures and word combinations. Still, there was no response from Aubrey. I was pleased. This was definitely going to show the doctor that she was not responding normally.

Another tester came into the room and Dr. Daniels left. I watched as Aubrey slid half way down her chair and looked at the mirror. Her eyes seemed so sad as she seemed to stare straight at me. Suddenly I felt overwhelmed with sadness and guilt. The doubts and questions picked away at me once again and though I wanted them to stop, I knew they were just getting started.

I watched as Aubrey followed the tester out of the room. I heard a door shut quietly and Dr. Daniels and Aubrey came walking down the hall to where I was sitting.

"Yeeeessssss," Dr. Daniels started speaking in her accent. "You little Aubrey are just a shy little guhhrrl, aren't you?" the doctor continued with a smirk. (Okay, now she was definitely smirking.) "She is ohhh kay," Dr. Daniels concluded, as her hands flipped to the sides of her body nonchalantly.

"What do you mean by *okay*?" I said bewildered. My heart had started racing the second I heard the superstar Dr. Daniels say that Aubrey was *just shy*. *Not* this again, dammit!

"When will you have the results from the testing?" I asked, knowing that there *must* be more to this than *just shy*.

"No, that is all," Pointy Nose said. "We see chillllrreen like theeese all the time. Parents think there is something wrrrong and then there is not. Just shy! She will be fiiinnne!" the too well dressed brainy woman with the pointy nose said.

"You don't understand!" I almost shouted. Then more quietly, "You do not understand, this, *these* behaviors are not *normal*!" I continued fully aware that my voice was rising above the hush of the hallway. After seeing that Aubrey had seated herself a bit further down the hall on another bench with a book, I decided it was safe for me to continue. I yanked at my purse and hauled out my *list of things that concern me* and shoved it in front of the superstar. I had thought briefly of not bringing it, hoping that there would not be a need for its presence.

"My daughter *does not* respond normally to people and it isn't just being *shy*! She won't let even her grandparents touch her, well, most of the time! She clings to me in public and screams non-stop in shopping malls. She tantrums sometimes more than twenty five times a day and they can last over thirty minutes at a time!" I was just getting started. I looked at Dr. Daniels who had switched on a "oh I will listen to you and send you on your way look." Superstar my ass! Who was she trying to kid anyway?

"Aubrey won't play with toys unless I almost force her to, and she will beg me for food hours at a time, even right after eating! She once asked me for a cookie over seventy-five times in row! And yes, I *did count*! Is *that* normal? Is *that being shy*? Look at my list! These are just some of the things that Aubrey has to have in order to have a good day! *No!* How about a good *hour*!" I could feel my hands going cold and my heart had started to race frantically, but I kept going anyway, "Why does she shred paper? Huh? Loads and loads of paper into tiny little shredded up bits? And crackers! She takes crackers and crumbles them into tiny specks and then tries to eat them! Then, to make matters worse, she then will scream because there are cracker crumbs stuck all over her hands and she can't get them off!" I concluded, almost shouting and definitely panting. Pointy Nose Superstar Brain woman did not look amused nor interested. Instead, she just looked at me absently and waited for me to stop my rant.

"All children are differrrrent, you know?" Pointy Nose Superstar in the white jacket spoke up, just as I was considering which form of torture would be best suited to administer. Under the circumstances, I figured a buffet of various techniques would do. I honestly could not believe what I was hearing. I was completely floored, but then again, I should have known.

It was always that damned thing called hope that urged me onward to seek out expert advice, to find the answers. I didn't know whether to trust *my gut* anymore, or have it bypassed altogether.

"I know all kids are different," I said as snidely as I possibly could. "Aubrey isn't *just* a different child. There are things that are not explainable that are making her sad and angry. Things that make her strike out and shut down all in the same instance." Didn't they know all of this already? Why did I have to keep explaining this, over and over?

Wasn't *anyone* listening to me? "I thought you would have the answers to these questions for me, but you don't," I said almost ready to cry. "I have to find out how to help my daughter. So, if you don't have any answers for me, then we need to go," I said emphatically, while collecting my things off the bench.

"Therrre is onnnne morrre thing we can try," Superstar chimed in. "I can recommend, you see, your daughhhhtter to see a specialeeest at CDMRC. You go? No?" Pointy Nose Superstar asked, looking at me quizzically.

She had caught me off guard and I was shaking. I was in no mood to either play games or make decisions. Why hadn't she mentioned this *before* I got myself into a lather and threatened to leave? I guessed she was having second thoughts to her original diagnosis of "she is okay." What was CDMRC anyway?

"What is CDMRC anyway?" I asked out loud this time, my voice trembling.

"It is a wonnnnderful place that has many expeerrrts that will help you," Too well dressed brain woman said. "The clinic speccccializzes in children with difficulitiesssss, uh, such as what you describe your daughter as having. CDMRC is a wonnnnderful place, yesss. Many experts," she stated again.

Oh huh? What? Experts like you? "Okay," I heard my mouth say, "I will take Aubrey there," I heard my mouth continue. "When can they see her?" My mouth had stopped paying attention to my brain at this point. I wanted to tell it to shut up.

"What was the point in dragging Aubrey to any more places?" My brain would say in defense to my mouth. The visit with Superstar Black Haired Pointy Nose had been useless...unless...(This is the part where the brain always won out) maybe, just maybe this was the *stepping-stone* that would get us into this CDMRC place that *would* have the answers? Everything happens for a reason, *doesn't it*? See how my brain was beginning to justify all the madness? See how hope kept taking cuts to the front of the line? See how pathetically stupid I was to keep trying over and over, after getting shot down a hundred million times?

My brain continued observing itself thinking and collected my daughter and drove it's body home. Two weeks and approximately one hundred and fifty tantrums later, my brain found itself driving its body, along with the reluctant mouth, into the parking lot of CDMRC.

I am sorry, baby girl, for what I have had to do
For what I have already done, they promise
Supposedly, and ironically, been put into place for you.
Somehow, these things they say
Will find your spirit free, and at peace, someday.

D.L. Clarke

Chapter 21

As the car pulled into the parking lot, a sign displaying the words Child Development Mental Retardation Center, stood set in concrete at the base of a giant gray building. I mouthed those words several times as a feeling of dread came over me. "Child Development Mental Retardation Center," kept silently flowing as I put the car into park and slowly released my seat belt. The words literally sent chills down my spine. Aubrey wasn't *retarded*! I already knew the "experts" would be way off with their diagnosis even before I entered the building. None the less, I found myself in the lobby waiting for the "experts" to arrive.

As Aubrey and I waited, I took the opportunity to observe the other families in the room. I couldn't help but notice that most, if not all, the children waiting with their parents had obvious delayed development and some sort of retardation either in speech or in physical movement. A couple of the children were sucking their hands while talking unintelligibly in highly amplified voices to whoever would listen. Another child sat and rocked on the floor, moaning repeatedly. The child's mother was engrossed heavily into a magazine, seemingly unaware of the rocking and moaning. I surmised that this was nothing out of the ordinary for her or the child.

The same feeling of gratefulness came over me as I watched Aubrey cram yet another book into her face. I didn't have it so bad, really. Did I? The foolish feeling came over me next as my child sat quietly looking at pictures in a book, and the other kids in the room created chaos and levels of noise that were beyond tolerable.

I met eyes with one of the mothers as her child rammed into her knees with his head, not once, but over and over again. As his head smacked into her bone, he let out a loud "weeeeeeeee." She pleaded with him to stop, and then (possibly embarrassed that she had no control), finally stood up with a sigh and headed over to a window. Her son followed behind, bellowing loudly after her.

As she stood, obviously admitting defeat, our eyes met and I immediately felt her angst. It was as if she were reaching out for help and understanding, but unable to speak the words. She looked completely defeated and worn, tired and about ready to give up.

I easily recognized that look. I had seen it a million times in my own face, having spent many nights gazing helplessly into my own tear soaked eyes in the mirror, searching for answers and help.

It didn't take too long before Aubrey and I were led down a corridor, (I say corridor because it was sort of dark and a little cold, different than your typical hallway), and into a small room without windows. It was also absent of one way glass, as far as I could tell anyway. Aubrey was fidgety and cranky. She was tired of sitting and flipping randomly through books. She had been up most of the night and the morning had started with her begging for a cookie over and over, relentlessly, despite my firm and constant refusals.

I watched as Aubrey toe walked all over the room, hopping up on my lap and then back down again. She was restless and it was making me feel restless too. I wanted this to be over with and be done with clinics and centers and expert's offices.

I was tired of being looked at behind one way mirrors and, furthermore, tired of observing my child being pushed beyond her limits. It really wasn't doing any good, and I had decided that this was going to be the last place I brought her to. There would be no more clinics or tests. No more watchful and dissecting eyes being cast our way filled with doubt and suspicions as to my integrity as a parent. I just needed it all to be over with.

If the experts at CDMRC didn't produce a diagnosis or a treatment plan, then I would just do my best to help Aubrey on my own. I hadn't been doing too bad of a job, really. I had tolerated her tantrums for two and a half years, hadn't I? Surely she would outgrow them at some point?

The pre-school seemed to help somewhat, so we would continue with that.

See? Everything was going to be great no matter what happened today, I concluded. I knew that I was just giving myself a line of bullshit, but I thought I would beat the experts to it for a change. Besides, it seemed a lot less disheartening hearing it from myself.

Aubrey was whisked away for what seemed like days. Hours passed and it took all I had to keep from pacing like an expectant father in a hospital waiting room. There were so many families waiting and talking and chit chattering away that it was making me crazy. Mother's were sharing their birthing horror stories and I do not know how many times I heard: "And that is why Mike, Johnny, Christy, etc. is the way he/she is."

They would all huddle together and say how sorry they were as the next mother would begin with her saga of misery.

I do not want to sound mean or spiteful, it just seemed like there was always a tragic story and one person's tragic story always outdid the other persons; and on and on. Most of the tales included blood and guts, (if you know what I mean); and please, the children were *right there* hearing it *all!* So, that is my resentment toward these tragic birthing stories. Enough said. I sat back down and tried to patiently wait for my daughter.

Aubrey appeared almost three hours after I had said goodbye to her and handed her off to one of the experts. She came walking into the waiting room looking very tired and not too happy about being there. The expert came over to me and informed me that I needed to make an appointment to come back in a week so they could go over the results.

I made the appointment with the lady behind the desk, who had watched me pace for the past three hours. Aubrey and I then walked out to the car. I didn't ask her how things went, I already knew. Aubrey's thumb was in her mouth and she was ready to sleep. I was ready for a nap too, but there was a two-hour drive ahead and one of us had to do the driving! I was actually looking forward to the quiet ride home, after hearing horror stories and children screaming for three hours in the waiting room.

I got Aubrey into her car seat and buckled myself in for the trip and turned on the radio.

"NOOOOO!" I heard Aubrey scream from the backseat. "NO NO NO!" she kept screaming. I immediately turned the radio off, and tried to shush Aubrey into calming down.

"No radio, sweetie, it's okay now," I cooed toward the backseat. What had I been thinking anyway? I knew she hated the radio on most of the time, and I should have figured today would not be a good day for it!

"NO NO NO! Eat eat eat eat! I wanna eat!" she hollered at me. I reached into the bag on the opposite seat and grabbed an animal cracker.

"Here, Aubs, have some crackers!" I tried being as enthusiastic as I could. I grabbed a couple more crackers and tried handing them back to her. She slapped my hand away and the crackers fell to the car floor. I could feel my entire nervous system gearing up for the onslaught.

"EAT! EAT!" she cried. By this time, she was arching her back in the car seat stretching the straps tight against her chest. "Eat, I wanna eat!" she kept screaming.

Trying to stay as calm as I could, I asked her if she wanted a hamburger or maybe some chicken? We would stop at Burger King, but I had to find one first. My seat was being pummeled from the blitz of Aubrey's strong legs, million dollar shoes, and writhing body.

"NOW!" she screamed. She was grunting and hollering and in an instant bit herself on the arm.

"Aubrey no! No bite!" I cried out to her, using Claire's choppy sentence method. "Be nice!" I continued, watching her from the rear view mirror. There was no way that she was going to calm down. This was her way of letting go of the stress of the day. Jackie had warned me often about this method of relieving stress when there had been *sensory overload*.

I wondered if it would be beneficial to me if I bit my arm, but since I was driving, thought better of it. I also knew from experience that Aubrey would eventually wear her little self out and then would sleep. I hoped it would be sooner than later, because the highway was packed with cars. There was little chance to pull over, if needed. My nerves continued to rile themselves up and I could feel my body begin to shake all over.

Aubrey's tantrum lasted an hour. I had tried everything to get her to stop. When we pulled into a Burger King parking lot, she screamed louder. I tried talking calmly; then briefly shrieking as I almost went into the other lane when her decibel level shot into unhealthy limits.

I had no tangible option other than to just keep driving. I knew that if I pulled over and got her out of the car seat, I would never get her back into it, without some Good Samaritan reporting me for kidnapping. I knew this because, though I hadn't been reported yet, (to my knowledge anyway), I am sure I had been very close many times.

Take for instance, our typical scene at the mall when I could be spotted madly scrambling out to my car, hauling over my shoulder a screeching child that was screaming "NO NO NO!"

Then when I finally got to the car, I would often be bitten and slapped, kicked and screamed at as I was trying desperately to buckle her in the car seat. I knew what all the Good Samaritans were thinking: "What do you think, Bess? Think it's one of them abductions? Think we should get involved?"

Then, out of the grace of God, my car would start and I would tear out of the parking lot as calmly as possible, hoping that I had not actually cleaned *all* the mud off the license plates. I was a fugitive in my own mind.

Although I was doing nothing wrong, it felt as if I was being put on trial, silently judged and sentenced every time I went out into public with my child.

Give your pain to me, for I can
take its wrath, for that is clearly
the only reason I am.
Truly the purpose I have been so carefully placed
Within your grasp, is for that, I no longer fear.
Place all the burdens you hold upon me
Let my attempts take your angst away
For then perhaps I, floating amongst your angelic wings,
will truly begin to feel free.

D.L. Clarke

Chapter 22

After Aubrey finished screaming for the first hour on our way home, she slept for the next. It was refreshing and I used the time to think and unravel my bundled nervous system.

As I let my mind drift and recollect, I couldn't help but remember other notorious tantrum scenes that would have been grand enough to make the ten o'clock news.

The best-produced and directed tantrum episode we experienced took place in Seattle, Washington at the well-known Space Needle.

Aubrey was almost two years old at the time, and my parents had come up to Washington from Oregon to visit. We unanimously chose to take the ferry through the beautiful Puget Sound over to the city of Seattle.

Shopping at Pike Street Market, window-shopping, and lunch were on the agenda of events and we were all excited for our adventure. Little did we know that one of the cast members had a secret twist up her sleeve and would pull it out at the least opportune time.

The ferry ride was relaxing and the scenery was so beautiful along the way that I almost forgot about things for a while. It was nice to forget about things and just not think. My brain took a little reprieve and my body unwound for a few minutes. Nice. I breathed in the salted air and smiled into the sun, letting it warm my face.

I had packed everything that Aubrey might or could possibly need for the ferry rides, shopping, Space Needle ride, and lunch. Things like a wet washcloth in a plastic baggy, crackers for before lunch came, and books for the hated stroller rides while shopping.

I was completely prepared and I was so proud of Aubrey as she sat and read her books on the ferry over to the pier. We were off to a very good start of the day and I was letting my guard down. I was sincerely hoping that she was going to have a "good day."

Once the ferry reached the Seattle pier, I began preparations to get Aubrey into her stroller. I knew she hated the thing, but we had a long walk ahead of us and she was too small to make the trip on her little legs. As I unfolded the stroller, she immediately started screaming and arched her back, completely refusing to sit down in it. I looked around at the other passengers and saw their faces of disapproval. I couldn't bear a stroller scene right then. I have to choose my battles appropriately.

Should I hold firm and get her into the stroller? Or, should I let her win *this* particular battle and try the stroller again later? What did the crowd want me to do? What did my parents want me to do? What *should* I do?

We walked off the ferry, all of us, with me holding firmly onto Aubrey's little fist. The crowd didn't want a crying toddler ruining their day. I completely understood that and agreed whole-heartedly that I didn't care to have a crying toddler ruin *my* day either. It was so nice that I could read minds and figure all of that out in a few seconds of dirty looks. What a neat gift I had!

Aubrey ended up walking a block or two and then said she was tired. I could only imagine walking the hills in Seattle *on tiptoes*. No wonder she was tired! I offered the stroller and it was flatly refused. I bribed her with crackers. She yelled and made it quite apparent that she was never planning on riding in the stroller, *ever*.

I could tell that my parents were thinking I was letting her "rule the roost" (remember, I have mind reading abilities) but there were only so many battles I could wager. I wasn't sure if this one was important enough to start.

Aubrey continued to walk and we all followed her lead and shopped the window displays at a painstakingly slow pace. I had let her get her way on this one, and it was okay, I thought to myself. We weren't in a hurry, and I knew she vehemently loathed her stroller, so what was the harm?

We decided to eat before heading up the Space Needle, so we stopped at a little café and ordered our food. The food never came soon enough for

Aubrey, whether it was me cooking at home or we were eating out. Today, of course, was no exception.

The crayons offered by the waitress were only a momentary distraction for her. She wanted her food NOW! Crackers were offered and after accepting them, managed to immediately crumble them into minuscule crumbs then demand more. It wasn't until her lunch arrived that she finally stopped repeating, "eat" every few seconds, while thrashing back and forth in her seat. My parents shifted nervously in their chairs, gazing woefully at their apparent, non-normal granddaughter.

I was getting sort of used to fellow patrons of eateries staring our way, but my parents weren't. I knew it was embarrassing and I felt defensive and awkward trying to explain, so I didn't. I just continued trying to eat and ignored the evil stares being shot across the room as my child repeatedly demanded more food, and to get down, squirming and screaming in her chair, all the while.

When lunch had concluded, I was so relieved to be walking out into the fresh air and away from the judging eyes and bodies that sat stuffing their gossiping mouths. I secretly wished some of them would choke. No not really, but people had really started to bother me and I saw most of them as the enemy. None of them were sympathetic to my child's angst.

Well, truly, how could they be anyway? They probably just thought she was being a "brat" or was "spoiled rotten" and behaved poorly because of the "lack of discipline" from the parents. Yes, I had heard it all so many times before.

But, none-the-less, they all still wanted me to do *something,* to make her stop *whatever* she was doing at the time to disrupt their peace. Knowing this only created anxiety in me, which I am sure, somehow caused some of Aubrey's distress out in public. What a crazy and vicious cycle we rode!

We arrived at the base of the Space Needle and got our tickets to ride the elevator up the shaft of the needle to the observation deck. Brittney was excited to be going and I loved seeing her anticipation grow, as our turn got closer.

It wasn't long before we all crammed into the glass elevator and zoomed up to the observation deck. Along the way, I pointed out the pier where we had been just a few hours prior and we could even see one of the ferries taking off across the sound.

Shockingly enough, Aubrey appeared to enjoy the ride and pointed and watched out the elevator glass, as the city appeared smaller and smaller below us.

Once the elevator finally stopped at the very top of the Needle, we all got out to explore the sights from the circular deck. It was at this moment that Aubrey started to scream. Being very crowded and noisy on the deck, her screaming was not too noticeable, *yet.* I tried to quiet her by diverting her attention to the gift shop.

"Look, Aubrey! There is a little plastic ferry like we just rode on!" I gestured toward the store in desperation. She was not interested, and the screaming got louder and more intense. I began to sweat.

My parents had taken Brittney over to one side of the deck and they were looking out onto the city. Brittney was having a wonderful time looking through the telescopes at the city and I was glad they were not witnessing the scene Aubrey was beginning to create.

What Brittney and my parents were missing, the *other* hundred people were getting a first hand look at. Aubrey was thrashing around at this point, still screaming. I could not contain her and I was desperate to do something to get her to stop.

I felt sick to my stomach, knowing there was little I could do. But nonetheless, I had to appear to have it all under control. People had started their staring sprees, and seemed to be almost expecting me to produce a wand, say something incredibly wise and magically quiet my child. I wondered if they would applaud. The magic 8-ball in my head gave me a definite "don't count on it" answer.

I talked to Aubrey in a quiet soothing voice. Getting on my knees to be eye level with her, only got me a swift punch in the face by one of her flailing arms. The crowd gasped. Then, more firmly this time, I raised my voice slightly and told her she needed to stop! There was no response from Aubrey, unless you consider screaming louder a valid response. The crowd grew thicker and their comments started to loudly echo in my head, easily shooing my magic 8-ball out of its way.

I suddenly remembered Claire's explanation of the "squeeze machine" technique that was invented by a well known doctor afflicted with autism, Dr. Temple Grandin. Claire had described her own modified technique and said she had even used it in the past on some of her more "excitable" students, with apparent success.

Claire had went on to explain that Dr. Temple Grandin had produced an actual device, often referred to as a "Hug Box" or "Hug Machine," or as previously mentioned, a "Squeeze Machine," which was designed to provide lateral and inward pressure by the use of foam padding, to both lateral portions of a person's body.

Throughout initial clinical and non-clinical studies, Dr. Grandin found that by experiencing the applied deep and even pressure to the body, many people, including herself, afflicted with autism and/or hyper-activity disorders, could find some relief from the anxieties and nervousness associated with such disorders.

Even though I didn't have any foam, and I was easily convinced that there weren't going to be any "Squeeze Machines" readily available atop the Space Needle, I decided to give the technique a try anyway. I would follow Claire's example, and use my arms as the "foam" as she had demonstrated on one of her students in the past.

As I grasped onto Aubrey's hand and led her to a nearby bench, she started to scream louder, yelling "NO!" over and over again, so loudly that at times, my ears would ring. Though she tugged and pulled at my hand, trying to break free, I was able to make it to the bench with her.

As I sat down, I held Aubrey and faced her body outward away from my own. I then held both of her arms tight against her body with my own arms. I then hugged her tight against my body. She could no longer flail her arms and there would be no way she could escape. I knew how much she hated being hugged or held tightly, but I had to try something that might help, regardless. Exhaust all means, try everything...

People had stopped looking through the telescopes and were now choosing to use Aubrey and myself as their choice of entertainment. I could have become rich that day if I would have charged them each a dollar! They stared and talked to each other by holding their hands in front of their mouths and whispering.

Of course this method was so much less rude than actually talking *behind* my back! I was getting used to it and I provided my own silent counter attack, by repeating, "Stop staring, go away, go away, GO AWAY!" inside my head. Come to think of it, I actually might have muttered it unconsciously out loud, but the jury is still out on that one.

Aubrey lurched and tried several times to break free, but she couldn't. Her screaming continued for what seemed an eternity. The elevator opened and closed every few minutes or so and spilled out a new mass of soon to be staring people. Not wanting to disappoint the crowd, Aubrey lurched and wiggled and screamed like a wild animal. The crowd hushed and then began talking loudly amongst themselves.

"Why doesn't she *do* something?" one woman dressed in tight spandex stirrup pants, which sadly exemplified her cellulite, would say.

"I left *my kid* at home so I could have a quiet day!" one bald man with bright red, almost sunburned cheeks and a big white fluffy beard, stated loudly. A little *too* loudly and purposely, as far as I was concerned. I immediately had an evil thought and wondered why he had left his station at the Santa hut at the mall. Surely his elves would be missing him by now?

His rude comment was quickly followed with a, "Yeah, she's one brave lady alright!" from a gentleman dressed brilliantly in an overpriced business suit. Well, I don't know if it truly was overpriced; he could have, after all, gotten it at Goodwill or...I then heard chuckles as the crowd directed their gaze at my bulging pregnant belly.

Because I felt like I was about to cry, I did not respond and tried desperately to avoid making eye contact with any of them, which wasn't so difficult since I had already begun to stare at the back of my bellowing daughter's auburn head.

I was so ashamed that I did not and *could not* get control over my screaming child. I didn't want to be there and yet, there was no easy solution of leaving the scene.

I knew that there could be no way that I could possibly let go of Aubrey. The millisecond she got free, she would run and be lost in the crowd within seconds.

The repugnant stroller was not an option either. She was flailing so madly that getting her into it would be next to impossible. The only solution I could even consider was to abandon the stroller, along with my purse and camera it carried, and try to walk her over to the elevator to make our escape.

After glancing around the crowded platform quickly, I could see that my parents were not within sight, so the stroller abandonment didn't seem to be the wisest decision either. Instead, I ruefully decided that my only choice, at the moment, was to wait out the tantrum and take the stares and comments as they cascaded from the crowds' mouths and surrounded us.

My mind flipped like a bewildered moth for a moment and then gently took a little stroll. My body clinging to my daughter even more tightly than before. "Okay, it really would be okay," I kept silently saying over and over in my head. "Everything will be okay, okay, okay, okay, okay..." I could feel my body instinctually begin to rock, as if it were trying to coax itself into subjugating the stress.

As soon as I started to envision beaches and tropical trees—my brain was rudely interrupted and brought back to the present scene by my parents coming over and asking me why Aubrey had been screaming for almost twenty minutes.

There! I then knew it had just been a mere twenty minutes! Good to know, for I knew that I had at least another twenty or thirty minutes left in me to ride out the tantrum. I wanted to go back to the place my brain had taken me. It was a good place and I could find calmness there. Any storm could be weathered in that place, and somehow I had found it right when I needed it the most.

As my parents and Brittney continued to observe Aubrey's raging tantrum, I noticed a large group of Chinese men heading our direction. Immediately upon their arrival, one of the men held out a wrinkled hand filled with candy and offered it to Aubrey.

"Here, little girl," in a thick Chinese accent, "here is some candy for your little girl," they said as they held the candy out to Aubrey.

Just then I heard my step-mom intervene, "No, she can't have candy. She is okay and not hungry. She is just upset and will be fine. Thanks anyway!" I heard her finish. I was so happy to have the support of someone who *did* know that yes, my daughter *was* just having a tantrum, and didn't need to be saved by a little piece of candy.

What I *was* doing was the *best* for Aubrey at the time. I was suddenly so grateful that my step-mom had stayed behind briefly while Brittney and her grandpa took another stroll around the platform. She had given me her support, and although she didn't understand what was going on with Aubrey any more than what I did, she had stopped asking me what was wrong with her, and stood up for us regardless. I don't think she will ever realize how much strength that gave me at that moment.

The tantrum had lasted nearly forty minutes and was finally dying down. Now, both my parents, one pushing the "camera and purse" stroller, were walking with Brittney toward another telescope on the opposite side of the observation area. My head hurt and I felt sick and exhausted. Most of the people on the deck had cycled through several times and new audiences had formed every few minutes for the "Aubrey and Mom" show.

I was sure the reviews would be very good: "Sad," they would say, "but raw and truly modern day life." Frankly I was shocked that none of them had called security. Wait! Who was that coming toward me?

"Uh, is this your daughter, ma'am?" the tall man in the police like uniform asked me.

"Yes, she is my daughter, and she was having a tantrum," I said smiling warmly up at him, hoping I didn't have any food stuck in my teeth. Thank God I had the "instant, no food stuck in your teeth, paint on smile" handy! I looked around for my parents, thinking I may need some back up, but they had disappeared in the crowd.

"Well, okay then. We have just had several people coming down the elevator, complaining about a screaming child up here. Not sure what was going on, thought I had better check it out!" he finished, while placing his hands in the front pockets of his "a little too tight to actually look decent" security uniform and sighing deeply.

"Probably a good thing to check out, I guess! One can never be too sure nowadays!" I said, still smiling, the paint wearing slightly thin. By now I was convinced I must have a sesame seed or some obvious food particle stuck in my teeth. Why else would he be looking at me so oddly?

The security guard had stifled whatever had been left in Aubrey's tantrum and she was now quiet. I gingerly released my grip on her and I watched as she took a few steps away from the bench.

She looked back at me and gave me a little smile. I smiled back at her and told her that we needed to find grandma and grandpa, and Brittney. With that, she reached up and grabbed my hand and led me on a hunt for the rest of the family. The storm was over, and it was time to head for home.

Take the tests and exhaust their leads
Take from it the noise, the pain, and agony.
What perhaps are you left with then
Just the facts, that tell you nothing
Leaving instead
An ever vast, blank emptiness of confusion deep within.

D.L. Clarke

Chapter 23

My thoughts came back to the present as I pulled the car into our home driveway. I felt relieved to be safe at home and out of the critical eyes of the white-jacketed professionals at CDMRC.

Aubrey had slept soundly after the Burger King scene and the drive had given me time to wind down, think, and refresh. Even though I was exhausted, I had hope that in a week we would get the results from CDMRC and be on the right road to help Aubrey. After all, that place was known all over the state of Washington for it's amazing results in developmental diagnostics. I breathed a sigh of relief and started to make dinner for the kids.

The week spent waiting for the CDMRC appointment was nothing short of literal hell. Aubrey slept one night out of the six, and screamed non-stop during the days. Tantrums came and went by the half hour and I had no power to stop them or even ward them off.

They came and I just waited them out. *They* always seemed to win, for I was beginning to get too tired to fight them anymore.

I was also too tired to figure out why they came. As suggested by the staff at CDMRC, I *did* take note of the time of day that they did come, how long they stayed, and what was going on right before they showed up.

Gazing at "tantrum list" I could see absolutely no pattern or justification for their visits. Why were they tormenting my child? Why did they choose her for their path of delivery? I saw them as the enemy now and they definitely were expecting me to throw in the white towel at any moment.

They knew they had me over a barrel, and better yet, I didn't care. I just sat back, rode them out, and waited for the white-jacketed professionals at CDMRC to give me the solution that would conquer them once and for all. They wouldn't even see it coming, and Aubrey would finally be free.

The moment came that I was to drive to the world-renowned clinic. I weathered the storm of dreaded car seats and screaming children, driving the miles in my own bubble of thoughtful silence. I really hoped that this would be the last day that I had to wonder what was going on with Aubrey. I was so anxious and excited thinking that I would finally know the answers that would unlock the puzzles that kept my daughter captive. A little smile formed on my face at that thought. Hope...

Upon my arrival, I checked Aubrey in at the front receptionist desk and was asked to have a seat. No problem. We sat and waited for a white-jacketed professional to appear. It didn't take very long before one arrived and asked us to join him down the hall. Again, no problem.

I gathered Austin up, and walked with Aubrey, following the white coat as it darted and dodged the other similarly dressed professionals in its path. We found ourselves in a room adorned with professional looking things.

Cherry wood desks, large informative looking books lining the sturdy and polished shelving, and plaques bearing prestigious letters after official and proper names; even the garbage can was trimmed in shiny metal that beckoned praise. Impressive enough, but let's get to the real reason why we are here, okay?

"The testing scores were inconclusive due to Aubrey's inability to reach basal scores. However, due to the frequent and unprovoked tantrums and rage attacks, we would like to perform an EEG as soon as possible to rule out any seizure activity," the white coat said behind the cherry wood desk that was lined in gold and silver and—

"What the—what? Okay, calm down. What? Okay... seriously take a deep breath. *Really? What the—*" I screamed silently inside my head. I had wanted to say it out loud, to scream it, in fact, but my kids were right there and I was a good parent. Right? At least I had thought I was at one point.

I had heard all of this before. This was nothing new. No miracle cure and no answers to the puzzle. Just more crap thrown at us from a perfectly white coat that I wanted to throw things back at just to muck it up and make less perfect.

"We will determine the brain activity during a sleeping EEG and also during a wake period. Then we will compare and hopefully have some answers as far as seizure activity," the white coat continued in a monotone voice. Robotic, I think actually. Maybe that is how they slept at night after delivering these messages to families daily.

"Your child is retarded, but we can't figure out why," or, "You need to go home and read this book, it will have your answers." And, my all-time favorite, "Perhaps we should have a 'home visit' and determine the child's setting and see if—"

See if *what?* That I am beating my children daily or no, better yet, by the hour. Yes! Of *course* my child has rage and tantrums all the time! They are simply striking out any way they can because of all the anger and rage that the family is creating around the child! Wow! I should have had *that* one all figured out and saved myself all the trouble and expense!

I made a mental note to myself to purchase a fine wooden desk made out of the richest mahogany wood that money could buy, and after setting it up in my home, I would hang a plaque showing how great I was. It would indeed symbolize what a genius I had become, especially to those that I seemed somewhat clueless to. Yes, my desk and plaque would back me up. A surge of something had rushed over me and I felt instantly and completely insane.

Not even knowing what letters I would add after my "important" name on my hand-made plaque, in my homemade office with fine mahogany wood, I had to logically, and however rapidly, ditch the idea entirely and I felt myself sink deeper into my chair and even further into the insanity that, temptingly so, beckoned my exhausted mind.

"Leave, leave...leave...just leave!" it taunted me continually, as I shifted uneasily in my fine leather chair. "Get up and leave, now!" it added fervently, finally concluding with a colossal, "Just do it, *NOW!*"

"I have a phone," I heard my mouth tell the white coat. "You could have just called me and let me know you needed to do another test," it continued spouting off as the white coat shifted uncomfortably in it's own fine leather seat.

I added to my mental note, "Must also get a fine leather chair, definitely in black, to go with the desk and plaque." I then wondered if IKEA might have an adequate ensemble. I imagined that they would, and with that, put my rapid thought to rest for the time being. But, my mind continued to slip into madness, and it would have gone on a little shopping spree if it hadn't been interrupted by the white coat's response.

"Uh, yes, I understand your frustration about this—" it started to say pathetically.

"You *do* understand?" my mouth said. I now realized it was on an unstoppable mission. "No, I really don't think you do. I have waited almost three years to find out what is going on with my little girl and have taken her everywhere trying to find help and I am getting absolutely nowhere."

I heard my mouth continue, a little muddled this time. "What? Do you think I am stupid? Do you think I am a bad parent? Do you really think that it is *my* fault my daughter is like this? *Is it* my fault? What have I done wrong? Tell me *that!*" My mouth continued to move but apparently had run out of things to say.

Probably a good thing, although judging from the look on the white coat's face, it wouldn't have cared either way. It was probably lunchtime or something and I was a huge distraction on the way to the cafeteria. It was probably some gourmet café like place with salads and freshly baked goods for the white coats to consume. Brain food! Ha!

I knew I had to get off this train of thought or I would likely end up requiring heavy sedation, which didn't sound like a bad idea at this point. But, there was the drive home, and it would take a rocket scientist to help me back through the doctor office maze. So, sedation was really not an option, but I did tuck the thought away safely for future consideration.

Aubrey was scheduled to have the EEG done in two weeks. They reassured me that if they had an opening sooner, they would let me know. The EEG was also going to be performed at a hospital that was even a further drive than what CDMRC was. Another long drive. Perfect!

"Please understand that because the results of the test will need to be transferred back over to CDMRC, it will take a few days longer than normal for us to know how things turned out," I heard the white coat explaining.

Okay, so, two weeks plus a few more days. It seemed like another eternity and I wondered if my nerves would hold out that long. All the waiting and testing seemed to become a ritual and it didn't appear that we were getting any type of tangible result that was actually going to help Aubrey.

Would we eventually? Ever? Was it worth it? *Would* it be worth it? Those are the questions without answers that kept me going.

The words filter and shine upon the blank pages
Almost beckoning my unobstructed gaze.
'Stop It! Stop It!' I want to scream, and yet I halt.
Amidst the chaotic lines of verse I stare
For within the smeared blue and black ink, my love
I find you quietly, hiding there.

D.L. Clarke

Chapter 24

Later that same day, as I was sitting on the couch in my living room watching the neighbor dog chew up a tennis ball, I decided to become more diligent with the daily "tantrum" journal. I would document, record, videotape, everything that happened on a minute-by-minute course. I wanted to have *something* for the professionals to look at and hold in their hands. Apparently, my *list of things that concern me* wasn't doing the job.

Perhaps seeing each and every tantrum and episode on paper and videotape would make it more real to them? Maybe if they felt a tiny bit of what Aubrey was going through they would feel compelled to do something, dig deeper, and come up with a solution.

The urgency to begin the new "minute-to-minute" journaling arrived at just the right time, for, seconds after my decision, Aubrey was awake and screaming in her bed. I grabbed for a pen, noted the time and date, and then hurriedly jotted the information down onto a hunk of newspaper laying on the coffee table. I could transfer the information later into a notebook I thought out loud as I rushed up the stairs to retrieve my daughter from her bed.

April 6
3:29 p.m. Aubrey is up screaming from her nap

4:00 p.m. has had several tantrums since she woke up, no apparent reason.

6:21 p.m. another tantrum, this time because she wanted to eat NOW!

April 7

5:02 a.m. Aubrey was up screaming most of the night. "Mommy help me," she screamed as she thrashed in her bed. I wasn't able to get her attention. Suddenly she began laughing hysterically. It really scared me since it has been awhile since she has woken so violently. Went back to sleep only after I brought her downstairs and rocked her in chair.

6:35 a.m. She's up now- eyes are very red- seems almost dazed- maybe just exhausted. Tongue is out- face is expressionless.

7:23 a.m. Went back to sleep after rocking her again in chair.

9:12 a.m. Aubrey just woke up screaming again.

10:00 a.m. Had three major tantrums since 9 a.m. She is just crying and screaming for no apparent reason. Didn't eat breakfast- maybe doesn't feel well?

11:30 a.m. Ate a good lunch. Eyes are very swollen and red from crying. Is quiet now- sucking thumb more today than usual.

12:30 p.m. Asked me to go lay her down in her bed. Slept until 2:30 p.m.

April 10

Having no time to write down events! Many tantrums and is angry all the time!

April 12

Last few days have been horrid. Aubrey screams and tantrums every hour or so. They continue no matter what I try. She shoved a pillow onto Austin's head then sat on it and laughed when he started to cry. I sat her in "time-out" and explained why she was taking time-out. She wouldn't meet my eyes and smiled the whole time. I am not reaching her.

April 15

8 a.m. Has occupational therapy today. Woke up screaming- doesn't' want to wait for breakfast. Wouldn't eat when I gave her cereal.

9 a.m. Hit Austin and is now pulling her own hair. Seems frustrated and angry at something?

9:35 a.m. Another tantrum. I don't know why.

9:45 a.m. Finally quieted down.

10:05 a.m. Tantrum! Why? Is now screaming into sofa cushion.

11:00 a.m. She is a little calmer now getting ready to go see Jackie for O.T.

11:30-12:30 p.m. Was very quiet with Jackie today. Seemed distracted and reluctant to interact. Wouldn't make eye contact with Jackie.

1:00 p.m. Aubrey ate lunch then I put her down for a nap. Napped well until 2:30

4:00 p.m. Had numerous tantrums after nap. Following me all over the house, crying, and whining constantly. Demands a drink and wants to eat all the time. Begging non-stop. I cannot soothe her. Wants me to hold her, when I try to, she wants down again!

4:15 p.m. Ate a good dinner

5:30 p.m. Took the kids on a walk. Aubrey rode in the stroller well and played at the park!

6:45 p.m. Screaming at Brittney- when Brittney yelled back at her, Aubrey laughed. Brittney is frustrated. Austin is crying because of all the yelling.

7:10 p.m. Aubrey taking time out unable to calm down on her own.

8:00 p.m. Put all kids to bed

9:20 p.m. Aubrey is up screaming for a drink! Woke up Austin. She doesn't want to go back to bed.

10:00 p.m. Rocked her back to sleep since she had become so agitated. All kids are back to sleep again.

April 17

5:55 a.m. Woke up screaming again- is up for the day. Won't go back to bed. Gave her breakfast- ate well. After breakfast is following me all over the house begging for a drink and to eat again. Is unwilling to wait for anything. Wants me to hold her constantly.

Screams when I put her down and gets angry when I tell her I can't hold her all day. Is angry when I try to hold her and almost begs to get down. Then wants back up!

6:20 a.m. Screaming and angry that Britt and Austin are still in bed. Screams louder when I ask her to talk quietly.

8:00 a.m. Had numerous tantrums already since 6 a.m.- mostly all because she didn't want to wait for anything or be told no. Even when I said she could have something, it was never delivered fast enough and she would tantrum. Time-outs are not working. She sits and laughs at me or just screams at me and tells me No!

As it turned out, the journaling became a gigantic inconvenient chore that I tried diligently to perform. But, I hadn't realized that just getting through each and every tantrum was stressful enough and then to throw in a hand written novel on top of each one, was too much. How ambitious of me to even attempt a feat I would think sarcastically to myself, and then follow the thought with a snort.

At first, the entries were lengthy and detailed, and rather unemotionally written. As the days progressed into a week and then into two, the entries became less detailed and scarcer. They also took on the emotions that I was feeling and though I tried to be clinical and unbiased, I couldn't. Some days I could only write down the time of the tantrum and one sentence following.

Other times, I would only write down the number of tantrums that occurred that day. It was becoming impossible to keep track of them. They would often run into each other and when I thought one was stopping, it would pick up and turn into a whole other charged event that eventually exhausted me. Even though the blank pages had become my greatest listener and best friend, they were also the enemy. Blank pages became ominous for I knew that I would soon be filling them and I wished for it all to stop.

In less than two weeks, I had filled in fourteen notebook pages, front and back, full of tantrums. I was happy that the time for the EEG had finally arrived. Though I had several haunting doubts about the procedure, I couldn't deny the fact that I was also very excited to see what it would unveil.

Your breath such a sweet flavor of a memory
Not yet faded, still bright
Your smile, yet your pain, such a permanent tattoo,
deeply set, imprinted amongst the tormented night.

D.L. Clarke

Chapter 25

The morning of the EEG had started out so peacefully that I almost felt guilty that I was about to put my daughter through yet another test. I wanted so desperately to believe that she was okay and that it was indeed just bad parenting. I once again started to vow that I would read, "The Defiant Child," at least once more and I would brush up on my behavior modification techniques. I gently began washing cereal from Aubrey's face and the thoughts raced around in my head. She looked up at me and smiled. A pang of doubt ran through me once again.

I loved the good days and dreaded the bad ones. I loved it when Aubrey was content and seemed happy. It gave me hope that she was indeed "normal," but then again, it made me second-guess myself to the point that I thought I was being ridiculous by dragging her from clinic to clinic to find out what was wrong.

The good days also made me think that there may *not be* something wrong. Perhaps I was just expecting too much? Expecting the perfect child? Wanting the perfect family?

Then I would think of how Brittney was at the same age, and then Austin. Weren't they okay? They were being raised in the same house, with the same rules, the same routine. Why weren't they acting out and seemingly miserable like their sister was?

The doubts were also thickened and made worse by the fact that the "professionals" were telling me that there was nothing wrong with her. Who was right? My mind drifted in and out of a fog as I loaded Aubrey and Austin into the car for the drive to the clinic.

The clinic was easily spotted through a grove of tall fir trees. It stood tall and sanitarily white against the backdrop of the Washington hillsides. Once inside the building, we were told to wait and pointed in the direction of a beautifully decorated room laden with plush chairs, and several varieties of ferns and tropical plants.

Aubrey found the fish tank on the far side of one wall and went up to it and slammed her hand against the aquarium glass. The fish within it, swam urgently to the other side and stared google-eyed out to the room full of us humans.

Perfectly good start, I thought to myself, as everyone in the room looked up to shoot me evil "control your child" glares. I then noticed the "Do not tap on the glass" sign that hung forbiddingly above the fish tank. Great!

As I walked Aubrey back across the room, she became irritated that I was taking her away from the "fwish," and proceeded to start stomping her million dollar shoes against the floor. I could feel my face turning red and the sweat under my arms being produced at an ungodly rate. No one had to say anything; it was obvious what they were thinking.

I was considering bolting for the door but was stopped mid-thought by a nurse calling us back to the testing area. Why did there *always* have to be a scene? Did my *own* anxiety out in public with my daughter actually *cause* her to act this way? I was convinced by now that I was, in fact, somehow to blame.

We were seated in a small hospital-like examining room and the nurse directed her attention toward me and politely requested that my children not touch anything. Ha! Why would she think that they would? Did my lack of parenting skills show *that* much? Of course they wouldn't touch anything. Of course I had complete control of my children. The sweat poured out of me as Aubrey insisted on getting down off my lap and wandered the small room on her tiptoes.

"Aubrey! Come here please," I dutifully requested, my upper lip turning into a small river of sweat. My underarms joined in and continued to soak my shirt. I wouldn't be buying *that* brand of deodorant again, I silently mused.

"No!" she almost shouted at my request.

"No touching," I informed her as she darted about the room trying to open the drawers and cabinets. I was pleased that they were all securely locked; at least they were on my side. I was also pleased to see that Aubrey was merely exploring and didn't seem to be in a "seek out and destroy" mood this morning.

I breathed a sigh of relief as the exam room door opened and a young man dressed in blue scrubs walked in. He introduced himself as Juan, and proceeded to explain the entire EEG procedure to me. It sounded easy enough, except for the wires.

The tech had pointed to about a hundred little electrodes throughout his explanation, and stated that each and every one of them would have to be placed in strategic places upon Aubrey's scalp and forehead. I had a nagging feeling that Aubrey would not be able to sit long enough for the placement of the wires, let alone the tech touching her head. I agreed numbly to what the tech was saying and within a few minutes time, Aubrey was placed on the examining table and the wires began their assault upon her little head.

Aubrey didn't budge for the entire twenty minutes it took for the tech to place all the wires. I sat in disbelief as she sucked her thumb and stared up at the ceiling. When he finished, almost her entire head was covered in small white dots with wires attached to them. She had been a perfect angel and the tech congratulated her for being so patient and laying still for him. I was so proud of her

The test began and I was told to sit next to where Aubrey was laying and go through a book with her. We flipped the pages and looked at the pictures together as the tape from the machine flowed out onto the floor in a quiet humming sound.

After almost thirty minutes, the tech instructed me that Aubrey would need to go to sleep so that they could record her brain activity while sleeping. I knew this part of the test was going to be the biggest challenge. Getting her to go to sleep in her own bed at bed time was tricky enough, let alone getting her to fall asleep in a strange room, on a strange cot.

I continued to talk to her in a soothing voice and stroked her little arm gently, as she would allow. She tolerated my touch and was appearing to relax in the midst of everything around her. It took just over ten minutes, and Aubrey was in a deep comfortable sleep. The tech gave me thumbs up sign and made some adjustments on the EEG machine.

The tape was making a circular mound on the floor as the machine kept humming. I was in complete shock at how well Aubrey had cooperated with everything thus far. The feeling of impending doom had gently lifted itself away from me as I watched Aubrey's little chest rise and fall as she slept.

After Aubrey had slept for nearly an hour, the tech asked me to wake her slowly. I was prepared for a tantrum that never happened, for when I gently woke her, she gazed up at my face and gave me a little sleepy smile.

It’s beautiful here, the flowers, the lake, and the sand
Come play with the children, my angel
And let the sun touch your face
Come softly, float in and gently
Find a warm safe place to quietly land.

D.L. Clarke

Chapter 26

"There is no evidence of seizure activity in the brain, which is really good news. If you have any questions about the test results, you can inquire anytime, we will be happy to assist you." The phone call had been brief and to the point, and it had cleared up yet another theory as to what was going on with my daughter. The EEG was perfectly normal.

So, what was next? What did I do now? Where could I go for answers? Who could I talk to now? I decided at that moment, to not do anything. Stop all the testing, try diligently to stick to the behavior modification techniques, and try my best to be patient.

Perhaps follow my own advice of not letting the tantrums "get to me," to try to relax more, go buy a treadmill, get into shape, start eating better, get out more. Yadda yadda yadda. Yeah, it all sounded so easy. I rolled my eyes and let out an enormous sigh.

I continued taking Aubrey to preschool. It was the one thing that didn't seem to be adding to her stress at the moment, and I looked forward to seeing Claire. She had such an ease about her that comforted me, and Aubrey liked her.

The weather had turned warmer and Claire had started taking the classes outside and onto the playground to begin some outdoor "sensory therapy" with the kids. The activities she chose all involved some sort of sensory interaction. Whether it be smelling the flowers or bits of bark, making sand castles in the sand box, or being pushed on the swing, it all had some sort of meaning and importance.

Teeter tottering with fellow classmates meant getting off the ground and having the sensation of upward movement, the merry-go-round supplied the feelings of spinning, and the balance beam (barely off the ground) gave the sense of balance.

Claire had a watchful eye and would pick up on clues as to when she needed to step in and assist her students. Some played effortlessly on the equipment, while others, were hesitant and not so willing to attempt the apparatuses.

Aubrey was one of the tentative ones. She didn't like being off the ground, so the balance beam frightened her. The merry-go-round seemed to confuse her, and the swings were never a consistent option of entertainment. An attempt on the teeter-totter only produced a tantrum, and the slide was "too sticky" to slide down.

One day, after noticing that Aubrey was not willing to venture onto the equipment that involved being off the ground, (which was, unfortunately, the majority of the equipment), Claire suggested we join her class for the next "after school" play function at a new park she had discovered. Because Claire often had children in her class that were in wheelchairs, she was always searching for new places for her class to play independently.

She described the importance for children, especially those with special needs, to experience independence that would, in turn, encourage their confidence.

Claire seemed confident that Aubrey would find several tempting options at the new park that did not involve being off the ground. It sounded encouraging to me and after I agreed to give it a try, she gave me directions to the park and stated that everyone was going to meet there the next afternoon at three.

The next day, after Brittney arrived home from school, I loaded all the kids into the car and we drove to the park. Once we arrived, I was thrilled to see all the shiny almost new looking equipment. There were plastic mazes designed in bright colors with clear plastic bubbles protruding from its sides (think hamster apparatus and you have an accurate picture), little brightly colored animals on largely coiled springs to ride, old tires to jump on and around, along with the usual playground stuff like swings, slides, and a jungle gym.

There was a covered picnic area filled with people, and more picnic tables and benches dotted the landscape. All of this was set within a grove of old growth trees with a large sparkling blue body of water lapping in the background. Even though it was a busy park, it seemed serene as well, and I immediately loved it! I could definitely see why Claire had recommended it!

I unloaded the kids from the car, and both Brittney and Aubrey ran over to the equipment. I followed carrying Austin. I spotted Claire talking to a group of moms and I waved to her. She waved back and gave me a "just a second" sign with her hand, letting me know that she would be coming over to chat with me momentarily. Once Brittney and Aubrey reached the equipment area, Brittney immediately started climbing the jungle gym and Aubrey watched her big sister make it to the top.

I picked out a shiny elephant on springs and sat Austin in its painted on saddle. He giggled and put his tiny little hands on the handle and almost instinctively started to rock it. I held him while he rocked and bounced and I called over to Aubrey that was standing just a few feet away to come join us. She glanced over to us and remained still. I was wondering if she was considering following her sister up the jungle gym! That would be a monumental achievement and I secretly began a cheerleading session inside my head hoping she would at least attempt the first couple of rungs.

Austin looked like he was getting a little "elephant sick" from all the bouncing, so I plucked him from the saddle and we joined Aubrey at the base of the jungle gym. By this time, Brittney was coming down the other side, ready to explore the "hamster cage" apparatus.

Claire had finished her chat with the small group of moms and was approaching me with a big smile. She was always so cheerful and I secretly wanted to be her, just for a day, well, maybe a week or two. I don't know what it was, but she just had this confident air about her that gushed happiness and comfort. I, on the other hand, saw myself as a wired mess that no matter how hard I tried to project confidence and joy, only ended up succeeding in sending out massive signals of anxiety and perplexity.

What was it? What ingredient did she possess that I lacked? Whatever it was, it seemed to make her job of helping children and their parents almost seem effortless. Was she just one of those people that was always in a good mood? I knew that had to be part of it. Or, was it because of all of her training? She was well educated and trained in the field of child development and special education.

That must be it! I vowed right then to start college as soon as I had a bit of free time. That thought made its delightful way to my nose and produced a slight humorous "honk." *Nice,* I thought to myself. *Real attractive!*

Claire had almost made it to where I was standing with Austin and Aubrey, but was suddenly diverted by a father having a question about his daughter. Claire's smile never faded as she spoke to him and I could see that she had a similar effect on him as she did myself. He seemed comforted by what she was telling him, and was soon heading back over to where his daughter was playing.

In the meantime, Aubrey had run to the other side of the playground and was standing near a group of small children. I had almost caught up to where she had stopped, when I watched in horror as she picked up a small handful of sand and threw it directly at the children playing.

Of course, some of it landed in a pair of eyes. *Of course* there was screaming and panic. And of course there were parents rushing from all directions of the playground to see which one of the kids had gotten injured. Everyone, including myself, was, of course, yelling "NO!" at my child. I saw every single one of the heated sneers that were, of course, in my direction. And, of course, I said how sorry I was a million and a half times and yes, of course, I got down and looked Aubrey in the eyes and told her "No throwing sand!" and then tried desperately so show her what she had done and why it was wrong to do it.

She stared right through me and while the parents tried to calm their children, and others were running for water to wash the offending sand out, she watched it all with an expressionless face.

It was obvious I was not going to be forgiven any time soon by any one of the afflicted parents, and after my continual apologies and offers to help were seemingly refused, I decided the best thing for us to do, was leave, of course.

Tears were trying their best to slam down my cheeks, but I somehow managed to thank Claire for the invite and tell her that we had to go. The tears begged to be released even more so when she tried to comfort me by telling me that everyone understood and that it was really going to be okay. I was shaking and I could feel my lip trembling as I tried to force my body to remain composed.

Brittney, even at her young age, seemed to sense my angst and grabbed her little sister's hand and started walking toward the car. Aubrey tagged along with her without protest. I forced a brave smile for Claire and almost whispered that I had to go. She nodded silently as her eyes squinted slightly. I knew she understood my pain. It was almost like she could feel it, and though she didn't have children of her own yet, it was as if she had been through the same things herself and knew.

As I turned in the direction of where the car was parked, the tears started shooting hotly down my cheeks and my upper lip trembled violently. I pursed them together in attempt to get them to stop, to no avail. They shuddered together and kept rhythm with the tears that had formed rivers down my face.

As we started to drive out of the parking lot, I glanced back over my shoulder and looked at the area of the park where the parents and their previously injured, now playing children, were gathered. Everyone was okay, and it was all going to be fine, just like Claire had said.

We continued driving out of the park and my mind fidgeted and tried to drift away. It did come back, however, long enough to order my foot to hit the brakes, in effort to avoid the certain death of a bushy tailed gray squirrel that had paused momentarily in the middle of the road. As the squirrel stared me down for a moment, and then decidedly scampered up a nearby tree, Aubrey, who had started to fall asleep in her car seat, jolted out of her near slumber and started to wail.

Austin followed almost immediately with a howl of his own and soon the entire car was one big flood of tears and blubbering. Through my tears I glanced in the rear view mirror and watched Brittney as she stared straight ahead, apparently trying desperately to drown us all out. Poor thing, I thought. I made a mental note to start looking into some sort of mental health savings plan for her future, sort of like the college fund thing, but .. well, you get the idea.

We exited out of the park gates, and in my mental attempt to avoid any future park scenes, silently vowed to never step foot in the park again. We soon found ourselves on the main road heading toward home. The crying had ceased almost as suddenly as it had begun. I breathed another collective sigh and wearily navigated the stretch of asphalt before me. Oh, what a lovely day it had been!

If it were up to me
Today would just always be today, never to be through
Being not yet tomorrow.
For today, I know what is to be
And tomorrow I haven't a clue.

D.L. Clarke

Chapter 27

Two days later, I was once again heading in the direction of the infamous park where the dreadful "sand scene" had occurred. Okay, I know what you are thinking, but Claire had almost *insisted* that we give the park idea another try.

"Perhaps Aubrey was just having an 'off' day and this time it would be different?" she had questioned me in her calming way. Well, I worshipped Claire, as I have already confessed to you, so I had to trust her again and give it another shot. Thus, before we realized it, we were entering the park gates.

As we rounded the bend in the park entrance, I slowed down and instinctively looked for my squirrel friend, my foot poised to hit the brake if needed. I think upon seeing my car, *he* instinctively ran the other direction, for this time he was nowhere to be found.

I spotted Claire and the rest of the class on the other side of the park. I hoped she would be right, that this was, in fact, a good idea. I had my doubts, and I was filled with anticipation and worry. But, I tried to be upbeat, none-the-less.

As we approached, Claire looked up and smiled. "You made it!" she exclaimed. "Good! You are just in time for the choo-choo train, Aubrey!" she continued enthusiastically.

With that, she grabbed Aubrey's hand gently and led her to the rest of the class where they were all forming into a line, one behind the other, some in wheelchairs and some even on crutches. As Claire went to the front of the line, she shouted back, "Okay! Let's go!"

The children giggled and started slowly forward, each making 'choo-choo' sounds as they wound down the cemented pathway of the park. I watched as they finally arrived at the tires, giggling and tired, some playfully bashing into each other as the 'train' came to a stop. I watched as Aubrey giggled and smiled. She was having a good day!

I wanted to jump to conclusions and immediately congratulate Claire at being right, again, but I hesitated. We were just getting started, after all. Things could head to disaster quickly in a downward spiral, but again, I tried to remain upbeat.

After the train exercise came to an end, the kids were instructed to jump through the tires and try to make it to the end without having to stop. The children that couldn't participate because of inability were designated as the cheer squad. They took to the duty whole-heartedly, screaming and clapping as the children, one by one, slowly made it over the tires. Hopping and jumping within each tire, they would finally reach the end.

When it came time for Aubrey to take her turn, she hesitated. "C'mon, Aubs," I heard Claire coaxing. I went over to the end of the tires and beckoned for Aubrey to try to reach me. She looked away, biting her bottom lip, and showing no interest in the whole tire idea.

Without hesitation, Claire grabbed Aubrey's hand and led her to a cement path. I watched as Claire crouched and then jumped! Jump! Jump! Aubrey stood watching her and when Claire asked her to join her, Aubrey did.

Tiny, little hops at first, but with each, "Jump! Jump! Jump!" that Claire exclaimed, Aubrey went a little higher. Soon, they were both jumping and hopping down the cement pathway. Aubrey was *off the ground!* Furthermore, she was *enjoying it!* Brilliant! What she refused to attempt in the tire exercise, she accomplished with the jumping. It was obvious to me that at that moment, that we *were* making progress. Little by little, we were actually getting *somewhere.*

The day continued onward, and with each exercise, I watched as my daughter attempted and succeeded at them. Playing in the "hamster" apparatus proved to be the most fun and at one point, Aubrey even summoned my attention as she pushed her face against the plastic bubble and waved.

I remembered back to the last time we were at this very same park. What a totally different experience that had been! It had definitely been one of those peculiar days when Aubrey was "off." I couldn't explain why nor did I even want to ponder the reasons, for it was all too baffling.

But then, not being able to stop it, I did start to ponder the reasoning. What had been so different from just two days ago until now? Why was she so interactive *this* time and so withdrawn the last? Why was she willing to try almost everything that Claire asked her to do, *this time*?

Could it have been the breakfast I gave her? Possibly the lunch? I had been doing a lot of research and reading on the effects of corn, peanuts, milk, egg, sugar, and, well nearly, all types of food allergies.

Within the last day and a half, I had cut out most of the sugars in Aubrey's diet. It was to be the first of the food allergy trials I had decided. Sugar, it seemed to be the easiest, at first, until I started finding all the "hidden" sugars in pretty much everything at the grocery store. But, I had to try it. I had to attempt all angles. Rule out all sources of her troubles, until I found answers.

So, maybe that was the reason she was so cooperative and happy today? Maybe I was really onto something? I decided to let Claire in on my little discovery. "Claire, do you know much about food allergies and children's reactions to them?" I asked her as she stood beside me and watched Aubrey running in the mazes.

"I know a little bit about them. I haven't really studied them too closely since it is really difficult to get very accurate findings. All children are so different and there are so many degrees of allergic reactions, I think," she stated. "I think it would be really hard to definitely rule out specific foods unless there were really obvious reactions," she concluded.

"I know," I replied, my heart sinking a little. "I cut sugar out of Aubrey's diet the other day. I was thinking that maybe that is why she is having a better day today, well, I was hoping anyway," I added after seeing her eyebrows rise a little.

"Well, you should stick with it then if you think it might be helping," she replied very encouragingly. I should have known that Claire would back up anything I felt compelled to try with my daughter. She was so supportive. So reassuring. So, as we watched Aubrey playing happily, I decided to stick with the food allergy experiment, at least for a while anyway.

When the time came for us to head for home, I called to Aubrey and we all headed to the car in an almost gleeful mood. This was a strange, almost foreign feeling, but it was wonderful. I didn't want it to ever end!

Once everyone was safely strapped into the car, I steered the car out the park entrance and onto the now familiar road toward home. Ah! It had been an absolutely wonderful day and I was almost up to cloud nine. Definitely up to seven or so, nearing eight, not yet quite there, but close. Nine still attractively loomed in the distance.

Once home, I gathered the children out of their car seats, we got to the front door without incident and upon inserting my key into the lock; I read the note that hung loosely on the door.

We regret to have to inform you that your home is in the Phase 2 section and has been scheduled for major reconstruction and remodeling. Because your home will not be habitable during this reconstruction, it will be necessary for you to vacate the premises within the month and locate alternate housing. Please be informed that the housing office will be happy to...

I ripped the note off the door and continued into my now "uninhabitable" house. Just then, Aubrey started whimpering and asking to "eat, eat, eat!" I fumbled around in the cupboard and pulled out a bag containing some of Austin's baby crackers. I handed her one and she gobbled it down, immediately asking for another. I grabbed a few more and absentmindedly handed them to her.

After settling my elbows on the counter to re-read the note in its entirety, I glanced half-heartedly at the cracker bag. It was now nearly empty and I couldn't help but notice the words, "Now with less sugar." *Less* sugar! Damn! There goes *that* experiment!

I folded up the letter, tucked it away, glanced around the house, and finished off the bag. We were going to have to move. A new house meant a new location. A new location meant different. More than that, shuddering as I thought silently, it meant *change*.

There aren't any words really
Left to describe
All the feelings of uncertainty hidden
For, so deep within my body
they diligently hide.

D.L. Clarke

Chapter 28

The month flew by, and though we had been tentatively assigned to another house by the Naval housing center, I didn't know which one it would actually be. It was a toss up between one of the older homes, that was also set to be remodeled in Phase 3 of the remodeling plan, and one that had already been remodeled during Phase 1.

After sitting on pins and needles wondering and worrying about the move, and spending way too much time and energy hoping to get into one of the Phase 1 homes that had *already* been completed, I got on the phone and pleaded with the Naval housing department.

I explained how change was such a drastic thing for my family and if we were to be moved into a home that was scheduled to be remodeled, just to have to move again in a short amount of time, that it could be very damaging to the welfare of my children.

They listened to me and then abruptly informed me that *everyone* has the same complaint, but they would do their best. After I hung up, I knew I would have to provide some sort of "proof" or back up to my claims.

I then called Clover Ridge and asked to speak to Claire. She wasn't there, but they promised to have her call me when she got in. I waited all day, and no phone call. I then called the Naval hospital and asked to speak with Aubrey's new pediatrician. Again, I was told to leave a message and that he would get back to me when possible. I waited and waited, still with no return phone call.

Not wanting to give up just yet, I called Clover Ridge again, this time asking for Jackie. I was put right through to her. On the phone, I explained my situation to her and asked if there was some way she could possibly help. What I really wanted was some sort of statement, a letter perhaps explaining some of the problems Aubrey experienced day to day, especially when it came to changes in her routines.

Jackie didn't even hesitate before asking me when I needed the letter. Before I could answer, she asked me if I could pick it up in the morning. I thanked her over and over and in the morning, I drove to Clover Ridge and picked up the letter that was waiting for me at the front desk.

I then immediately drove to the Naval housing office and asked to speak with the manager. I was asked to wait. I waited. I was asked to calm my child, I did my best. I was asked to come on back. Obediently, but with a definite plan of attack, I followed the receptionist to the manager's office.

Once inside, Aubrey and I waited on the plush chairs while Austin slept in his carrier. I was nervous, but determined. When the manager appeared, I introduced myself and then explained my situation briefly. She looked incredibly bored and I could tell she had heard this all before. I was not making an impact and I feared that I was going to be easily forgotten. She sighed, but before she could make up an excuse to get me out of her office, I presented her with the letter I had received from Jackie. "This is a letter from my daughter's occupational therapist," I explained as I almost thrust the letter toward her direction.

I watched as she read it, or at least appeared to. She looked incredibly bored and completely non-interested. I suddenly wished that I hadn't handed her the letter. It would have made one heck of a paper spit bullet collection. Too bad I had forgotten my straw!

She then looked at me, then to Aubrey, then down to where Austin was sleeping. After attempting to clear her throat, she pulled her file cabinet open and pulled out a file with a set of numbers on it. As she thumbed through the papers it held, I saw my house number at the top of one. She pulled it out and sat it aside.

Another attempt at clearing her throat brought about a loud auditory display of "hurrrrrrrrrrr eh eh eh." Looking as if she were satisfied with the results of her "hurrr eh eh" session, she again looked at me, her eyes slightly damp and red. As she picked the file back up, she started to speak with a slight rattle still in her voice. She apparently had left one of the "frogs" intact.

"Ma'am?" she began, then went into another "hurrrr eh eh eh EH!"

"Yes?" I answered quizzically, wondering if I should offer her some water or perhaps a lozenge? I figured I would wait and see what she had to say. If it was favorable, I would offer her some gum or something easily scrounged up in my purse. If it was not the answer I wanted, I would let her choke. Not really.

"Ma'am, you have already been assigned a unit," she continued. "Your family has been assigned to one of the remodeled homes from Phase 1. It is just up one street from where you are living now, about the equivalent of a block," she stated after closing the file with one hand and plopping her glasses on the table with the other. I watched as she rubbed her reddened eyes viciously. I surmised at that point that she was probably battling some sort of allergy, rather than a horrible cold, so I was able to relax a bit. Nothing I, or my children, could catch. Excellent! Her office suddenly took on a new aura of welcomed germless ness.

"Oh!" I said a little sheepishly. But, I thought quickly in my own defense, how was I supposed to know that anyway?

"A letter explaining your housing assignment was sent out yesterday, you should be receiving it today," she concluded with another outrageous "huhhhhhh huhhhh huh!" and then a rapid pounding on her chest with her closed fist.

"My gosh! Are you okay?" I asked rising out of my chair a bit. That last display of coughing was sufficient enough to wake Austin, who was now starting to squirm in his carrier. Aubrey hopped down from her chair and started exploring the room, stopping momentarily to look at her little brother.

"Ye-es, I am fine, thank you," she answered haltingly, wiping her eyes with a tissue she had ripped from its box.

"Can I get you some water or something?" I gingerly inquired. See, I could help her *now*; she had given me one of the remodeled houses. Thank goodness *she* didn't have mind reading abilities.

"A moving crew will assist you," she said, handing me a sheet of paper with listings of moving companies on it. "You may call them and see which one has an opening soonest, and then schedule to have your belongings transferred to the new home," she continued.

I wondered if it would be possible to actually go and see the house, inside and out, before we moved into it. My reasoning behind this was to take the kids there as much as possible before the move. It would hopefully assist in acquainting them with the idea that that would be our new home. I was concerned mostly about Aubrey's reaction to the move, and new surroundings, so I knew the more prepared we were, the better off we all would be

I asked the housing manager, if it would be possible to get the keys, and was amazed when she got up, went to a small locked cupboard, opened it up, and pulled out a set of shiny keys. I was more amazed when she reached across her desk and handed them to me.

"You can go there anytime, ma'am," she said, then went into another long coughing session.

I thanked her over and over, wished her well, and (realizing they would need to be sanitized before use), placed the keys in a quarantined pocket of my purse, gathered up the kids and we drove to our new house.

Through the chaos I see your little face
Looking up at me
Confusion fills your eyes
And your pain, unable to hide
I want to take you away from here
Quiet and peacefulness
to somehow replace your sad little plight.

D.L. Clarke

Chapter 29

The coughing, allergy challenged Naval housing manager had been right! The new house was just one street up from our old home, and it was beautiful! I opened up the front door and took the kids inside.

Upon entering, a very large, probably almost huge, smile came across my face, and I took a deep breath in, sniffing, sniffing. Aubrey had started up the carpeted steps, so I followed her. I could see all the massive improvements already. Where the old house had cold and sound amplifying linoleum, the new house offered brand new, comforting carpet. It was definitely going to make things a little quieter. Well, I hoped so anyway.

The closet doors were freshly painted a crisp white, as were the doors and trim of the bedrooms. New windows and fixtures were in place, as well as new tubs and shower enclosures.

I stood and soaked it all in. I was truly overwhelmed and almost felt like pinching myself except Austin was doing a good job of it for me at the moment.

"Owww eeee!" I giggled and poked at Austin's tummy a little while I held him. He smiled at me and released his involuntary pinching session.

"Oh! Oh! Oh!" I heard Aubrey shouting in one of the bedrooms. As it resonated against the bare walls, I joined her in the room and saw her standing by a window. She was standing on her tiptoes and pointing at a dog that was running crazily in the neighbor's yard.

"Is that a dog, Aubrey?" I asked her. She turned and looked at me with a smile.

"Nnnnnn iiiiii cccce!" she said quietly, patting her hands as if she were actually petting the animal. She repeated, "Nnnniiiiicccce." Her little face had taken on a gentle, yet serious look.

I instantly made the connection, and I laughed a little as I joined in with her, "Nnniiiccce, yes!"

I asked Aubrey to wave bye-bye to the niiiiiccce, and after she felt she had sufficiently said her good byes to her new friend, we headed back down the steps and explored the rest of the house.

After I locked the front door, I heard a little voice calling to me from the neighbor's yard, "Hello?" I looked up to see a little girl sitting in a wheelchair.

"Hi!" I replied. Just then I saw a woman with shoulder length sandy blonde hair come around the corner of the house with a handful of clippings she had apparently just cut from her garden. "Hi there!" she said, smiling. I watched as she unlocked the child's wheelchair and started pushing her to where we were standing.

"My name is Paulina, and this is my daughter Rebecca," she said, as she bent down and re-locked the wheelchair wheels.

"It is nice to meet you both!" I replied. "These are two of my kids, I have three, but she is at school now, her name is Brittney. This little guy is Austin, and this is Aubrey!" I said patting Aubrey, without thinking, on the top of the head. She immediately cocked her head away from me and rubbed it as if I had just hit her with a sledgehammer.

Paulina didn't seem fazed by Aubrey's reaction and I was glad. I had patted her so gently; at least I thought I had anyway. Hadn't I? I hated the taunting games my mind played with me.

After the introductions, including my own, I explained that we were moving in because of some remodeling they were planning to do on our old house. Paulina said they had just gone through all of that too and was happy to be getting some neighbors. She said our new house had been completed several months ago and had sat vacant ever since.

I was happy, too, to be getting a new set of neighbors. Hopefully they wouldn't come with a new set of problems, as always seemed, unfortunately, to be the circumstance.

I had long ago tired of Cheryl's horror stories about her son Timothy, and the neighbors on the *other* side of me had become a chore as well.

I guess it wasn't so much *them* as it was their dog, or niiiccce, I should say. They would habitually leave for the day, chaining their poor, matted-haired collie, Billy, (or Silly Billy as I liked to call him) outside in the dirt. Unfortunately, it happened to be right outside one of my side windows and I could hear every whine and whimper it made.

But, fortunately for the dog, I had decided that I loved it regardless and I would take it water and treats.

Okay, let me explain myself a little. Reason number one, because it was often left without a sufficient water supply, two, because I felt sorry for it and three, I wanted and desperately needed a break from its persistent barking. *That* was probably the biggest and most selfish reason, but it did work for brief periods of time, and it helped me feel better about the whole situation. Besides, reporting the incidents to the housing office never got me far, so I had pretty much given up the thought that the cavalry was going to arrive and save the animal from its neglect and boredom.

After saying goodbye to our new neighbors, the kids and I drove to our old house. It looked worn and pretty pathetic after witnessing the fresh newness of our new place. Such a traitor I was! Yeah, yeah.. You would have felt the same way, really!

Every chance I got I took all three of the kids back to the new house. We hung pictures, and even started decorating their bedrooms. I tried everything and anything to ease the stress of the new house, and all the changes that would come along with it. The children always seemed excited to be there, and one of Aubrey's favorite things was to watch out her bedroom window and babble at her "niiiicccce" in the neighbor's yard.

When moving day came, I really felt like we were prepared. I had gotten the kids up early, gave them a good breakfast, loaded up a diaper bag filled with crackers, washclothes, a few books, some small toys, and even saved out a few blankets for a potential "nap time" later.

Once the movers came, however, my confidence rapidly started to crumble. There were about five movers that worked inside the house, while three others worked outside loading boxes and furniture into the van. There were virtually people moving and scampering everywhere. Boxes were put together in mere seconds. Items were wrapped in paper and stacked for eventual packing. Tape was stretched and pulled with loud "rips" and was used to secure the packed boxes. They were definitely a very efficient team, but they were also very noisy. Noises that I hadn't anticipated.

As the house emptied, the louder the noises echoed and bounced off the bare floors and walls. Workers hollered at each other with instructions, and their mere footsteps sounded like thunder. Every single sound seemed to be amplified.

Although Austin did not seem to mind the chaos and noise, Aubrey was not handling it so well. Panic had set into her little body and I could tell by the look on her face that I needed to get her out of the house and somewhere quiet.

I found one of the workers in the kitchen packing the dishes and told her I had to get the kids out of the house. She merely nodded and kept wrapping and packing the items out of the cupboards. Aubrey had started to wail by this time and was getting obviously frantic.

As quickly as I could, I gathered up the kids and we made our way through the maze of boxes and out to the car. Where would I go? I had been informed that I would have to stay at the house while the movers were there, but I HAD to get Aubrey out of there. It was enough craziness to make an adult nuts, let alone a small child. After loading the kids into the car, I peeked around the corner to where the moving van was parked. There were several workers loading up furniture and boxes and I was surprised to see how much had already been loaded! It didn't look like it would be too much longer and they would be unloading it all at the new house. I asked one of them how much longer they thought it would take, and after hearing that it would be another hour and a half or so, I told them I was going to take the kids over to their aunt's house and I would be right back. He nodded and wiped the sweat off his brow and onto his shirt.

It was a huge fat lie, but what else was I supposed to say? "I am leaving because you guys are just being waaaaay-hay-hay too noisy, so, could you keep it down a little?" I got into my car, turned on the ignition, and drove the .2 miles to my new house. Once inside, I immediately felt a sense of relief. I had done the right thing by leaving. I should have done it sooner, actually, but I was trying to "follow the rules."

Both the kids were cranky now and I didn't blame them. I was too. I was glad that at least Brittney had been spared the chaos by being at school. Aubrey had started asking me to "Eat! Eat! Eat!" in the car on the short drive over, so without argument, I gave in and supplied both kids with small handful sized zoo of animal crackers. That seemed to help a little, until the supply ran out. Then it was back to "Eat! Eat! Eat!"

"You just ate, Aubrey!" I tried reminding her, somewhat patiently.

"NO! Eat! Eat! Eat!" she replied angrily. Then, the crying started. She slammed her fists into the floor and then onto the walls all the while screaming to "EAT!" Austin started crying and as I bounced him and tried to calm him down, I repeatedly tried to soothe Aubrey by telling her that we could eat again in a little while. By the loudness of her screams, I could tell she wasn't ready to accept that as a solution.

"Shush shush shush! Sweety! C'mon!" I tried, pleadingly. It was ignored. Her screaming tantrum had escalated into official ear blowing levels and I was afraid my new neighbors would think I was hurting her!

Oh gosh! I just realized that though my *old* neighbors knew about Aubrey's tantrums and screaming, my *new* neighbors didn't know about them yet! I had to go explain our situation to Paulina and whoever else was within immediate earshot!

Just then, in the midst of screams and wailing, I heard the doorbell ring. A little knot formed instantly, flipping crazily in my stomach.

Letting you into our world
Such a chance we were taking
But hope was all we were living on
And hope is what you
were somehow awakening.

D.L. Clarke

Chapter 30

I miraculously got the new house set up within just a couple of days. It was more out the need to get things back to normal for the kids that kept me going. It had been such a stressful week and we were all tired and grumpy. But, with every box that was unpacked, a little more ease seemed to settle in, replacing the upheaval.

After Pauline had come to the door that first day of the "big move" with a plateful of freshly baked cookies for the children, she had become a source of comfort to me for which I was so grateful.

Her daughter was at pre-school, so she was able to sit and talk with me awhile. We both ended up sitting and chatting for over an hour on my bare wooden floor, all the while trying to patiently wait out Aubrey's tantrum.

When I asked her if she had brought the cookies over to "investigate all the racket," she reassured me that she hadn't. At one time, during our chat, she had reached over, grabbed Austin out of his carrier and began playing with him on her lap. She was a natural.

I heard myself explaining to her about Aubrey, and I watched her face as I described some of the difficulties we were experiencing. She listened intently and reassured me that she would not be bothered by the tantrums, *really*, so I had no reason to worry.

I warned her that Aubrey's tantrums could easily exceed twenty five times in just one day, and there were often several throughout the night, Paulina again reassured me that it would be okay.

I then listened to her as she explained that Rebecca, her daughter, had been born with Cerebral Palsy. I was amazed when she told me that she too, attended Clover Ridge and that Jackie was her Occupational Therapist as well!

Paulina shared her story with me and it was exciting to hear about how much progress little Rebecca had made! At just two and half years old, she was already expected to eventually walk with the use of crutches, something Paulina was told, she would never accomplish. Like myself, Paulina had persisted in trying to get help for her daughter, and in her case, it was definitely paying off!

Before she left, she asked me if I was going to take Aubrey to the fair event that Clover Ridge was sponsoring. In all the chaos of moving, I had completely forgotten about it! Paulina reminded me of the date, and I told her that I would definitely try to make it. She seemed excited by my answer and we agreed to follow each other there in our cars and experience the fair together. I had made a new friend.

We pushed you too far
We all thought that you could take it
Insane thought processed for a moment
Somehow we purchased it and packed.
Now there is no way of faking it
Saneness sadly, is the one thing of many
We momentarily lacked.

D.L. Clarke

Chapter 31

The day of the fair was beautiful, sunny and hot. I dressed the kids accordingly and as planned, I followed Paulina and Rebecca to the event. Upon our arrival, Aubrey spotted some cows out in a field grazing. She pointed her fingers and exclaimed, "Niiiiicccce!" Brittney giggled and I smiled to myself.

"Is that a cow, Aubrey?" I asked her, watching as she continued to point out the car window with her fingers.

"Niiiicccccce," was her reply.

I got Austin loaded up in his stroller, Brittney held Aubrey's hand, and we walked with Paulina while she pushed Rebecca in her wheelchair. There were huge white tents set up everywhere and the smell of barbequed something filled the air. Cotton candy tubs overflowed with their sugary temptations, and horses whinnied in the background.

We passed by sheep and lamb stalls, pigs with their piglets, and live ponies hooked up to carousels for riding. Brittney was ecstatic and couldn't wait to ride the ponies. I was glad she was able to come along. We were all definitely in need of some fun.

Brittney was first on the ponies, and after asking Aubrey to join her and being refused, she went around the circles alone, her little head bobbing under the weight of the helmet. After the pony ride, we all trekked over to the pigs and after getting over the initial "smell shock" the girls took an interest in their babies and watched as they rooted around in the straw.

Next there were baby chicks to visit and then a litter of puppies. As the girls bent down to pet the first puppy, Aubrey got a face full of puppy slobber as it jumped up and licked her. She stood up and brushed herself off rapidly and wiped, and wiped, and wiped at her face.

I immediately snatched a washcloth out of my bag and handed it to her. She wiped at her face, smearing the rag all over until she felt she had cleaned herself sufficiently. Brittney giggled at her sister, telling her that it was just puppy kisses and not to worry. Aubrey responded with a "NO!" and then kept wiping.

Not wanting this to be the end of the day, let alone the "puppy visit," I asked Aubrey if I could have the rag back so that she could pet the puppy if she wanted to. She actually handed the rag back almost immediately, much to my surprise, then bent down next to Brittney to pet the little black puppy.

I watched as Brittney stroked the puppy's back and said, "Nice, you have to be nice, Aubrey, like this," and continued to demonstrate to her little sister what 'nice' meant.

Aubrey started petting the puppy with little pats, saying, "Nnnniiiiiicccce, nnniiiiicccccce." the entire time. She was being so very gentle with the dog and I was quick to congratulate her and reward her with verbal praises.

Things were going so smoothly and I said a silent prayer of thanks. I couldn't have asked for a better start to the day.

We ended up visiting almost every single animal at the fair and in the midst of it all, managed to stop for a few minutes to eat some lunch. That too had gone pretty well, as I had come well prepared with several wash clothes, extra crackers for Austin, and a change of clothes for Aubrey.

It wasn't until we tried to get pictures at the photo stall that trouble started settling in. It was just a small wave at first, nothing to get too excited about, but then it quickly advanced into a giant tsunami that none of us were prepared for, not even little Aubrey.

At the photo stall, all the kids from Clover Ridge were taking their turns getting their pictures taken in the "hay loft." It really didn't look like a big deal, but everyone had to do it, including us.

So, one by one, children were brought up by wheelchair, on crutches, by foot, or carried by their parents, and sat down on the hay bales for their photo. The photographer was a jolly older lady who was a little "too" happy, in my opinion, but we will let that notion go; just simply my non-clinical observation.

With every child that appeared before her, she would present a "genuine, really worn by cowboys" cowboy hat for the child to wear, along with a "real life, that every cowboy wouldn't be caught without" bandanna. Okay, so she loved her job, and the kids. I was happy about that, but did every child have to wear the hat? Was every child required to wear the bandanna? I heard one of the parents ask that question, as if they had read my mind. Hey! That was my trick!

"Yessssss sirrrrrrr eeeeeeeeee! Yup! You gotta be a *real* cowboy to be in the hay loft folks!" had been the jolly lady's reply as she snap, snap, snapped picture after picture.

Oh. Okay. That mystery was solved at least.

When it came time for Aubrey's turn, she hesitantly followed her sister up to the hay bale, but even after Brittney took her seat, Aubrey would have nothing to do with the "pokey" straw seat. I couldn't blame her, that crap could be painful! But, nonetheless, the jolly lady wanted her photo.

I considered the fact that this was indeed a fair for children with developmental disorders; surely she would understand and make allowances? Uh, no, I guess I was wrong with that assumption, because she didn't.

There were a few hundred kids in line, and *my kid* was holding it up. Okay, let's go then. Nope. She apparently wasn't ready to "lose" a customer, even though the photos were, uh, free.

Crap! Crap! Crap! Now what? Aubrey would *not* sit on the straw, and I didn't want to make her, but the lady was *insisting* she get a photo. So, problem solving genius that I was, I quickly plucked Aubrey away to the front of the line with me and let Brittney hold her little brother on her lap.

Bandannas in place, cowboy hats intact, the jolly old lady met her quota. I just wished she wasn't soooooo nice! Geeesh! She was making my dislike of her completely unjust! Or was she?

She, as nice as she *seemed* to be, was not to be deceived, however.

Upon the completion of Brittney and Austin's photo, she almost *demanded* that Aubrey join her in the "hay loft" and get her cowboy picture taken. "Last chance folks! Last chance! Get yer peanuts here! Popcorn!" Damn! There was my mind playing evil tricks on me, yet again.

Because Brittney was still seated on the bale of straw, I gently placed Aubrey on her big sister's lap, then gingerly placed a "genuine really worn by cowboys" hat upon her little head, and quickly wrapped a "real life that every cowboy wouldn't be caught without" bandanna around her tiny neck.

She writhed and pulled at the bandanna and immediately threw the hat off her head. Okay, this wasn't going to work, I immediately realized. I had already known that, but now this was my proof.

The jolly old lady wasn't so quick in her judgment though. She wanted her subject to *succeed* in having a nice little photo taken. Success was the motto of the day, by the way, and, didn't I *know that?*

I watched as she walked up to Aubrey and gently sat the "genuine really worn by cowboys" hat *back* on her head, and straightened the "real life that every cowboy wouldn't be caught without" bandanna around her neck. Because it had been the lady, and not me, Aubrey allowed her to do it. And, alas, the jolly lady got her flippin' picture.

I knew it was time for us to all head for home. The kids were tired and I was spent myself. Dealing with clowns, stinky animals, and demanding photographers had just about done me in, let alone the smell of the overcooked corn dogs and the sticky sweetness of the cotton candy machine.

Since Paulina and Rebecca were nowhere to be found, we had all gotten separated after the "photo session," I decided to make our way toward the fair grounds exit, only stopping momentarily by the ponies after I heard Aubrey exclaiming, "Nnnniiiccce! Nnnnnicccce!!!"

Just then, I heard a voice from behind me ask, "Do you want to ride the ponies, Aubrey?" I turned to look and saw that it was Claire.

"Hey there!" I said, trying my best to be cheery. "We are all really tired, Claire," I explained. She responded that she understood, but then asked if I thought Aubrey might "attempt" the ponies if we encouraged her to do so. I told her I didn't know. I honestly didn't want to try.

I was done for the day. I wanted to go home, to be somewhere quiet without noise and odd animal and cooking smells. I wanted a bubble bath and maybe a manicure, even though I had never had a manicure, it still sounded good at the moment. Oh, and a massage, and perhaps a facial? No, never mind, too much stimuli. I wanted to be left alone. *Really alone*, and my kids needed naps. We *all* needed naps.

Claire, however, was noticing how intrigued Aubrey was with the ponies. She asked me again if I thought she could attempt to get Aubrey on one. I told her no, but then thought about it for another second. I again came up with the same response as before, but when my brain said, "no" my mouth immediately disagreed and gave the verbal "okay" to Claire.

Within minutes I was standing on the side of the carousel watching my daughter being placed on a very much alive pony. I then watched in utter amazement as my little girl was walked around the circle on the pony's back by a staff member. She was off the ground! No, she was *really off the ground*!

As the pony's back swayed back and forth with the movement of its hooves, so did Aubrey in her little white and blue polka-dotted shirt, and striped cotton shorts. Back and forth, without so much as whimper.

She wasn't smiling and I couldn't tell if she was enjoying the ride, but *she was riding!* And, she wasn't crying so? My mind raced and dodged within itself, pondering thoughts over and over, circling within itself.

Again, Claire had been right. She had picked up on the cues my daughter was giving and acted upon them. I, on the other hand, was the one wanting to remove her to some place that was safer. A place of quietness and solitude. Somewhere we could all be without obstructions and obtrusions from the outside world. This is what I thought would be best for my child, but I had obviously, been wrong, again.

As I aimed my camera toward the gray and white speckled pony that carried my daughter and managed to snap a photo, I scolded myself for not wanting to give Aubrey the chance to ride the pony.

Was I *insane?* Was I too protective? Was it *me* that had the problems with the crowds and smells and sounds? Was *I* to blame for her difficulties? At that moment, I truly believed that I was. My mind taunted again, picking and poking into the depths where it could hurt me the most.

At that moment, I made a vow to myself silently that I would stop being so unnecessarily protective. After all, it had been just a stinky little pony! It wasn't the Trojan horse for crying out loud! If it hadn't been for Austin's stroller blocking my angle, I would have kicked myself all the way to my car.

After getting all the kids strapped into their car seats and seat belts we headed for home with an exhausted little sigh. As we rounded the bend out of the fairgrounds, Aubrey started to writhe in her car seat.

Within a minute, she was screaming and yelling so loud she was beginning to choke. Before I could pull over, the choking had turned into a bout of vomiting.

As the car came to a lurching halt at the side of the road, I quickly unbuckled my seat belt and opened the rear door to where Aubrey was strapped in her car seat.

I grabbed at the extra washcloths I had brought and began cleaning her up, ever so gently, and ever so thoroughly. With a soothingly soft voice whispering to her, I wiped. I had to get all the sticky off. I had to get it all.

I pulled at another washcloth and went through the routine again, precisely getting every bit of "sticky," every little bit of "messy' off of her little body. I wiped her little face, got under her chin, and replaced her soiled shirt with a fresh clean one that I had packed.

I could hear her crying as she lurched forward, spewing yet another round of vomit forward and into the towel I thankfully held. I then heard Brittney asking if her sissy was okay.

But, most of all, I heard myself saying over and over, "I am so sorry, sweetie, I am so sorry. Aubrey, I am *so* sorry! I knew it was too much. It *was* too much. Mommy knew, I *knew*, and I am so sorry." Brittney was looking at me, and when our eyes met, we both started to cry. Little Austin slept though it all.

I only wish that I already could foretell
What tomorrow would hold for you?
For what tomorrow bears
I could already begin to reveal the clues.
But, alas, I cannot foresee,
What troubles lie ahead, in the vastness ahead of me
So stay with me now, trust that I will find
Everything I can, about tomorrow, dear
To help ease and unburden your troubled little mind.

D.L. Clarke

Chapter 32

Aubrey's graduation day had come, which in a nutshell meant, Clover Ridge was ending. Which, in another sense meant, that I, who had become dependant on their support and guidance, was about ready to go into a full-fledged panic.

What were we going to do *now?* Even though they didn't have the answers I needed, they had given me help and support over the course of time that Aubrey had been in their care.

What Jackie couldn't accomplish in occupational therapy with Aubrey, Claire would attempt to in her class. It was a tightly knit circle of support and therapy.

Although Jackie had offered to continue occupational therapy for Aubrey in the form of private sessions in our home, I knew that financially, it was not even going to be an option. The reality was, that after today, all services and support would end. *All support would end.* That thought taunted me all morning and eased itself smugly and unwelcomingly into my morning.

Just getting the kids ready for the ceremony at the Clover Ridge was turning into a nightmare. Austin was crabby and had already soiled two of his outfits with spit up, and Aubrey was refusing to take her bath. I already knew we were going to be late, and I thought for a moment that maybe we shouldn't even go. It would definitely be *easier* to just stay home, but something inside me said no; I really should go. I knew that Claire and Jackie were expecting us, and I really did want to thank them and tell them goodbye.

After finally succeeding in getting Aubrey bathed and dressed, I attempted to brush her hair. The very first contact of the soft-bristled brush on her head set her off into a screaming tantrum. "NO!" she screamed loudly.

I tried to coax her into letting me try again, and after what seemed like forever, she did. I eventually succeeded in getting some of her hair into a ribbon and the rest; I left hanging to dry on its own. We were officially late.

We made the short drive to Clover Ridge and once there, found a parking spot half way down the drive. Upon walking up into the main parking lot, I could see that it was overflowing with cars.

Wow! I hadn't realized it was going to be so crowded! I found a few empty chairs toward the aisle in the back row, so the kids and I sat down and waited for the ceremony to begin. A lump formed in my throat and my chest felt heavy. This was a good day, a *very* good day. I repeated inside my head.

"This is a very wonderful day," I heard the male voice say. "All of you children should be proud of yourselves! And moms, dads, grandparents, aunts and uncles, brothers and sisters, you all should be so proud of what your child has accomplished!" the voice continued over the loudspeaker.

Out of the corner of my eye, I could see Aubrey covering her ears and bending her head down. I reached over and gently patted one of her legs with my hand. "It's okay, honey," I whispered to her. She immediately took one of her hands away from her ear and plucked my hand off her leg.

"Today marks the end of one small chapter in your child's life, and begins another. Today, your child moves onward, and again, you should all be so proud!" I heard coming from the sound system, and then the sounds of spattered clapping throughout the audience began.

As I joined in with the applause, I repeated the speaker's words to myself. "The ending of one chapter, and the beginning of another." I knew I should have been ecstatic, but I wasn't. What *exactly* would that new chapter hold? At this point, I didn't like not knowing what was going to be happening. I wanted time to prepare. Time to organize my thoughts and emotions. I also needed time to prepare Aubrey. I had to have a plan; I had to know what to tell her. And yet, I knew at this moment, that I could not.

So many little details that I had planned out so carefully and organized. They had formed into rituals and they had become our way to get through the days. Knowing what was going to be happening and when. If Aubrey asked me when we were going to the store, I could show her on the schedule and tell her,

"After lunch," or "Before dinner," and that would satisfy her momentarily. When she would repeat the same question, ten minutes later, I could tell her again when we would go. Every day had its plan and I did my absolute best not to alter it.

The schedule itself was even posted on the same wall at the same time, which was every night before bed. And, even though Aubrey had easy access to the schedule that she could easily decipher because of the "story board" method I had used with pictures instead of words and numbers, she always seemed to prefer asking me, "when, why, how?" I didn't mind repeating it to her either. So I would, over and over, over and over again, sometimes thirty or forty times a day. It seemed to make her happier, and it obviously eased some stress, so I didn't try to alter it in any way.

I was brought out of my thoughts, when Aubrey hopped down from her seat and headed off into the parking lot. I hurriedly collected Austin and went after her. I called to her, but she didn't look back. Instead, she kept going, now almost running. As I tried catching up to her, she dodged in and around the parked cars.

"Aubrey! STOP!" I demanded. Holding an almost one year old in your arms, while trying to run, in order to catch your almost three year old, was not proving to be too advantageous.

I again shouted at Aubrey to "STOP!" this time adding a "NOW!" I was sure we had attracted the attention of the audience by now and I could feel my cheeks flushing into bright red hotness. "*Please please please please, stop! Please please..... Please,*" I repeated in my head. "*Don't do this now, Aubrey, please stop,*" I continued to beg inside my head.

I could hear the audience intermittently clapping, and I assumed that they had started handing out the graduation certificates.

"This was such a mistake to do this," I scolded myself under my breath, which had now turned into a slight pant. I was starting to pit out in my dress and my upper lip was decorated with little sweat balls. Yuck! Looking really lovely today! I continued to scold myself over and over again for even attempting to leave the house in order to participate in this ceremonial day. "Why? Why? Had I done this?" The questions taunted and pulled at me. How could I answer them? What would I say? Other than the fact that I had thought that we *should* go, and that it had been the *right thing* to do, I had no other explanation.

I suddenly heard Aubrey laughing, and at that moment, I made the decision to stop in my pursuit. No one was leaving or arriving by car, yet, so there wasn't too much danger with her being hit by one, at the moment. I let my initial panic subside and I walked to the edge of the parking lot and waited, my eyes scanning around each car for evidence of my child.

I wanted to tell Aubrey that I was going to go sit down now, or I was going to get in the car and go home, or I was going to go talk to Claire, and she would ultimately be left behind. I thought it might ruin her fun a little if she no longer felt as if she held the deck.

But, because of all my "self-training" sessions from all the wonderful parenting books I had read, I knew that if I *did* tell her a plan, then *I would have to do it*. There could be absolutely no backing down, at all.

Any reversals or hesitations on my part would mean weakness. Therefore only reinforcing the fact that *she* was in control, not me. (See? I *had* actually read those books and had absorbed the material!) So I made no threats, yet. I wasn't ready to desert her in the parking lot; it just wasn't safe.

The audience again exploded into applause and I momentarily looked over to where they sat. Flash bulbs were firing and I could see video cameras being pointed in various directions, each one capturing a different moment and memory of the event. I was suddenly very relieved that none of my family was there. Why? I simply hadn't invited any of them. I wanted absolutely no videos, no cameras, other than my own, and no one to have to explain anything to. Yes, that had definitely been the right decision and now was proving to be quite a correct decision after all. Brilliant!

"They are handing out balloons Aubrey!" I called out into the lot of cars where my daughter was hiding. "You will need to come back and sit down with me if you want one!" I continued with the bribe.

Okay, I knew, and you know, she didn't deserve to be rewarded, but it was all I could think up at the moment, so give me a break! I just needed the stand off situation to end.

Austin was beginning to feel ten times heavier than he was, and my arms were starting to shake from fatigue. Why hadn't I taken my sister-in-law up on her offer to baby-sit him for me? Why? Well, simply put, I didn't want to burden anyone. I knew she would have done it for me, happily, but I had refused. Now I was wishing I hadn't.

Tanya, my sister-in-law, had in a sense, become my surrogate support system. She was my only respite, as Aubrey didn't seem too troubled being baby-sat by her. Well, some of the time anyway. But, at least it was help that could be there at a moments notice if needed, and I was grateful for that.

I was suddenly distracted by something moving in the corner of the parking lot. It was Aubrey, running. "*Shit!*" I said silently in my head. She hadn't yet tired out and I knew I was going to have to just grab her and *make* her come back with me. My arms ached as Austin squirmed in them, trying to free himself. I felt completely helpless and utterly frazzled. Why? Why? Had I even bothered to do my make up and hair today?

I slowly started walking within the parked cars and decided that I would try to get Aubrey cornered so that I could get the chance to grab her. I wanted to cry, but didn't. I knew I was not the one in control here, but I was *supposed* to be.

Sadly, I knew that *I* was the one *being* controlled, forced to go beyond my comfort zone in order to gain control. This was not the way I wanted to handle things, but it was what I chose to do at the moment.

Once I spotted Aubrey, I started to slowly approach her, all the while keeping my eye on the section of the lot where I would eventually trap her, hopefully. That was my plan anyway. Did it work? Um, sort of.

Once I got Aubrey into the little corner, I approached her quickly and grabbed onto her arm.

"NOOOOOOOOOOO!!!!!!!" she started screaming. Great! Now it looks as if I am abducting my own child.

"NOOOOOOOOO!" she continued to scream, more loudly than before. Through her screams I could hear footsteps behind me. Click, click, click. I immediately knew they were either ladies shoes, or a policeman's? I couldn't tell, without further deciphering, and at the moment, I really didn't care to continue my investigation.

As I held onto Aubrey's arm, she continued to scream at the top of her lungs yelling "NO!" and had begun to twist and writhe at the end of my hand. At one point, she even fell onto the ground briefly. I was not going to let go of her arm.

"Stop it, Aubrey!" I demanded. "You need to STOP!" I said again, trying to utilize Claire's "direct and to the point" sentences. My requests were loudly denied.

"Would you like some help?" I suddenly heard behind me. I spun around for a moment, and as I did, accidentally released my grip on Aubrey's arm. Within mere seconds, she was off running again into the depths of the parking lot.

I then watched in awe as Jackie with her shoes rapidly click, click, clicking, caught up to her. It was obvious that Aubrey had not been prepared for it, for she had a look of complete confusion on her face.

As Jackie held onto her, she quieted down and stared straight ahead, breathing hard in an out. Her little face softened and as I walked up to where they were standing, she smiled at me sweetly. The storm was over, once again, for now.

Let's hide here just you and me
Hiding so far out of sight
Up in the safe shadows of the trees.
Don't come down yet
For it isn't just the forest I do fear.
It is the shadows that lurk so closely
So dangerously and threateningly near.

D.L. Clarke

Chapter 33

As long as we didn't have to leave the house, things were a little more tolerable, I could rationalize. We had a routine at home, and things didn't really have to change there.

Sticking to the routine was easier than in the outside world. In the outside world, we were subjected to traffic lights and unexpected trains, unplanned stops to the gas station, wrong turns, loud trucks, and blaring horns.

It began slowly, but I soon realized that I was beginning to cut ourselves off from the outside world, or as I called them, the enemies. Anyone who gave us stare downs in the grocery store, or asked me if I could "control my child," in the mall, had become the enemy. As long as we didn't go out, we didn't have to deal with people staring at us, nor were there opportunities for rude and dreadful comments concerning my "Oh, my God, what a brat!" child.

It was amazing to me how terrible and insensitive people could be. Aubrey wasn't a brat, nor was she "spoiled rotten" as one person had commented once without a moments concern to anyone's feelings.

I wanted to make a t-shirt for Aubrey that could explain why she was acting the way she was, but sadly, I wouldn't have known what to write. *I* didn't even know why, but what I *did* know, was that she wasn't doing it on purpose. I only wished that *they* all could realize that and have just a smidge of compassion.

I thank God that I had that insight instilled within me for without that bit of knowledge, I would have surely gone mad. Yes, I absolutely was convinced that there was *something* that was making her miserable; I just needed to find out *what* it was. Until then, I just wanted to keep her away from everyone, which meant keeping her safe and protected.

Being alone was okay, as far as I was concerned. I had convinced myself by now that it was definitely safer and much less stressful. The only times I went out were to get groceries, and even at that, I waited until the very last morsel of bread had been consumed, the last of the formula mixed, and the milk in the jug drained to its last drop. We were doing fine, I would demand of myself to be convinced.

After all, it wasn't *that* bad. I *did* make it to every single one of Brittney's school functions, even if it meant leaving after only a minute or two. The point was, I *had been there*. She had seen me. Even though it often meant that I would have to spend the majority of the event rocking and walking, a seemingly very troubled little toddler back and forth across the entrance hallway of the school.

But, I was *there* and, I had to be satisfied that it was enough for now. Even though I wanted and needed more, to be that mom sitting in the front row snapping hundreds of pictures of every movement of my child on stage, I knew I couldn't. I had to settle for everything that I could get at the moment, and so did she. I *was* doing the best I could. But, it *had* to get better, somehow. I couldn't even entertain the thought that it might not.

Austin was now one year old, Brittney eight, and Aubrey three. Time was rushing by. With every hour, day, week, and month, I waited for things to get better, become smoother, but they really didn't seem to be.

Chaos had just become the way of life for us. Tantrums, lack of sleep, missed appointments, forgotten lunches and homework, this is what we had become, our definition. But, it was okay. We didn't have to be the perfect family did we? At least we *were* a family.

Wrongness possessing no rightness
Within itself, something so oddly normal
Ultimately moving onward as it progresses
Rapidly growing deeply within its very own madness.

D.L. Clarke

Chapter 34

"There is something seriously wrong with Aubrey," my sister-in-law Tanya, informed me one day during the course of one of our phone conversations. I knew at that moment, that she had seen it too. The strangeness of Aubrey's behaviors, the oddities. The things that didn't seem to make any sense to myself, were also now not making any sense to others; anyone who spent any amount of time with her anyway.

"She ate candles at my house the other day," Tanya continued on the phone, matter-of-factly. She explained that she had started a list of strange behaviors that she observed while around my child. Well, I know that that isn't really *normal* to want to eat candles, but Aubrey was just three, so considering that aspect, I wasn't too concerned by that observation. And, I let Tanya know that I wasn't too troubled about it.

But then she continued to tell me that Aubrey would often slap at her kids, and sometimes try to bite them and pull their hair. Often, she said, Aubrey would just end up biting herself, or pulling at her *own* hair. She wouldn't play with the toys she offered her, but would instead, pull toys *away* from her kids that *were* playing with them. She said it was like Aubrey *wanted* to make them mad, or make some sort of a dramatic scene.

Aubrey would often sit and tear up pieces of paper into tiny bits and leave them lying all over her floor. Tanya went on to explain that Aubrey constantly asked her for food, even after she just gave her a snack, or lunch, or dinner.

It sounded much like the continual stream of begging for food, much like what I experienced at my own home. The list continued, on and on, of all the concerns Tanya had about Aubrey.

Most were not a surprise to me, as they were on my "list of things that concern me" as well. She said she could see that I was stressed, and encouraged me to continue to seek help.

I knew I needed more help, but I didn't know who to go to now. All the services that Clover Ridge had offered, no longer were an option. Even my attempts to get social security benefits for Aubrey in order to help fund private occupational therapy had been denied. Hiring a babysitter was not even a reasonable option for me, as I could not possibly trust someone else to have the patience needed to tolerate my child's tantrums and odd behaviors. I knew that *I* could barely tolerate some days, so, how could *they* be expected to?

Pre-schools would not consider taking Aubrey into their classes until she was toilet trained. It was a definite requirement of all the schools I had called, and it was one obstacle that was becoming a major hurdle.

But, I kept trying. Toilet training sessions came and went as I only attempted them when Aubrey was having a "good day," otherwise, it was proved to be pointless. The only thing the sessions would accomplish on her "off" days were more tantrums. It just wasn't worth it. She could wait a little longer to join pre-school. I knew she would get out of diapers at some point, so I stopped worrying about it.

But, even in the midst of my desires to be left alone, shielding Aubrey from the outside world, I knew I needed the help and support from the outside sources.

Something in my gut kept urging me to make more calls, despite the negativities, make more appointments, see other doctors, *someone, something, anything* that might help. I knew that I was battling something that I had no control over and that realization scared the hell out of me. If *I* couldn't help my daughter, *who could?* Keep on...keep on...my mind would urge me.

Shattered, and shatter,
Break and break
The mold that once held
Your truths so forlorn
Boldness envelops the mindless
Thoughts now left unborn.
Where are you now?
Shattered amongst the ruins, do you quake?
Of the mind that no longer seeks, I warn
Is the mortal that no longer appears to matter.

D.L. Clarke

Chapter 35

After yet another day of listening to Aubrey scream and tantrum, and after another sleepless night, I finally broke down and decided to call the Naval hospital. I could not take it anymore. I knew it and more than I wanted to admit, felt it. If one could truly be at one's "wits end," I had truly found the proverbial, ending of the wits. (Still looking for the damned infamous, pot o' gold, but that is another story, another time).

Though I didn't know what to say as the reason for the visit, I knew I had to see *someone*. We were scheduled to see a new pediatrician, and within two days, we were on our way to his office.

Sitting in the waiting room, I watched as Aubrey buried her face in book after book. She would sit for a second, flip the pages, get back up, grab another book, sit back down, and the flipping would begin again. In the course of just a few minutes she had exhausted the supply of children's books.

We didn't have to wait too long, thank goodness, before we were called back. Butterflies were fluttering around in my stomach. I didn't want to hear another, "Oh, your daughter is very normal, stop worrying about it," from another person in a white coat.

But, I knew the reality of that possibility was great, so I was nervous and sick with apprehension by the time the exam door opened. As I watched the door swing widely open, my anxiety levels rose, but then fell immediately upon seeing that it was just the nurse coming in to record the reasons for the visit, and to check Aubrey's temperature.

I kept it brief and to the point, "I am having some problems with some behavioral issues." was all I said. The nurse looked at me quizzically lifting her "a little too detailed with, a little too dark eyebrow pencil," penciled eyebrows and then let them fall when she went to write my statement in Aubrey's chart. After letting me know that the doctor would be right in, she, along with her horrible artificially designed eyebrows, shut the door.

Aubrey immediately wanted down from the examining table. "DOWN DOWN DOWN!" she shouted.

"Shhhhhhhhhh!! There are sick kids here, sweetie. You have to be a little quiet," I responded as I went over to the table and asked Aubrey, before letting her down, if she could ask to "get down, *please?*"

"Pfflease?" she responded.

"Gooooood girl!" I responded back. I wondered if we were going to have a good day today.

Within a few minutes, the doctor appeared and sat on the little round stool across the room from me. He too, wanted to know what the reason for the visit was. I started slowly with the explanations, expecting him, at any moment, to brush off my concerns with a wave of his hand. But, to my surprise, he didn't. I continued to explain Aubrey's first few years of life, and all of my trepidations.

I watched as he wrote, and wrote, and wrote in her chart. He was listening intently and I was impressed.

After I was satisfied that I had covered almost every one of my concerns, he asked me to put Aubrey back up on the table. I did. He then checked her ears, looked down her throat, listened to her heart, and lastly, gave special interest to the tendons in her legs.

"Has she always walked on her toes?" he asked me as he pushed her little feet up and down, testing the tendon's capacity.

"Yes, she has," I replied. "I was told that it could be because I used to put her in a baby walker? That some kids get used to pushing with their tip-toes, so then they walk on their toes?" I continued, readily accepting the blame for the abnormality.

"No, I don't think so," the doctor replied frankly, as he finished with her tendons and once again concentrated on writing in Aubrey's chart.

"I do not have any distinct answers for you, but one thing I am sure of, is you need some respite," he stated. "Is your husband here? Or—" he started then stopped mid-sentence.

"No, he *isn't* here, he… *hasn't* been here, " I answered with a sigh. "He actually isn't supposed to be home until four months from now."

"Ah! Doing the West-Pac deployment?" he asked.

I answered with a quiet yes, but reassured him that I was definitely *doing okay*. I was completely surprised when his reply back to me was, "No, no—you are *not* doing okay!"

Oh no! Here it was coming as expected, the blame, the accusations, and the list of parenting books that I should read and live by oh so diligently. I braced myself for the onslaught.

"C'mon, you can take it!" My own personal cheerleading squad yelled and then, "Give us a D!"

Then my own personal psychologist, apparently seeing the irrationality of the whole process, chimed in with a bit of reason and took inventory of the whole situation. It had easily decided right then and there that I had gone seriously and completely mad.

"Oh well," my split personality would chime in, offering to give us a much-needed break. I had let it butt right in, voicing its own opinion, after all, it was offering asylum that seemed exceptionally tempting. Should I take it? Or—

"Wait! Where are you going?" I witnessed a slightly vociferous whimper from my own throat as I reached for it frantically. It continued to glide slowly but steadily out and away from my attainable reach.

Lunacy was not to be had today, I surmised. But, I had witnessed it, however briefly. I knew it was attainable nearby, and I also knew that if and when I needed it, I could seize it. With that, my hands fell to my sides in silent capitulation.

"I would like to prescribe some sleep medication for Aubrey. It will benefit her by allowing her to get some continual sleep, possibly even breaking her habitual night waking and tantrums, and *you* need to get some sleep as well," he said while writing feverishly on a prescription pad.

"Is it safe to give her sleep aide?" I inquired. He reassured me that it was a form of Benadryl and was completely safe in the doses he was prescribing. I felt comforted, but was still wary.

I was also comforted when the doctor informed me that though my daughter's physical health and development seemed excellent and right on schedule, he definitely had some major concerns with her social and behavioral development.

I assured him that I had tried everything that I or anyone else could think of to help her. From pre- pre-school for developmentally delayed children, to speech therapy, occupational therapy, to sensory integration. He seemed satisfied with my attempts and congratulated me on being so diligent in my quest to help my daughter.

He then asked if I wouldn't mind coming back in a few days to check on how the sleep aides were doing. He also said that in the meantime he was going to consult with some of his colleagues about a future plan for Aubrey. As we were heading out the door, he asked me to not expect miracles, but he did want to help. That was all I needed. The willingness of someone to help me find the answers.

As we left the medical clinic, I felt a little better emotionally. The doctor hadn't blamed me for anything that was "wrong" with my child, nor did he hand over the usual stack of parenting books. A little wave of hope swept over me just then and my heart quickened. Maybe, I would find out how to help Aubrey after all? I said another silent prayer, and headed for home.

The stars are out again tonight
How can you not see them there?
Dancing and gliding
Crazily into the crispness of night.

D.L. Clarke

Chapter 36

Sleep didn't come as promised, nor expected. If anything, the medication just seemed to make Aubrey more hyper at bedtime. After calling the doctor to double-check on the dosage, I was encouraged to give it a couple of more days to see if it would help. It didn't.

When the doctor called me two days later I was almost in tears, and ready to break down. It had been nearly three days since Aubrey had slept more than a few minutes at a time during the night, and we were all frazzled and stressed. Tantrums only intensified with her lack of sleep, and they would often rage on deep into the night.

No plan or behavior modification techniques worked. There was absolutely nothing to do but try desperately to wait the tantrums out and more importantly, remain patient. But, my patience had worn thin long ago and it was becoming more and more difficult trying to soothe my screaming child that was so obviously completely out of control.

More nights passed, and with every sundown, my anxiety and worry would begin. With every sunrise, I would thank God that I had made it through another sleepless night without losing my mind or patience. I would also pray for solutions, for some help, or knowledge, *something*. I prayed for Aubrey's happiness and for something to take away whatever it was that was making her so miserable.

After almost a week and a half of no substantial sleep, I figured I had given the sleep aide idea enough of a trial, and called Aubrey's doctor to schedule another appointment.

I was told to come in on Thursday. That was two more days! I couldn't do it. I asked if I could come in sooner, and the receptionist informed me that there weren't any appointments, but that she would put me on a waiting list. I suddenly wished that I *had* scheduled the followup appointment *before* leaving the office last time, as the doctor had recommended. But, Aubrey had been made cranky by the visit, and I had just wanted to get her back home and out of the public's eye as quickly as possible.

Later that same day the phone rang and it was Aubrey's pediatrician's office. They had a cancellation. It took me a matter of seconds to gather the kids up and drive to his office. I was desperate for help.

After waiting for what seemed like an eternity, the doctor finally appeared in the exam room doorway. "Not doing too good today?" he asked sympathetically.

I replied that, "No, we weren't doing good, *at all.*" I continued, "She won't sleep at all now, even after discontinuing the sleep aide."

"Really?" the doctor replied in utter amazement. He then asked me if I wanted to try something else, and before he could finish, I broke down in tears. Without a moment's hesitation, he handed me a Kleenex.

"Do you have anyone that can come in and help you? A family member? Someone nearby?" he asked earnestly.

"No, I really don't," I managed to say between sobs. Kyle, who had since finished his enlistment requirements, had been honorably discharged from duty a few weeks ago, so he and my sister-in-law Tanya had moved back to Oregon. My little support network was dismantled almost as quickly as it had been constructed. I missed Tanya terribly, and the mere thought of her departure, now sent me into another huge round of sobs. Damn!

Why was I *so weak*? I got instantly pissed off at myself for showing such a lack of control. The sobbing was just going to have to stop, I tried convincing myself. They didn't listen though, and went into another long bout.

The doctor's expression then got very serious as he looked at me. He explained that whether I wanted to admit it or not, *I had to get help*. He wanted me to see if I could get my husband home for emergency respite. I told him I didn't need it. He argued that I did.

"I am going to write a letter and make some phone calls, and as your daughter's doctor, I am telling you that something needs to be done, immediately." he stated emphatically.

I knew, without telling the doctor what I thought, that there was no way the Navy was going to allow Darrin to come home to play babysitter or supportive hubby. The Navy wasn't exactly the best career choice for a "family man" and they surely had made that quite obvious so long ago, as early as boot camp, actually. After all, he *was* in the Gulf for crying out loud! It wasn't exactly a hop and skip type of plane ride home, besides, we didn't have the kind of money it would take to fly him home. It was not going to happen, I knew it.

I could be stronger. I knew I was just tired and things would make more sense after I got a little rest. I would come up with a plan, and things were going to be *just fine.* I glanced over to where Aubrey was sitting with a book, flipping pages back and forth, muttering something to Elmo.

"I will forward a letter about your situation to the right people, and we will get you some help, okay?" the doctor said reassuringly, handing me yet another Kleenex.

I told him thank you, over and over, and after blowing my swollen red nose for the hundredth time, left his office. We never saw him again.

It only takes a moment to start believing
But forever for it to impossibly stop.

D.L. Clarke

(And no, I didn't get that from a church's reader board!)

Chapter 37

For those that are believers, you will certainly find the next few paragraphs very interesting and perhaps a bit enlightening. For those who are skeptics, you can chalk it all up to delirium from my lack of sleep, if you must. Nonetheless, I feel compelled to share this part of my story with you, believers or not.

. It was the middle of yet another sleepless night. As I lay in my bed listening to Aubrey, she rustled around in hers. I knew that at any moment, she would awaken completely, and heave into a full-blown scream session. Even though I had just laid her down a mere half hour before, I knew the pattern and was trying to mentally prepare for another night of tantrums and screaming.

My stomach felt sick and my head ached. I *had* to find help for her! But, I was out of resources and ideas. As I lay quietly, I felt my breath flow in then out as it escaped into the stillness of my room. I had to remain calm, but as I heard Aubrey's whimper, I felt my pulse quicken, and knew there were only going to be a few minutes more of rest.

"Lord, *help me*," I whispered as I stared up at the shadows being cast by the beams in my ceiling. The only light coming in was from the street lamp, that flickered slightly, making faint humming noises as it did I felt my breath go in and out, as I lay, trying to stay as calm as possible in the midst of the off-and-on whimpers coming from Aubrey's room.

"Please, God? *Help me!*" I whispered again in earnest. Then lay in silence listening to my own breath. Then out of the stillness of the night, came a voice:

"Rest my child, for he will be home soon," the voice spoke ever so quietly. But, I *had heard* it! And, perhaps I should have been, but wasn't, afraid. Nor, did I even have to question where it had come from, or from *whom* it had come. I just somehow *knew*.

I closed my eyes, and the entire house, including Aubrey, slept straight through the night, for the first time in two weeks, until morning.

The second I opened my eyes, I had a sudden panic and shot straight out of bed. I raced into Aubrey's room and found both her and Austin still sound asleep. Brittney was up watching cartoons on the downstairs television.

I then thought about the "voice" I had heard in the night and in the morning light, was able to easily stifle it with a simple explanation of "wishful thinking," for I rationally knew, that there was no way we could afford to fly Aubrey's father home to help me out. I had been merely exhausted and had "dreamed up" the "voice," I concluded as I walked into the kitchen.

As soon as I started to make Brittney's breakfast, the telephone rang. I quickly picked it up, hoping it hadn't woke Aubrey or Austin, and it hadn't.

"Hello?" I said into the receiver.

"Hello, this is the American Red Cross calling," I heard on the other end and immediately thought about how I would tell them that I really didn't have the money to donate right now.

"We are calling to let you know that your husband has just received the necessary paperwork that will enable him to fly home for a period of at least two weeks. You should expect him to arrive in the States within two days," the voice continued. "Furthermore, the Navy has stated that you will not be required to provide funding for his flight," the voice concluded.

I was dumbfounded and stood in complete disbelief, my knees feeling as if there were going to buckle at any moment. Then the words, *"Rest my child, for he will be home soon,"* came flooding over me and as I realized just exactly what those words had truly meant, I immediately felt the flow of goose bumps begin to riddle my skin.

And, after thanking the caller, I hung up the phone, collapsed to my knees and between sobs of joy and immense relief, thanked God over and over and over again.

More changes, my dear
Please try to remain strong
All of this is to someday help you
My sweet little one.

D.L. Clarke

Chapter 38

As promised by the Red Cross, Darrin did arrive home, free of charge. Though it took a little longer than expected for his arrival, he was *home!* When I asked him how he was informed that he would be coming home, he simply said, "I got read some orders by the ship's chaplain explaining that I was needed home immediately. They told me it wasn't a life threatening emergency, and I sort of knew it was because of all the trouble Aubrey has been having, but that is about all they said."

I then described to him what I had experienced that fateful night that seemingly had changed everything so rapidly. After listening to my story, he reassured me that he too, believed that it *had* been a miracle and with that, we both began a prayer of thanks and guidance.

We knew we would have some major decisions to make, and we didn't have a clue as to what we should do or even which direction would be the best. All I knew for sure was now that he was home; there was no way I could handle him leaving again. Two weeks was not going to be enough. I desperately needed him to be there to help, *every day*.

With some guidance from the career-counseling center on the Naval base, rather than seek and an honorable humanitarian discharge from military duty, we both figured our best direction would be to request humanitarian shore duty for the remainder of time Darrin was enlisted, which was less than one full year.

So that is what we proceeded to do. We got all the paperwork together and with it, included twenty-five pages of statements and letters from therapists, teachers, counselors, doctors, neighbors, friends, family, and finally both Darrin and myself, describing Aubrey's difficulties and the overall situation.

We also explained to the Navy, making it perfectly clear in all of our written statements, that we could not financially afford to be discharged at the present time. We hoped that they would, instead, consider and grant Darrin's request to fulfill his military obligations and commitment on shore at the Naval Hospital.

All our requests were denied. We *were* given thirty days notice, however, by letter, that Darrin had been granted an honorable "humanitarian discharge" from active duty. Which really meant to us, no job, which meant, no money, no health insurance, and no place to live. In a matter of a week, we were granted the honor of being jobless and homeless. I guessed that we had made a wrong choice, and almost waited for the "gong" to go off, but it never did.

Instead, we figured, there had to be a *reason* they wouldn't grant shore duty, right? So, what was it then? We pondered that question and finally, without coming up with any answers, decided to just follow the most obvious path, which was, go home, back to Oregon.

Within three weeks we were officially discharged and all we were waiting for now was the moving crew. Once they arrived and packed up our belongings, we would be ready for the trek back to Oregon. I was still waiting, suspiciously, for the "gong" to sound.

Our plan, once we arrived in Oregon, was to stay with Darrin's parents temporarily until we found work. I had already scoured the employment ads where we would be living and had sent out nearly thirty résumés for Darrin and myself combined.

We would just make all of this work somehow, we had already decided. Besides, with two of us working as a team lately with the kids, things had become a *lot* smoother. Not to say that the problem behaviors that Aubrey displayed had disappeared, because they hadn't, they just were more manageable when you weren't the only parent dealing with them.

As the moving van arrived and the workers piled out to pack and load up our belongings, a sense of renewal washed over me, followed by feelings of sheer panic. Did we really know what we were doing? Or was this all a big mistake? There was only one way to find out, I surmised. Once the last box had been packed and loaded into the moving van, we loaded the kids up in our car, bid our house goodbye, took a few last pictures, and started out on the road to Oregon.

Tomorrow is here
And I do not know what to say
How can I try to explain something to you?
When my words cannot even possibly begin
To find their way?

D.L. Clarke

Chapter 39

Though I was excited to be "back home," I couldn't wash the feelings of sadness away. As the road signs whizzed by and with each mile became more and more familiar, I knew what we had known as our little routine and life, was going to be replaced. It is the 'with what' that caused the acute sense of anxiety within me. I wanted reassurance that we had made the right decision. And for the time being, there was none to be found.

We had taken a leap of faith, and once the leap had been leapt, there was nothing more to do but wait and see what it would entail. I just could not escape the feelings that everything happens for a reason, and there was a definite reason for all of this. With that, I let my mind drift off in aimless thought.

I thought about Paulina, and then Rebecca. They had made such an impact on me; even in the short amount of time I had known them. I wondered if she would keep in touch as promised. She said she would send letters and photos, and so did I. (She didn't, and neither did I).

I then thought about Claire and Jackie. Claire had just accepted a special education teaching assignment in Germany. She was due to leave within a few weeks of our move to Oregon. She promised to write and so did I. (Both of us never did).

Jackie was moving to Montana and promised to send pictures of her new place. I am still waiting. I promised to send her pictures of our new place in Oregon. (I don't know if she is still waiting, but I never sent them either.)

I then thought about the last doctor I took Aubrey to see, my hero, Dr. Johnstown. I thought about his intelligent and inquisitive way of just knowing that what I had to say was real and without validation of any "proof" he had accepted what I had had to say. And, furthermore, he had seemed to truly understand. He had been such an amazing amount of support for us, and I never got the chance to thank him. I hoped that he would know how much I appreciated what he did for us.

I laughed a little under my breath when I thought back to all the times in Lemoore. Shy and quiet Janice and flamboyant, outspoken Gwen. What a pair they were! But they too, had helped me in their own separate ways. (We all too, promised to write and keep in touch, but sadly, none of us ever did.)

The lumps formed in my throat and with each passing road sign, it was becoming more and more obvious that I was nearing my hometown. I don't know why I was so sad. We were definitely making some really positive changes, weren't we?

I pulled my seat into a more upright position and glanced around my shoulder to the backbench of the car. All three kids were sound asleep. Little peaceful sleeping angels.

As I turned around to face forward, a sign reading, "Welcome to Albany" greeted me.

What is it?
This little secret you hide
Clearly hidden from anyone's view
Protected there; safely hidden
Deeply inside of you.

D.L. Clarke

Chapter 40

Within two weeks of our arrival back to Oregon, Darrin had gotten employment at Hewlett Packard. I too found a job at a local medical clinic, and though I was working only fifteen hours a week, it was enough to supplement our income. Better yet, it got me out of the house enough to where I felt myself growing again as an individual, rather than just "mom." Days spent with my fellow "office ladies" did me an amazingly amount of good. I needed it and relished it and I actually looked forward to my three, five-hour days, of work.

It took just a matter of weeks before we were able to move out of Darrin's parents house and into a place of our own. Though they had been wonderful hosts, it was still nice to have our own space.

I also had to hand it to the kids. They had adjusted seemingly well after all of the chaos of moving. Aubrey's tantrums had all but ceased, Austin slept through the night, most of the time anyway, and Brittney had started school at the local elementary school. Everything was falling right into place.

But, I couldn't help but wonder, *why?* Why was Aubrey allowing *them* to hold her? Why was she accepting baths and having her hair pulled into ponytails and ribbons? Why was she allowing herself to "get messy" at dinner times? Though it was all wonderful, I couldn't help but wonder, WHY? And, what had made the transformation possible?

Was the move responsible? I knew that by just having more people around to care for her, to provide her with the necessities she needed without delay was part of it. But that couldn't possibly be the explanation for everything, could it? It also didn't help validate all of my earlier complaints to them about Aubrey's difficulties. Obviously, if they didn't exist now, they never did, uh, apparently.

Music would be played in Grandma's car, and my daughter would dance in her booster seat. Gone was her usual "covering her ears and shrieking" routine. All of my concerns, therefore, were "blown out of proportion" and rendered "unreliable." I had been just "too stressed" to properly care for my children, and even though I didn't like hearing it, I started to slowly believe it. What else could possibly be the reason?

During the three weeks we co-habited with my in-laws, Aubrey had seemingly transformed into a more enjoyable and tolerant toddler, (not that she had ever been anything less in their eyes, after all, they were *grandparents!*).

The fact that she was so easygoing with them was in itself so strikingly odd to me. What had caused all the drama and sleepless nights *before* then? Was it me? Yes, yes, yes. All answers pointed to me. I was the problem, for now, my daughter was fine. I felt as if they truly believed that as well.

Well, I grasped that notion for a moment and really thought about it. Good! If she is cured, then excellent! The hard part is over and now she is completely normal and happy. Gone are the days she spent crying miserably, and here now are the days she spends playing happily. Excellent!

My gut still said there was something "up," but I could now easily ignore what it was trying to say. We all could brush off incidences of drama and tantrums again as having a "bad day" or "being too tired," and now, for some reason, it all made perfect sense.

I felt relieved and scared all at the same moment. Somehow, I knew the dam might burst, but then guffawed the idea and scolded myself for even venturing to think it. But, none-the-less, it was still there, nagging, nagging.

And just as if it needed some proof to back up its insistent nagging, one week after moving into our new upper level three bedroom townhouse, we received a note from our landlord informing us that: *because of all the complaints he had received pertaining to the extreme noise level coming from our home, specifically, screaming children at all hours, he had no choice but to ask us to "keep the children's noise levels" under control,* or *we would be asked*, nicely, but forcibly, *to vacate the premises, permanently.*

The storm had reared its ugly head again. My gut gleefully lurched and began chewing a hole in itself, for, it had been right all along. There was still something really wrong with my daughter, and for some unforeseen reason, all the problems had resurfaced immediately upon our departure from my in-law's house.

They sting, they burn
No salve will help
pull away the poison
But the bites are still there
Achingly throbbing, each taking their turns.
Silently stabbing into the night's air.

D.L. Clarke

Chapter 41

Winter was approaching quickly and Aubrey's behaviors had continued to worsen over the past few months only to reach new intolerable levels with the arrival of the holidays. I didn't know if it was the crowded situations at the stores that bothered her or if she was picking up on other stress, but she cried nearly all of the time.

And, when she wasn't crying, she was stomping mad and angry at everything. She would storm around demanding to "EAT! NOW!" And when I refused to give in, because she had just had a meal, she would demand even more, getting louder and louder with each request. Nothing Darrin or I did could please her. She was once again, apparently completely miserable. Zardar had sadly, yet abruptly, returned.

It finally all came to a head when one morning upon opening my front door was greeted with a "please find other housing," notice from our more than tolerant landlord. He truly was trying to be understanding and sympathetic, but under the circumstances, I could understand his predicament as well, his hands, were in a sense, virtually tied.

We quickly obliged and luckily found a three-bedroom house in a quiet neighborhood that held a good reputation. We were especially pleased when it meant both Brittney and Aubrey would be in a better school district. The only problem was, Aubrey was still not toilet trained. Even though she was over three years old, she could not grasp the idea of the "potty."

The holidays came and went, and though it was great being home and having the family gathered, it also made it more apparent to me that other people were noticing Aubrey's odd behaviors as well. There were moments when they just could not be ignored.

Gifts would be presented to Aubrey, and upon opening them, there would be no reaction from her, and I truly mean, *none*. She would rip open the paper, and upon revealing the contents of the box, observe it, possibly hold it to her nose to smell, and then more often than not, it would be dropped to the floor with a definitive thump.

I would try to explain to those that were confused by her reaction, but I didn't really know what or how to explain it. "She really loves it! Really! She is just really tired today," would be my usual response at birthdays, and holidays.

I knew the gift giver's feelings had been hurt, after all, aren't we all trained to act exuberant upon opening a gift in front of someone, especially the gift giver? Even though we might hate the color, or dislike the gift all together, we are still programmed to "love it" and smile convincingly, aren't we?

And, aren't we all so damned happy when we can return the gift the following day and get the cash to either cram into our pockets or buy what we *really* think we want? Well, what about those that *don't* have the "programmed skills" automatically in place that enable them to skip forward to the happy-go-lucky side of getting a crappy gift? Then what? You too would sadly be forced to sit with a blank stare on your face not knowing what in the world to say, all the while wishing you somehow did.

One day, after spending part of the afternoon at my parent's house with my kids, I was again confronted by the two of them with, "Have you checked into the possibility that Aubrey is autistic?" That, again, had immediately pissed me off, and upon arriving back at my house; I vowed to never speak to them again. Obviously, they had hit a nerve that I didn't want to have hit.

The next day, I was on the telephone with the Early Intervention program for our county, and before I knew it, I had made an appointment for the "intake" director to make a home visit to observe Aubrey. I could feel the recently hit nerve pulsating quietly in the back of my mind.

Again, you are let in
To find the secrets she bears
Holding tightly and securely,
Into the light we hope and peer.
Only within your grasp, this will we dare.

D.L. Clarke

Chapter 42

About two weeks and a thousand tantrums later, Joyce, the Early Intervention specialist arrived at our front door. I was so happy to have someone finally arrive that I had to fight back the urge to give her an earth shattering bear hug. Notepads in hand, pencils in place, she sat down at my kitchen table and began her observations.

I was told to carry on "like she wasn't even there." Though that might sound a bit hard to do, I was, by now, a pro at it. Throughout Aubrey's short three year life span, I could not even begin to count how many "specialist" and "observers" had sat at my kitchen table or on my living room sofa and instructed me to "carry on as normal." Each with their own agenda as to what they wanted to find, each never finding anything really "substantial" enough to come to any "definite conclusions."

It was okay, though. I truly didn't *want* anything to be wrong with my daughter, so when they would come up with "inconclusive results" I would, in a sense, feel a little reassured that perhaps it *was* just a phase and that she would eventually 'outgrow' it.

But, along with every "inconclusive result" came another slew of questions and uncertainty. And then, there was still my nagging gut that refused to shut up.

I was more than ready to either rule out the fact that there *was* something wrong, or ready to accept that there *wasn't* anything wrong and *never had been* anything wrong with Aubrey. Just please, someone, finally tell me *something* that *was "conclusive."*

I did carry on like Joyce wasn't even there, for really, I wanted to believe that she wasn't. I wanted to believe that there was never a *reason* for her to be there in the first place. But, when I looked over at my kitchen table, she *was very much so,* sitting there. Her hands scribbled madly at the paper with her pen, and she made little "uh huh" noises as she wrote.

Aubrey had been especially agitated that day, asking for food constantly and I, trying to show Joyce that I was a good and "trained" parent, repeated often and firmly, that she could not have a cookie. I reminded Aubrey several times throughout Joyce's hour-long visit that she had just eaten. When she switched to requesting, "Drink! Drink!" I had dutifully fulfilled her request and gave her a tippy cup full of apple juice. After the juice had been drained, however, Aubrey went right back to requesting food, "EAT! EEEEAT!" she demanded over and over.

Even the toys I offered Aubrey, trying to distract her from the "eating" idea, were not interesting to her and she would shout and throw them to the floor. Then she would climb on my lap, and then back down. After grabbing a book, she would again climb on my lap, and then before I could even get the book open, she was down again and back over to the bookshelves, still asking me if she could, "Eat!"

I suddenly felt a flush come over my body. I felt like a failure. Surely Joyce would see that my daughter's behavior was out of control and somehow, my parenting techniques were to blame. I mean, it was so obvious wasn't it?

Then, it was apparently time for Joyce to leave. As she started collecting her notepads and paperwork, she told me she was going to over some of the notes she had taken, as well as the visual observations she had made. As she spoke, I tried to read her expressions, but I couldn't. There would be no insight as to what she was thinking today.

She then informed me that she would be giving me a call soon to go over some "things." In other words, I was just going to have to be patient and wait for the results. When the phone call finally did come, three days later, I wasn't shocked at how apprehensive I felt. We had been through this so many hundreds of times before, and I had already mentally prepared myself for the news. I knew that there would be "nothing wrong" with my daughter, and they would feel bad and wish they could help, and then end the conversation bluntly by offering to give me some titles of some "really great" parenting books.

This time, however, I was not *at all* prepared for what I heard coming from the other end of the phone. It was Joyce, and I listened in shock as she told me she really wanted to bring a team of specialists over to my house to do some more observations on Aubrey. One of them was specialist in Autism. *Autism!*

Joyce waited for a moment for my reply, and when I told her that it would be okay to have the team come over, she wrote us down on her calendar for the following week. As soon as I hung up the phone I had to sit down, for my legs had turned to mush. *Autism!* The word circled around in my head for the rest of the day, and when I awoke the next morning, it was still there. *Autism.*

On this day
The light finally beginning
To shine outward of the night
Casting rays out of the shadows
Turning darkness into light.

D.L. Clarke

Chapter 43

The team arrived right on schedule, and it had been right after Aubrey had woken from a short nap. Her little face was slightly puffy and her eyes were sort of glazed. As the team sat down in various places of my living room, Aubrey continued to wander around, slowly coming out of her previous slumber state.

I wondered if I shouldn't have let her sleep prior to the team's arrival. It had been my fear that if I hadn't, she would be completely out of control and possibly unwilling to cooperate with them if asked.

I also wanted her to be cooperative with *me*. I was still not out of the woods with the "lack of parenting skills" accusations, as far as I knew, so it would be in my best interest as well, to have my little girl as rested and happy as possible.

The nap, however, seemed to have had just the opposite effect on Aubrey. It was either that or the fact that there were four strangers staring at her. I guessed it was most likely the latter of the two. They made me nervous too, so I could understand.

As the team asked me questions one at a time, Aubrey would come between the team member, and myself and demand my attention, often by shouting or once again, demanding food or drink. When I would try to get her to lower her voice by saying, "Inside voice, Aubrey!" She would return my requests with a loud, "Cookie! COOKIE! *I want a cookie!*"

When I would try to distract her with some wooden blocks one of the team members had brought, her fixation on wanting the cookie, only seemed to intensify. "Cookie! Cookie!" She was hanging on my lap now and grabbing at my arms, continually begging for a cookie. I wanted to put her in her room and shut, no actually *lock* would be more of an honest description, the door. (And no, I have never actually done that; so don't get all disconcerted with me).

I was mortified. What was I supposed to do? What would the *team* of experts want me to do? If I seemed "too nice" to Aubrey, then I would be apparently "allowing" or "enabling" her to behave this way. The team would surely write that down and call me later with a massive line of good parenting books.

If I seemed "too harsh," again, they would jot all of it down, and I would get a similar phone call with the book suggestions. I felt like I couldn't win. Nothing I did at the moment would be right.

I was no longer confident of *anything* I did or didn't do as a parent. Since I was convinced that most of Aubrey's difficulties were brought on by my horrible parenting techniques, being judged by a jury full of experts in my own living room, just made the whole thing nearly unbearable.

Question after question I heard from each member of the team, and one by one, (throughout Aubrey's demands and tantrums), I answered them all the best I could.

We went back to Aubrey's birth, to her first stages of development, her first tooth, when she got toilet trained. Whoops! That one was still an issue, and they made note of it. Then onto when I had first started noticing things that couldn't be classified as "normal behaviors."

They wanted to know how long she had walked on her toes, and if she ever *didn't* walk on them. The questions were intensive and very inquisitive. I had to stop and think several times pulling from every possible memory that I had. My brain cramped and dug and I made it think and rethink everything my mouth said or started to say. Be sure, be accurate, help them, *and help us!*

No one, and I mean literally, *no one* had ever dug as deep as this team was. Though it was exhausting and I had a pounding headache by the time they left, I was glad. I felt like we had not missed one thing. My "list of things that concern me" had been thoroughly discussed and dissected. It had finally, after years of following me everywhere I went, become apparently useful.

The burdens, little one, you bear
Will surely leave you now
your wings, will finally repair
Soon to be soaring, reach now
Into the beautiful weightless air.

D.L. Clarke

Chapter 44

"You did it, Aubrey!" I exclaimed one morning after she successfully utilized the "potty" chair. "Yeahhhhhhh!" I continued my praise. Aubrey looked up at me and giggled.

"Yeahhhhh!" she said and clapped her hands.

"You are such a big girl now! Mommy's sooooo happy!" I said encouragingly as I ran some warm water for her little hands. I watched as she scrubbed and scrubbed and scrubbed on her hands until they turned bright pink under the running water.

"Honey, I think they are clean now! Let's dry them off, okay?" I said, handing her a towel. I then watched as she took the towel and one by one, diligently wiped each individual finger over and around until every drop of moisture was off her hands. Then, I watched as she repeated the entire process all over again.

Wiping, wiping, wiping. I stood and patiently let her finish. No sense in interrupting the process, besides, it was going to be another busy morning; the team of specialists was due back with their results.

As the doorbell rang, I once again got the usual apprehensive and sick feeling in my stomach. What if—stop it! I did not even want to think about the fact that they would have nothing, not even a list of suggestions that might help us.

They all filed in, greeting me happily, smiling down at Aubrey as they entered and found seating in my freshly cleaned and vacuumed living room. Jo, the autism specialist, was the first one to speak.

Looking straight at me, she began by asking me more questions like, "You remember when you told me about Aubrey's dislike of change, and that she did better with set routines?" When I said that I did, she continued speaking. She talked and explained, and with everything she said, the light started to shine a little brighter, my heart pounding a little harder and stronger.

Routines, and dislike of change, lack of eye contact, certain textures of fabrics and foods that bothered her, loud noises that crazed her senses, and even Aubrey's dislike to being held or touched, all made perfect sense to Jo. The shredding of paper and the crumbling of crackers into tiny bits, even the fact that Aubrey preferred walking on her toes, made sense too. I wondered, silently to myself, *why* it all made sense to Jo, and never did to anyone *else?*

When I asked her why Aubrey usually showed most of her worst behaviors in *my* presence, she reassured me that I should be honored. *Honored? Really?* I let that soak in for a moment, not quite ready to accept the trophy, just yet.

Jo explained that while it was pretty typical of us all to fall apart emotionally when we needed to, usually just with select people, it was even more so with a child that was afflicted with "certain" disorders. She explained that even though Aubrey could often "hold it together emotionally" while visiting *other* people's homes and being in unfamiliar situations, such as school or physician's offices, it was her fear of how they would or wouldn't respond to her that kept her from falling apart. So, usually Aubrey would choose to "hold it together."

Her choice to "hold it all in" would be so exhausting to her, that when she did arrive home after a visit to Grandma's house or school, for example, she would then feel as she could finally unravel and release. And, she would.

Sometimes that meant a very livid and ferociously long tantrum session, or it would simply come in the form of a very long, self-induced, nap.

Now, it was all starting to make perfect sense to me. It also was starting to finally put to rest the proclamations that others had decidedly declared that just because Aubrey was okay at *their* house, she was indeed perfectly and completely normal, everywhere *else*. Even though I too desperately wanted them to be correct with their assumptions, I knew in my gut, that they weren't.

Everything that Jo had witnessed and read in Aubrey's history of therapy sessions, tests, and psychology reports, as well as the findings she had gathered personally from the interviews and meetings we shared, all pointed toward the fact that Aubrey showed definite signs of autism.

Autism. That word *again!* I felt it sting a bit, but nonetheless, I let it soak in a little, and continued to absorb everything that Jo was explaining to me.

Jo then went on to explain that people affected with autism have a wide variety of sensory issues as well as social/communication, and emotional difficulties. Because of this, Aubrey most likely screamed and would tantrum because at times, she may have felt as if that was her only means of communication and stress relief, as she mentioned before.

Also, because of the sensory issues, Aubrey was very uncomfortable being involved in anything that produced movement that challenged her physical comfort level. This included swings, teeter-totters, slides, and other playground equipment that required "being off the ground." The nightmarish bath times made sense to Jo as well. Being wet often made Aubrey miserable as did having her hair touched.

Aubrey's dislike of textures and her reluctance to put her hands into goopy things like shaving cream, finger paints, as well as gritty things like glitter and sand, all made perfect sense yet again. Even the toe-walking was because of her sensory issues, (not wanting her entire foot "feeling" the floor), and was quite significant in the world of autism.

Not laughing at cartoons and things that were supposedly funny, fell under the social difficulties autistics experience as did the situations where Aubrey would go into a "daze-like" state and stop communicating for hours or sometimes days at a time. The repetitive asking for food, or certain objects, and her frequent lack of eye contact, was also a red flag for the diagnosis of autism.

The list of things went on and on, and as Jo explained them all and made connections between the symptoms and Aubrey's experiences, I felt the weight shifting a little more and gently begin to lift.

"So, dear," she said quietly to me, "it absolutely is not your fault." I watched Jo as she sat back a little in her chair, letting her words take a moment to soak in. *Autism.*

But, I still had some questions. I had to be completely *sure* that I had not left anything out, that what parenting techniques I had used in the past *really hadn't* caused Aubrey to be the way she was.

Nothing I said, convinced Jo that there was anything I did that had caused any of the difficulties Aubrey was having, nothing. She assured me that under the circumstances, I should be *proud* of what I had accomplished. More so, she said that I should be even *more* proud of how well Aubrey was doing.

Proud? I sat in utter amazement and let everything unload slowly. How *well* my daughter was doing. *How well.* I wondered what the alternative *would* have been. I didn't even want to consider the fact that she could have been much worse, as Jo implied. She also stated matter-of-factly, that everything, every single little thing, that I had done up to this point, had helped Aubrey in *some way*.

Wow! That took several minutes to make sense to me. This was completely opposite of the usual "results" meetings I had grown so accustomed to. My gut turned and chirped happily within my body, slowly giving up its usual and persistent nagging that had kept me going for so long.

Just then, Aubrey running by me interrupted my thoughts by her hollering, "I have to potty!" The team looked over at me and smiled. "Good job!" one of them mouthed silently.

I guess I should have felt utter gloom and sadness at the fact that I had just been informed that my daughter was autistic, but I didn't. The diagnosis did not bear the "expected doom" upon me at all, and oddly enough, it actually bore quite the opposite, for when I stood up and walked down the hall to assist my little girl on the potty, a sense of complete and ultimate euphoria washed over me.

You thought you had the last words I think
But I thought that I should just let you know
Last words don't just happen overnight
They continue to expand, fester, and grow.
Within your body they boil and finally become rotten,
And when the last words are finally spoke
Just where within those last words, have you really gotten?

D.L. Clarke

Chapter 45

I wanted to share the news with everyone. I knew that those who had supported me all along would be ecstatic to hear that we finally had some answers. But, I almost feared the responses I would get from the ones that hadn't given their support. Nonetheless, I felt that I *somehow* had to get some sort of validation from them. That yes, it *had* been wise to drag Aubrey all over from therapist to psychologist, from clinics to pre-schools, anywhere and anything that might help her.

I made a few phone calls and was thrilled to be able to share Aubrey's new treatment plan with those that wanted to hear it. Then, because of my inextinguishable desires for validation, I made a personal visit and delivered the news along with the future treatment plan, to some that didn't want to hear it.

But, I made them listen. I had needed them to. I also needed them to know that what I had done with my daughter *had been the best thing*. Even though they had never believed it to be. As soon as I had finished talking, I watched as they stood up and after letting their front door slam them bluntly on their buns, they took a very, very long walk. I was not invited. The only thing they allowed to accompany them was, a big balloon bursting full of disbelief and doubt, anger, disappointment, resentment, and themselves.

It was obvious at that moment that they still did not want to acknowledge nor hear anything that was "negative." And at that moment I had to accept that they never would, so I did. No sense in popping their damned balloons. So, I shrugged my shoulders briefly, then put my pin away.

Yet, in the very stillness of the darkest of nights, with my pin still temptingly near,

I can still hear that front door slamming its denial in such obdurate finality in my ears.

"My little girl is flying!" I scream into the night.
"Flying? How?" Is all they want to ask.
"Flying is not possible," is also their disconcerted retort.
"Only if you never try," just is simply mine.

D.L. Clarke

Chapter 46

Under the guidance and advice from the Early Intervention team, I got Aubrey enrolled in a pre-school program that had both special needs children and those that weren't. Although Aubrey didn't like going, and she would often kick and scream upon arrival to the school, I still took her three times a week, dutifully, as scheduled.

Often, her screaming would be so loud that the teachers would come off the playground, help me get her out of her booster seat, and then, with her still kicking and screaming, they would carefully haul her off into the classroom.

Brutal? Yeah, I thought so too, at first, and then I had to decide quickly that it wasn't. Even though I would drive off feeling washed out and sick from the scenes of my daughter being carried, screaming at the top of her lungs all the way into the school, she *had to go.* Staying at home where it was comfortable and safe was not going to help her. She was still safe, at school, but she wasn't *comfortable* there. I had to accept that, and eventually, so would she.

As pre-school became a routine for us, so did everything else. Charts, schedules, and daily storyboards posted throughout the house continually reminded Aubrey of the day's events. Charts, schedules, and daily storyboards at her pre-school, also provided reassurance of what was coming up next. It was becoming more and more obvious that the more structured our life became, the more it seemed to ease Aubrey's stress.

Since Aubrey loved books so much, I learned from the Intervention team how to utilize them as tools to explain any changes that were going to take place. The change could be drawn out descriptively with pictures and words, in a simple homemade book. Aubrey could then look at the book, flipping the pages back and forth as often as she wanted or needed to.

Everything was helping a little bit at a time, and with each one of Aubrey's successes, I could see something emerging within her that I had never seen before. It was confidence.

Don't try convincing me
That you were strong before
I already knew it, for I could see
It shone so deeply in your eyes
Before even you, knew it to be.
D.L. Clarke

Chapter 47

Though there were often little, and at times major, setbacks nothing ever went back to the hopeless and panicky way it was before we found the Early Intervention team. Their constant support and almost daily guidance enabled me to start being a "mom" again, instead of the raving lunatic advocate for my child that I had somehow become.

When the occupational and sensory integration therapists would come to the house, I was now able to let my guard down and actually enjoy and learn from the sessions they had with Aubrey. I was even asked to occasionally join in on some of the sessions and I welcomed the invite readily. I felt as if I was no longer being judged and placed on some "worst mom of the year" chart, and it was a very comforting feeling.

I also no longer felt that panicky fear that had once consumed me about Aubrey and her unknown future. When pre-school ended, and kindergarten was just around the corner, we already had a plan in place, thanks to the Intervention team.

Even before the first day of the new school year began, the school would be visited several times by Aubrey and myself and the new teacher was introduced.

I often would even take along my camera to take pictures: of the classroom, where Aubrey would have her lunch, the new teacher, and her new cubby where she would put her backpack. Aubrey could then have the pictures at home to look at whenever she got anxious about the new school. Practically everything that was new or different would be prepared for and known, before she had to encounter them.

As time went on, as busy lives go, things became less of a routine, and schedules were apt to change at a moment's notice. When Aubrey would become agitated or upset because of it, I would sometimes apologize and quickly write up a new schedule and post it for her; but sometimes, depending on how agitated she was or wasn't, I would try to just brush it off with a quick explanation, "Sorry honey, Mommy was really busy today, and I just didn't get it done." I was, most of the time, becoming more and more able to get away with the sometimes forgotten schedule or "daily plan," and it was a welcomed relief.

It just was not possible to foretell the future in every situation, nor be able to prepare her for them all. Though I really tried to stick to the event schedules, sometimes I just had to shrug off my failures, always letting Aubrey know that, hey, its okay to have to stop for gas because Mom forgot to do it this morning. In other words, it really didn't *have* to be a big deal, especially if we didn't make it into one.

When Aubrey would insist on sitting at the table after an art project to pick every single solitary piece of glitter stuck to her hands, I would try to accommodate her by *acknowledging* the fact that she had glitter on them, but also showed her all the glitter still adhered to mine. "It was okay for it to be stuck there, silly ole' glitter," I would say, and then follow it with, "Maybe it wanted to be our friend and hang around on our hands all day?" Okay, so *that* one hadn't worked out so well, because she remained seated for over an hour picking at the stubborn specks on her hands. But, I did know that some of my "brush offs" *had* worked. I was continuing to still trust in and follow my gut instincts and what they were telling me to do.

She was beginning to depend on the schedules less and less, looking at them fewer times a day, and instead of always reaching for a book to shove in her face when encountering someone unfamiliar to her, she would watch them instead, often out of the corner of her eye.

Yeah, they were little things, but they were *there*. We *were* finally making progress. Christmas and birthdays would come and gifts would be opened and paper strewn about, and Aubrey dealt with the mess. Though she hated the tape that would get stuck on her fingers and would scream until it was removed, the screaming was often not as intense as it had always been. I knew then that the sensory integrations and occupational therapies at the pre-school and private counseling sessions were working.

When we would venture to the playground, instead of her usual greeting in the past of "throwing sand at the kids," she was beginning to show signs of "parallel play." It was another big step of progress, and I knew it was because of all the therapies and skill training put into place by the intervention team and school system.

Aubrey's love of books was apparently paying off well too, for, from second grade on, she had become known as the best reader in all of her classes! Her love of books also helped her become one of the top spellers, possessing a huge vocabulary of words.

All along, with each success she had, I knew that we had done *something* right, that *something, somewhere* all down her lifeline, had made a difference.

Even though I wanted you to be in the right,
you know, it wasn't until tonight
That I figured it all out.
Simply put, you were so afraid of what might have been that
Your true fears and emotions, you never did show.
But more simply put, I was more afraid of what might have
been
If I hadn't of been so unafraid of the fight.
Unafraid of the ever-vast unknown.

D.L. Clarke

Chapter 48

Aubrey continued to flourish within the Early Intervention team's direction and guidance. Their phone calls kept me updated, and home visits by the team reassured me that my daughter was continually making not just little, but giant leaps into a very promising future. After only just a year and a half in the Early Intervention Program, Aubrey was no longer considered simply "autistic" but rather a highly functional individual with "autistic-like" behaviors.

(I later learned that this would have been categorized as Asperger's Syndrome. But, the syndrome was just beginning to be realized in the medical and educational fields at the time. Even though a doctor in Austria, Dr. Hans Asperger had identified the syndrome in 1944, it hadn't been translated into English until 1991. It also took until 1994 for the syndrome to finally be defined in the medical world of American Psychiatric Association's Diagnostic Statistical Manual.[1] Thus, it had been nearly impossible to diagnose or treat individuals with the disorder. It also helped in explaining why Aubrey's symptoms had not made any diagnostic connections with anyone in the medical field, until just recently.)

Speech therapy sessions continued until they had been deemed unnecessary, as did the Sensory Integration therapies. Once she got into the third grade, Aubrey could be discontinued off of Occupational therapy. She was also re-classified as having an "Autism Spectrum Disorder," which was still a form of autism, of course, but to a much lesser degree.

Everything, in a sense, was becoming more and more manageable on our own. I knew the team of helpers were still there, but knowing that they didn't have to monitor my daughter's every step, was helping me to become more and more reassured that she would someday become independent.

School years came and went, and as friends were made and girl "dramas" at school were reported, I knew we were making progress. When parent teacher conferences came around, and I would be informed that though Aubrey really needed to stop "talking so much" to "all her friends" in class, her math scores were high and her spelling and reading even higher. I definitely knew we were on the road to a very successful and normal future for her and yeah, I know normally one would cringe at the report of "too much talking in the classroom," but to me, it was reason to be overjoyed!

"Uh, how many friends did she have? Oh! Wow! *That many!* Okay, I will talk to her about it." Yeah, that was definitely something none of her therapist or doctors had ever thought to warn me about! Snicker snicker, glee, glee, my heart would tippy tap-dance.

With each and every "normal" milestone that one would just expect to have happen in their child's progress, that actually ended up happening in Aubrey's, I rejoiced and celebrated. I took absolutely nothing for granted.

We continued monitoring her progress throughout her early elementary school years with the use of the IEP, or Individual Education Plan administered through the school system's special education program, and her teachers and staff. Individuals trained in certain fields would monitor Aubrey's progress and tests would be administered throughout the school years.

I would be called in to have meetings with the intervention teams, and with each one, fewer and fewer members of the team were needed and/or utilized. Aubrey was becoming more and more independent. And, with each team member that was crossed off the list, I rejoiced and felt my heart swell.

She was doing it! Growing and maturing, expanding her knowledge and senses. She was becoming a little miracle before everyone's eyes. She was now officially diagnosed with Asperger's Syndrome. Again, a form of autism, as explained previously, but to a lesser degree.

The only problem I had now was that I couldn't find the words to actually *tell* Aubrey what was going on with her. I mean, *how could I?* Here she was, outsmarting the best of the best, proving herself over and over again, showing herself to be way above average and far brighter than anyone could have ever imagined.

Who was I to *now* tell her that she had a deficit of some sort? I couldn't, and there was no way I was going to break it to her, not now, not ever. So, I didn't. I kept putting it off, for the timing never ever seemed quite right.

The years passed, and she became brighter, sharper, more confident and less dependent on outside sources to get through her days. The intervention team slowly dwindled away for her lack of need, and the hope now was that by the time she entered the eighth grade, she could stand completely on her own two feet.

She entered the sixth grade with just a monitoring plan on paper, in place. No big team of experts, no home meetings to be held, no big school conferences between professionals to be scheduled. Nope, just Aubrey, and her notebook covered with every "normal" teen girl's décor of rock and roll stickers of the latest "alternative" band, and phone numbers of all her "best friends."

In every sense of the word, Aubrey was completely and ultimately "normal." And I couldn't be happier or more satisfied. Drawing a deep and cleansing breath had once again become a part of normal everyday life rather than a "coping" mechanism to get through a tough moment or episode of stress.

It was amazing at how much weight had gently flowed away without my apparent knowledge. I don't even remember when it all had drifted so silently away. I was just so happy that it finally had, for it meant that I could finally relax a little.

Besides, Aubrey was just eleven, not even close to being thirteen yet, so what did I have to be afraid of anyway?

"Come sit with me awhile"
The old man beckoned me with his weary eyes.
As the campfire spit and crackled, I sat.
"Have a bite to eat and tell me,
What all in this life, do you wish to be?"

"A weary moth will land into the fire
If he follows too closely his dreams," was my reply.
"Careful to cling not too tightly
To his instinctual desires.
We all want and need certain things," I continued.
"And dream to follow what we start.
If you truly believe in that, old man,
You will know then, what's inside my heart."

D.L. Clarke

Chapter 49

"Camping is messy, Aubrey, you are just going to have to get used to that idea, and please, honey, try to have some fun!" I said while setting up the first of the two tents we had packed. It was the summer before Aubrey was due to start her seventh grade school year, and because it was summer and the kids had never been, we had decided to take them camping. But, even before we got the last of the supplies out of the van, I was beginning to think that it hadn't been such a great idea!

"There are bugs everywhere, Mom!" Aubrey shot back in my direction. I looked up to see her swatting at all the bugs that were apparently "getting all over her and sticking in her hair."

"Honey, I told you there would be some mosquitoes, remember?" I replied. I had abandoned the tent and was now digging in one of the Rubbermaid tubs I had brought full of supplies. Where *was* that bug spray! I really hoped that I hadn't forgotten it. No, I wouldn't have forgotten something as important as that. I tried to keep thinking positive as I continued to dig. Ah! There it was, hiding underneath the, AH! Better yet! Washcloths! I pulled out the large zip-lock bag of pre-wetted washcloths, handing the bag over to Aubrey with one hand, while shaking the can of bug spray with the other.

"MOM!" she said as she dropped the bag and started waving her hands around madly. "There are BEEEEEEEZZ!" As I looked around where she was waving trying to locate the offending insect, I noticed that it was a dragonfly and not a bee. I let her flap madly at the aberrant air around her.

"Aubrey, that wasn't a bee, it was a dragonfly and they don't bite," I said, trying to get back to the task of putting the tent up.

"NO! It was a BEE!" she said matter-of-factly. Austin chimed in then, agreeing with me that it had been in fact, a dragonfly. As the two kids started to argue about the specific species of insect that had tried to "bite the crap out of" Aubrey, I continued to get the tent upright.

"It was a stupid dragonfly, Aubrey!" Austin said, almost yelling this time.

"No it wasn't, Austin! I think I should know what a flippin' bee looks like!" Aubrey frustratingly replied back. I could easily see the look of disgust on her face.

The tent pole slipped out of its binding and I felt like stomping my foot, but didn't. I wondered if I had made a huge mistake by trying to take the kids camping. Gary, the kids' step-dad, had had to work part of the day, but was due to arrive shortly and I thought momentarily that I should halt my attempts to set up camp until then.

"Where is the pop at?" Austin asked.

"Yeah, I am really thirsty too!" Aubrey chimed in.

"You guys be patient! Geesh! Can't you see Mom is busy?" I heard Brittney say.

"There's that bee again! MOM! It is *chasing* me!" Aubrey yelled as she waved and swatted at the dragonfly.

"It is a stupid DRAGONFLY, Aubrey!" Austin proclaimed, seemingly determined to convince her.

"No, it is not!" I heard Aubrey retort as she kept swatting. "It is a flippin' bee!"

I eventually got both tents up, and with the help of all three kids, (I had to finally bribe them with squished marshmallows) we were able to get most of the camp all set up before Gary's arrival. It was now time for relaxation and fun!

"MOM?" I heard Aubrey ask.

"Yes, honey?" I replied.

"I have dirt in my shoes," she stated ruefully.

I replied back to her that, "Remember, camping is messy? You are *supposed* to get dirty while camping, honey!" She told me that she didn't remember, and she still didn't like the dirt being on her. Okay. But there hadn't been a scene, and there was no drama, yet, so I was pleased so far.

"Mom? How do we wash our hands?" was her next question. I pointed to the dishpan that unfortunately, unbeknownst to me, had claimed the life of several small gnat like insects. Crap! Crap! Crap!

"I am supposed to wash my hands in THAT?" Aubrey almost shrieked, her face contorting into a little scowl.

"Um, yeeeess," I started to slowly say, then thought of another option. "Would you rather wash your hands in the river?" I said pointing toward the rippling flow of water that was just about a hundred feet or so away from our camp. I watched as Aubrey looked over at the water and then back to the dishpan.

"No, that's okay, I will use this water," she said, and gingerly dipped her fingers into the "if it hadn't been for the bugs" perfectly clean pan of water.

"People pee in that water down there," I heard her inform Austin later. Aha! That explained her decision! I giggled to myself.

"When can we eat?" was the next question I heard, it was from Austin.

"Yeah, can we have something to eat?" Aubrey joined in on the request.

"Guys! Goshhh! Leave Mom alone!" Brittney said, coming to my defense as I explained that my hands were full of twigs for the fire and that I couldn't possibly prepare a snack. However, if they wanted to help me, we could all sit and have a snack as soon as we had enough twigs to start a fire.

It didn't take long before our fire was crackling and we were placing pathetically smashed marshmallows on our terribly scrawny twigs to roast. Our entire camp was together and looked good enough that Jeff Propst would be pleased. Well, maybe not quite that good.

For one night and two days, bugs were battled, hands and lips got chapped and sore, faces couldn't be "properly washed," the pit toilet got "more and more disgusting" and even got to point of "who can use those things without barfing," which *was* used without barfing, and cuts and scrapes had to be "unhealthily" cleaned with whatever Mom had brought along from home.

But, along with the millions of complaints, and several thousand reasons from the kids as to why we "should never, *never* have come camping, and *never* want to come back," there were also hotdogs that had been roasted beyond recognition, (on purpose), and marshmallows torched and burned, (again on purpose), cups of hot cocoa drank cozily around the fire, and long pondering gazes to the night sky that seemed to hold zillions of twinkling stars. The "pee" river had been swam and rafted in, joyfully and voluntarily, and the forested hillsides explored for lizards and frogs despite the snakes that were "for sure hiding there," and the moths that were "the size of flippin' bats!"

Then it was time to pack up the camp and head for home. As we loaded up the cars, I caught a glimpse of the kids collecting the last of their belongings. All of them were covered with dirt and their hair and bodies in desperate need of showers.

Aubrey had dirt stuck under her nails and I knew she was more than ready to "get it out of there!" I had a feeling that this would probably be the very last time any of them wanted to go camping again.

I knew that Aubrey especially had been pushed past her level of comfort and her thresholds crossed many times even within the short amount of time we had been there. I felt sort of guilty, in a way, but I had wanted her to at least try the whole "outdoorsy" thing. Even if we never came back, at least we had tried it.

With that, we started out the winding and graveled road that led toward home, Aubrey picking at her fingernails in the front seat. Once the car passed through the campground gate, Aubrey looked up and matter-of-factly said, "I am going to miss this place! When can we come again?"

"Soon, honey, soon," I replied quickly as my eyes started to well with tears. I drove on in silence and reflection.

Everything about her amazed me. Here she was, out in the dirt, with really nothing that she was used to. No storyboards to explain the daily events, no schedules, just me, giving her little suggestions at what we should or might do during the day. Routines were set aside and even her physical comfort had been compromised and tested beyond her liking. But, she had still dealt with it and coped.

The night had been chilly, and though she complained and wanted her "blanket from home" because it is the "warmest flippin" blanket ever, she had accepted the one I handed her and managed with the fact that it was not "her blanket from home." I had actually left it on purpose because of its vulnerability, being handmade by my grandmother several years ago. I had wondered if that had been a wise choice after all when all the "blanket issues" arose, but I guessed now that it had actually been okay.

She muddled through, she dealt, and she pushed herself, and tried new things. She was brave when I didn't think she would be, and laughed at things when I was certain the situation would have induced tears and anger instead.

I looked over at her sitting in the car next to me. She had stopped the persistent picking under her nails, and was now watching out the window. The miles zoomed past us and as she leaned forward to put on "some tunes," I smiled.

A couple of tears streamed down the side of my face and fell to my lap just as the first notes of music filled the car. Then, as if on cue, we all joined in with the radio singing the Avril Lavigne song. We continued singing at the top of lungs all the rest of the way home. The song was, ironically, called "Complicated."

I have only just started to see
So, please don't yet say goodbye
just say a welcome hello
To all that is only beginning to be…
The last chapter
But, alas, only just the beginning.
As we all now can so plainly see.

D.L. Clarke

Chapter 50

It was the summer before Aubrey was due to start the eighth grade, and though the morning was already starting to warm rapidly from the sun as it slowly lit the sky with its orangey hue, I couldn't help but feel a little panicky and nervously cold.

We were already well on our way to the Portland airport and I was thankful that the traffic was light on the Interstate.

Though Aubrey seemed perfectly comfortable, and I knew that I had double and triple checked that I had packed everything she would need for her trip, I still couldn't find any ease for my mind.

My feelings were valid, after all, because this was going to be big. Aubrey's plane was due to take off in a mere couple of hours and, get this, she would be flying alone, back to Illinois to visit her grandparents for ten days! Her only source of assistance during the flight would be a flight attendant that was specifically designated to get her from point A, which was me, and point B, which were her grandparents in Chicago. So, yeah, I was more than just a wee bit nervous! But I was trying my best not to let on that I had any concerns at all.

I looked into the back seat where she was sitting and saw her watching out the window as the miles rolled by, and I wondered what she was thinking.

"Are you nervous, honey?" I asked her. Thinking that she might shoot back a quick answer that she was, I watched her as her face crumpled into a perplexed expression.

"No! Why would I be nervous? I am *excited!*" she exclaimed, her eyes growing wide with anticipation and joy, as she glanced over where her brother Austin was. Her answer comforted me temporarily as I silently went through the checklist of travel preparations in my head again.

I had packed away a few snacks in the backpack which she would be carrying onto the plane, as well as a couple of juice drinks. Extra batteries for her Walkman were in the side pouch, I recalled with a silent, check! Then continued on down my mental list.

A packet of hand wipes and hand sanitizer, (check!) her toothbrush and toothpaste, (check, check!) and extra change of clothes just in case her luggage got lost, a list of phone numbers and a calling card, lip balm, a book, (check, check, double check!) and lastly her drawing pencils and paper, all safely secured in her backpack, (check, check-) Okay, now we are being neurotic! Stop it! Check!

"I will e-mail you everyday, okay?" I reminded her, still going over my mental "check list" in my head, unable to stop the apparent madness spree my head "needed" to complete.

"And, I will try to get on the chat thing so we can talk online too," I heard myself start to ramble. Stop it! She will be fine! Gawd! My brain would not listen to reasoning now and rampantly kept spitting off its lists of "things I needed to remind myself of," and on and on. My hands were ice cold and I felt my level of anxiety rise sharply as our van made the exit and continued onward toward the airport parking lot.

"I probably won't have a lot of time to write, ya know," I heard Aubrey say from the back seat. "Grandma said we will be really busy every day doing stuff, but I will write stuff down so I can tell you about it when I get back!" she promised in an excited voice.

"You can still try to chat with Mom online, Aubs," I heard Brittney coax her.

Ten days, I mused to myself. Ten days and then she will be back. But what if she doesn't even get on the plane? That was just one of the million scenarios that ran through my head. My brain, of course, had all the scenarios in place, organized and ready to counteract or assist if or when needed.

They all had pretty much the same thing in common, and that was Aubrey backing out of the airplane screaming with her luggage wildly swaying from one wheel to the next as it tried to keep up with her fleeing. And then there I would be, intercepting her and the stuffed and floundering suitcase, all the while trying to tell her just how proud I was that she even *tried* to go.

Once Gary found a parking space in the short-term lot, we all hopped out of the van and proceeded to enter the busy airport. I watched Aubrey and when she saw me looking at her, she smiled at me and restated how excited she was. Everything was going really smoothly and I was beginning to relax a little.

We decided to get some lunch and wait for Aubrey's plane to arrive, so we chose seats by the window and watched as the planes taxied during their arrivals and departures.

Austin sat quietly while Aubrey produced a flurry of questions about the planes, the pilot, and whatever else popped into her mind. She didn't seem nervous or scared at all, and that comforted me too.

Time passed quickly, and before we knew it, it was time for Aubrey to board her plane. Since I was the only one who could walk her past security, Gary, Austin, and Brittney all gave her a big hug and told her goodbye.

I took Aubrey through the security checkpoint and we found her gate easily. We didn't have to wait at all before an attendant approached us and asked us what our names were. I heard Aubrey tell her name to the attendant, and she in turn, told Aubrey that she was going to be her helper on the plane during the flight. She then gave Aubrey an "Unaccompanied Minor" identification badge on a string to wear around her neck for the duration of the trip.

"Ready?" I heard the attendant ask Aubrey brightly.

"Yup!" Aubrey quickly replied, and started following her helper toward the walkway to the plane.

"Hey!" I called after her. "What about my hug?"

"Oh yeah! I almost forgot, Mom!" Aubrey said, giggling as she hurried back to where I was standing. She threw her arms around me and gave me a quick but tight hug accompanied by her trademark pat-pats on my back.

"I will miss you, honey!" I told her as a lump formed in my throat. My legs felt like wet noodles and my eyes were considering crying, but I firmly talked them out of it, for now anyway.

"I'll miss you too, Mom! Bye!" I heard Aubrey say as she hurried back to her helper and quickly disappeared down the walkway and into her plane.

I took a very deep breath, and then another. I waited for a few minutes, watching the door where Aubrey had gone through. I wondered if she had found her seat yet. I wondered if she was scared. She certainly hadn't let on to anyone that she was.

I watched as the attendant who took the tickets slowly shut the door to the walkway.

I took another deep breath. Okay. It was going to be okay. Okay, okay, okay...

I hurriedly walked back through the security checkpoint and over to the cafeteria where the rest of the family were still sitting. Gar and Brittney watched as I walked up and I heard Gary ask how it had gone. I reassured them that she had done really well, and we watched out the window as Aubrey's plane backed up and taxied out onto the runway.

Austin had his face buried in his hands and I encouraged him to watch his sister's plane take off. He hadn't wanted to go with Aubrey, but I was wondering if he had changed his mind now.

"I feel like I don't have a sister anymore," I heard Austin say quietly. I looked over at him from across the table and saw that he had tears in his eyes.

"Thanks a lot, buddy!" Brittney exclaimed jokingly at him while playfully jabbing her elbow into her brother's side. He smiled at that and turned his face toward the window to watch.

It took just a few more minutes and Aubrey's plane had left the ground and was departing quickly into the clear mid-morning sky. I watched and watched, waiting until the last little speck of her plane had left my sight. As we all stood up to leave, I glanced once more into the sky.

A million emotions and feelings engulfed me as I let my eyes scan the sky again, seeking the speck that held my daughter. I was glued to the windowpane, unable to move, my mind and heart colliding in a million different directions.

"C'mon, hon, let's go," Gar said as he gently touched my arm and started leading me away from the window.

"She did it, Gar," I replied, choking as I took his hand and we started to walk away from the window.

"Let me look one last time," I pleaded. I needed another moment to let it all soak in. I could see from the look on Gar's face that he understood.

I went back to the glass and stared out the window. The lump that had formed earlier in my throat made its return and my eyes were brimming with tears. As I let them free themselves and purge their way down my face, I thought back to the day in Washington when at just eighteen months of age, Aubrey was being "diagnosed" with some unknown condition that was supposedly going to impair her for life.

The hot tears continued as I remembered being told that she would never dance or play like a normal child, and that she would either need to be institutionalized or at best, attend a "special school." I grimaced, and after retrieving a Kleenex from my pocket, (yeah, I *told* you I was prepared!)

I continued to remember the way I felt when I was told she would merely succeed in one thing and that was to tear the family apart. God those words had stung, every single one, and I was recalling them all.

They had left deep wounds and scars that I thought for sure might not ever heal. But they had eventually. I reached up to my eyes then and dabbled the Kleenex carefully around them.

When Aubrey had done the seemingly impossible task of becoming a normal and happy child that had joined dance class and performed in front of large audiences with her teammates, the scars had started to fade a little.

When, at just age four and half, she bravely stood up with her big sister in the middle of a large and noisy crowd at our local pizza place, to go to the stage to sing Barney's, "I Love You" song, the tears that had brimmed my eyes erased more of the wounds.

As she courageously thrust herself down a seventy-foot water slide one summer while we vacationed in Palm Springs, a whole new world of possibilities seemed to be opening up for her. And, each time she climbed the water park's sky-high ladder then bravely slid down, not once, but *three* times, I could almost feel her flinging the doors to her exciting future wide open. A future that I had only dared to silently hope and dream that she would someday experience.

Then, as she stood on stage in front of her entire elementary school and sang a Faith Hill song at the school talent show, every joyful tear that ran down my face erased another scar.

She hosted countless slumber parties and got invited to and attended endless numbers of birthday parties and sleepovers. There were countless amounts of friends and endless hours spent on the telephone talking about the latest and greatest happenings with her girlfriends.

Not only did she attend a regular school, she was at the top of her class. A proud little giggle escaped me just then as I thought back to the doctor that had informed me that she should only be expected to attend a "special school." If he could only see her now!

Already, at just twelve years of age, she had accomplished so much more than she, nor anyone else could ever begin to even realize or fathom.

I turned away from the airport window and saw that my family was standing patiently waiting for me to join them. My family. I knew that in just a little over a week we would all be back up in the same airport to retrieve Aubrey, but until then, we were all going to be missing our little link.

Soaring high above the clouds
Such strong wings gently grasping the air
Tell me, little one, my little angel
What all did you see, way, way up there?
No need to come back down just yet
Let the wind continue to unfurl your sails
Fly higher little one, and rejoice
Land, little one, only when you're ready.
We will wait to hear of your amazing tales.
Tell me, tell me, did you see the stars afloat
Deep within the darkened night sky?
Or did you see all the promises laden
Within God's angels, very own eyes?

D.L. Clarke

Epilogue

Exactly ten days later we all found ourselves up at the same airport waiting for Aubrey's plane to arrive back home. I had made sure we had arrived earlier than necessary, but I didn't want to be late in case her flight had been early. It wasn't.

With each speck in the sky that eventually got closer and grew into the formation of a plane, I would lean forward in my seat and wait with growing anticipation.

Aubrey's ten-day journey back to see her grandparents in Illinois had been a wonderful success, and from all the emails and phone calls home, I could tell she had been having the time of her life!

As one of the dots in the sky grew closer and its shape evolved into a shiny American Airlines jet, I hurriedly stood up, my heart thumping loudly, and went down through the security gates to wait for her arrival. The rest of the family would wait in the main terminal for us.

I could hear the plane as it arrived to the gate where I stood waiting. Butterflies encircled my stomach and I rocked a little back and forth in my flip-flops. Oh! I was so anxious and excited to see her!

Once the attendants opened the walkway doors leading out to the plane, I began to hear voices funneling out. I soon saw that it was Aubrey and an attendant! As soon as she saw me, she gave me a very big smile, and her step quickened, ever so slightly. After I provided my identification to the attendant, I quickly stuffed it away and reached around to give Aubrey a big hug.

"Hi, honey! Long time no see!" I said through damp eyes.

"Yeah! You too, Mom!" she replied with a smile. We hugged briefly, she giving me her signature "pat pat pats" on my back with her hands, and then made our way through the security gates to where the rest of the family was waiting.

Everyone was so full of questions about what all she did, where all did she go, and did she have a great time? She told us she would have to take a minute to think up everything she did.

Before she left Oregon, her original plan was going to involve writing all of the events down daily and keeping track of her activities that way. But she said she had to quickly ditch that idea because she got way too busy! She was so excited, and I could see her little mind working to organize her thoughts. We reassured her that it was okay and we didn't expect her to remember everything she did every day!

As we drove home from the airport, details of her wonderful trip started to emerge, but at one point, she stopped abruptly, giggling a little and said, "I have to start over! I got it all out of order!" We all reassured her again that it didn't matter. We just wanted to hear about her wonderful time.

She then started again giggling and informing us that, "Okay, I will try tell you everything I did, BUT it is definitely *not* going to be in order! So, if you don't care that it *isn't* or *won't* be in the right order, I can tell you!"

Both Gary and I smiled as we continued to look out the front window at the road winding and stretching before us. We then turned toward each other and gave one another a little smile, we had our little Aubrey back!

To Aubrey From Mom

I finally found the words
They came a little easier than I thought
When I told you what a miracle you are
And what battles you so bravely fought.
All the courage you showed me and the world
And what you've overcome.
I finally found those words,
Never thinking that I would
But, my little one
I am so thankful that I could
Describing everything you've accomplished
the amazing miracle you have become,
Was something I've waited long for.
Now the found words, simply
Are all said and finally done.

D.L. Clarke

Aubrey's Poem

I used to be extremely shy, but now I am more open
I just didn't know
about all the people out there.
I love to dance now, and I always want to
Do something fun, and not be stressed,
by girlfriends, family or drama.
I want to be an actress someday, though,
Or a model, or to sing
in a rock band with my friends.
It just has always been my dream.
I can't wait for high school, to see all my old friends.
And that means middle school will finally end!
I like my life, and even though things go bad once in awhile,
Like stuff in life always seems to do
I just try my hardest and work my way through.
The only things I need to stay the same now
Are my family and friends, but most of all, me.
Cuz' my friends all say, "Don't ever change"
Because they all like me, just the way I am.

Aubrey P.

(Part of) The Infamous *List of Things That Concern Me*

1. Will only let me hold her, screams when anyone else tries to hold her
2. Usually hates the bath—doesn't seem to like to be wet.
3. I cannot wash or comb her hair without her screaming
4. Walks on her toes all the time
5. Hates her hands to be messy or sticky (have to have a wet washcloth for her at all times)
6. Does not like runny or mushy foods, gags easily even on soft foods
7. Screams and tantrums in public, especially malls and open spaces
8. Does not make regular eye contact
9. Seems sad most of the time
10. Does not sleep through the night
11. Wakes up in a tantrum several times a night
12. Shreds paper into tiny bits
13. Crumbles and/or tears crackers or toast into tiny pieces
14. Asks for food constantly
15. Lines up toys on floor to resemble picture of toy on display box
16. Seems to "get stuck" or "fixated" on certain words or objects, repeats them over and over.
17. Likes routines and everything in the house to remain the same.

18. Screams when I have to change plans such as: stop for gas when I didn't tell her ahead of time
19. Does not like to wait for anything, wants things *right now*
20. Doesn't laugh at cartoons or things that are supposed to be funny
21. Acts aggressively toward baby brother and others in the family
22. Tantrums and then will laugh immediately after
23. Does not like to touch certain textures like: rough paper, sand, dirt.
24. Does not like her hands being wet, will spend thirty minutes or more trying to dry hands
25. Acts aggressively toward animals; pulls their fur, squeezes their bodies
26. Does not like to swing or use playground equipment, doesn't like being off the ground or off-balance.
27. Will not initiate play with other children
28. Moods change quickly and drastically, often by the minute, or hour
29. Bites herself and/or others when frustrated or angry
30. Seems to prefer being alone or wants to be with me constantly—no in between.
31. Throws rocks at other children on the playground as a greeting
32. Follows me around the house crying all day, I cannot soothe her.
33. Often stops talking or communicating and will go into a "trance-like" state for several hours at a time.
34. Experiences "rage" attacks several times a day for no apparent reason.
35. Touches objects with her fingers first, then puts her fingers to her nose to "smell" the object instead of just picking the object up to smell directly with her nose.

There were eventually over fifty items on this list in 1993…as of today, there are none.

To Whom It May Concern

There were times, you told me just to ignore
All the "certain things"
That baffled you and challenged your heart.
You wanted comfort and the quick promise
That things were "A Okay,"
You wanted me to bury my head also,
In the sandbox you so conveniently made.
But what was I to do? Ignore all the "certain things"
That tugged at my gut without relief
Things that pushed me forward and moving,
Despite all of the grief?
But that, I could never have forgiven myself doing,
And will not apologize, remember, my heart was aching too
Such impossible things I was construing
For, it was my daughter, my beautiful child
Being tormented, pulled to pieces, and torn into two.
I moved onward, not trying to hurt anyone,
only trying to find help
And, simply pretending there was nothing there
It was a hand to her, I couldn't have dealt.

D.L. Clarke

Autism and Asperger's Resources

Internet Sites:
www.campmakebelievekids.com/AspergerSyndrome.htm
www.aspergers.ca/about_as.html
www.autism.org/
www.autism.about.com/
www.aspergers.com/

Autism Society of Amercia
7910 Woodmont Ave. Suite 300
Bethesda, MD 20814-3067
Tel: 301-657-0881

[1] www.aspergers.ca/about_as.html

LaVergne, TN USA
16 December 2010

208952LV00004B/25/P